Lily's Sister

Karen J. Hasley

KAREN J. HASLEY

Outskirts Press, Inc.
Denver, Colorado

Lily's Siser
All Rights Reserved

Outskirts Press
http://www.outskirtspress.com

ISBN-10: 1-59800-540-5
ISBN-13: 978-1-59800-540-0

Library of Congress Control Number: 2006927898

Outskirts Press and the "OP" logo are trademarks belonging to
Outskirts Press, Inc.

Printed in the United States of America

PROLOGUE

My father died in my arms, an experience difficult to accept at any age, but for the young woman I was then, smart and confident and happy with life, especially hard. He died in the family store stocking shelves, a common task done without a thought of danger or death. Father had placed one foot on the ladder to lift up a sack of flour, and I heard him make an odd, choking sound. When I turned, I saw the pallor of his face, reached for him to break his fall, then cradled him in my arms as he died. I suppose his death was an omen of sorts, but I was just nineteen at the time and of a practical nature with little patience for the intangible. Besides, omens are revealed as truth only after the fact, and I'd have to wait six years before I realized that the store held life and death for more people than my father. Me, for example. I nearly died inside the family store and still have the scar to prove it. More than one scar inside and out, truth be told, but scars, even ones that heal clean and smooth, have their place in the telling of this story, and I'm not complaining.

I remember the beginning of the story as if it happened this morning—little Jeffy Hansen calling for help, poking his head just inside the door of the store to tell me Billy was in trouble, then taking off without further details to find his father. Catching Jeffy's urgency, I picked up my skirts and rushed outside, turned the corner, and came face to face with two toughs who might as well have had the word TROUBLE, all in capital letters, stamped on their foreheads. Grown men tormenting my Billy and my temper rising at the sight, since I have never been able to tolerate a bully.

That alley altercation was how I met John Rock Davis, a man who brought a different kind of trouble into my life—and heart—although never a bully, thank God. Anything but. If it hadn't been for that morning and the seemingly random intersection of simple-minded Billy and two thugs and John Rock Davis, Civil War veteran and man with a past, only God knows how my life would have turned out. But I did meet John that morning and loved him practically from the first moment I caught the full force of his clear blue eyes. For better or worse, that meeting set the future course of my life, and I believe now it was never random, couldn't have been, the way things turned out. The hand of God was busy in Blessing, Kansas, not that I realized it at the time. Too young. Too content with life. Too blinded by other loves, past and present. Too independent to admit any man held appeal. Too afraid of change. Too stubborn. A woman of excess and proud of it.

In the end when it came down to choices, I made mine although the memory still causes heartache, and I wouldn't wish what I had to go through to make that choice on anyone else. All hell broke loose that summer of 1880, but heaven, too, and it's the touch of heaven that makes even the worst times worth remembering.

CHAPTER 1

When I first heard the sudden bang of the door and the simultaneous loud jingle of the bell that hung there, I was in the middle of the store accounts, checking on Tom Furlong's order for a new plow and anticipating a delivery of staples from Topeka: coffee, sugar, canned fruit, molasses, things we kept in stock even in hard times. Early morning though it was, I had already sent Billy out to run an errand before I sat down in the back room to see what orders were still outstanding.

Young Jeffy Hansen's urgent voice interrupted me, sounding high-pitched from panic. "Miss Lou, Miss Lou, you'd better come quick."

By the time I pulled off my apron and hurried outside, Jeffy was racing down the street toward his parents' hotel. I heard a sound from the opposite direction and stepped quickly around the corner of the store into the alley, surprising two armed men intent on malicious mischief.

One of the men, who stood over Billy as the boy lay sprawled face down in the dust, said with a smirk, "You better watch where you're going, boy. You can't be as clumsy as you are stupid." He nudged Billy with his foot, and as Billy pushed himself up on his hands and knees, the other man stepped forward to plant a boot on Billy's behind and kick him back down. The disdainful gesture made me more furious than I had ever been in my life.

Grabbing the broom from the corner of the porch, I ordered, "Go bully somewhere else," and swung it at the knees of the man closest to me, hitting him hard against his shin. He let out an oath and reached for the broom, twisting it away from me.

The other man looked over at me and with a wolfish grin of nasty yellow teeth said, "Well, what have we here?" He had a broad, pock-marked face and wore a seaman's cap pulled down low on his forehead.

Fury, not fear, made my voice shake. "I don't know who you are," I told them, balling my hands into fists at my side, "but get out of here and leave him alone."

"Or what are you going to do, girlie?"

The other man stood upright from rubbing his leg where I'd struck him and muttered, "Maybe it ain't the dummy that needs teaching, Cobb."

"You aren't welcome here," I retorted fiercely. "Go back where you came from."

"And who's going to make us do that?" asked the man in the cap, still grinning. "You?"

He moved toward me, and as I looked around for something to defend myself with, a man behind me inquired, "Trouble here?" in a mild, almost uninterested voice.

The two who had accosted Billy froze, their hands moving in a clear and deliberate manner away from the weapons they wore. Both of them stood very still as if they had become part of a photograph.

"I believe you've been asked to leave." The voice went on pleasantly, inexorably, with a slight Southern drawl and the same mild tone although I admit its very quiet caused me to hold my breath. I dared not turn around to see who was speaking since I feared taking my eyes off the two philistines in front of me.

Billy had raised himself once more to his knees, shaking his head as if to clear it, and I saw a trickle of blood running down his cheek. I was outraged that they had dared to lay a hand on him and, saying his name, started forward, my temper at an edge. To keep me from moving, the man behind me grasped my upper arm firmly so I couldn't move without wrenching free. He said nothing, but I was very conscious of the strength of his grip.

The nasty-faced man in the cap spoke. "Just having a little fun, is all. No harm meant. We're here to pick up supplies for Mr. Harper."

"Tell him he'll have to make other arrangements," I snapped. "You two are not welcome here. Don't ever set foot on my property again, either of you. I don't sell to thugs and bullies."

His black eyes narrowed, and I was even more aware that he was wearing a handgun. People in Blessing did not carry firearms, never had to my recollection.

The man behind me said very quietly, "Tell the boy to stay down."

I realized he was trying to keep Billy out of harm's way if violence erupted, so I spoke clearly and calmly. "Billy, lie face down, and don't move unless I tell you." Poor Billy, used to doing what he was told, didn't ask questions, just plopped down on his stomach and wrapped both arms over the back of his head.

The moment seemed very quiet to me, time suddenly halted and no noticeable street noises or activity, only the five of us in a posed tableau. With a smooth motion, the man let go of my arm and casually stepped in front of me. From behind I was conscious of a tall man, taller than I by half a head at least, blue denim shirt on a broad back, black flat-crowned hat on dark hair.

"I wouldn't chance it if I were you," he advised in a friendly tone. He wore a firearm as well, a long-barreled Colt strapped to his leg by a narrow band of leather. The gun was worn and deadly, obviously tailored to his grip with the trigger guard cut away to fit his hand. I had never seen a gun quite like it before. His speech sounded easy and relaxed, a man out for an afternoon stroll, but I sensed a focused tension about him that told me he was very much aware of what was happening in front of us. The next moment everything deflated. The man I'd whacked with the broom held up both hands.

"No use getting riled. Misunderstanding, is all." He held out both hands in a gesture of innocence. "No harm meant. We gotta get back anyway. Mr. Harper'll be expecting those supplies."

"Mr. Harper may expect those supplies until hell freezes over," I stated distinctly, spitting out each word. "You and your friend are not delivering them." Still furious, I stepped out from behind my protector to face the tormentors.

The two men, keeping their eyes on the stranger beside me, edged their way past us, careful not to turn their backs to us until the last minute, and unhitched their horses. It wasn't until they rode off that I realized I had been holding my breath.

"You can unclench your fists now," the man next to me said, a hint of smile in his voice. "They're out of the ring for the time being."

I turned to look at our rescuer full-faced, and for the very briefest moment, my breath caught in my throat and I was unable to say a word. When his gaze met mine, my heart thudded so loudly I thought he must surely hear it or see it beating through the cloth of my dress. It was just a momentary reaction, one breathless second, a sudden, strong attraction that was over so quickly I thought I must have imagined it.

Behind me, with his face still against the ground, Billy asked, "Are they gone, Miss Lou? Are they gone now?" His plaintive words brought me back to reality. You're acting like a smitten schoolgirl, I scolded myself mentally. How childish!

I went to Billy and crouched down next to him. "Yes, they're gone." He looked up at me, dirt and blood smeared on his cheek and eyes wide with fear and confusion. "Oh Billy, honey, I'm so sorry this happened." I helped him to his feet and put my arms around him in a big hug.

His face pressed to my chest, his words muffled, he asked with the bewilderment of a child half his years, "Why'd they do that? Why were they so mean? I just went over to help them. I didn't intend no harm."

"I know," I answered, then paused, searching for the right words. How to explain to this simple boy that some people took pleasure in hurting others and enjoyed the thrill that came from bullying someone weaker? I didn't know how to express it. Billy had never been exposed to that side of people before. Blessing had protected him for all his thirteen years. "You go inside and wash your face. I'll come in in a minute and fix that cut. Change your shirt and wait for me." He sniffed and wiped his nose on his sleeve, and I laughed. "You definitely change that shirt now, young man."

When he was gone, I said to the tall man who still stood there, "I don't have words to thank you, Mister—"

"Davis," he filled in. "John Rock Davis."

"Mr. Davis, I'm Lou Caldecott, and Billy and I are beholden to you. I don't know what I'd have done if you hadn't come along." I put out my hand and he took it in a firm grip, his own hand smooth. Not a man who worked at hard physical labor for a living, then, I thought.

"Remind me not to cross your path when you're wielding a broom, Miss Caldecott. I believe you could do serious damage with it."

John Rock Davis had the clearest, bluest eyes I'd ever seen on man or woman and the strong, lean, weathered face of someone who had spent a lot of years riding against the elements. Clean shaven and all of him muscle, without a pinch of fat on him. Close to thirty, I thought, because of the sprinkling of silver at his temples, but life might have aged him beyond his years. It was hard to get the measure of his age from his face. Not a handsome man in any traditional sense, but attractive in the way the clean, fierce lines of a hawk can be both austere and beautiful. He smiled when he made that last remark, and it changed the whole look of him, took years from his face, smoothed out the furrows in his skin, and wrinkled up the corners of his eyes. His was a slow, rich, warm smile, and for whatever reason my heart literally skipped a beat, causing another brief bout of breathlessness. I gave myself a mental shake. This had been too serious an incident for me to become suddenly moonstruck as a schoolgirl. I needed to concentrate on the issue at hand.

"It would have taken more than a broom with those two, I'm afraid, but I cannot abide bullying."

"So I noticed," he said dryly, "but if the situation happens again, you shouldn't try to handle it by yourself."

I looked at him in amazement. "Mr. Davis, if I don't handle it by myself, it doesn't get handled. Who would I have called on? This is Blessing, Kansas. We've been at peace with the world for years, and we have no local law enforcement. We've never had a need to carry firearms in town."

Without meaning to, my glance dropped to the deadly weapon strapped to his leg. When I looked up, I met his gaze again, and all the warmth that had been in his face was gone, no smile in those eyes now.

"Times are changing, Miss Caldecott. You've just experienced it. I recommend you keep a rifle handy yourself." Then he touched the edge of his hat. "Ma'am," he said by way of goodbye, inflecting the word with cool courtesy. He turned, walked down the alley and out into the street, untied his horse, and led it toward the other end of town.

I watched him from the porch until he disappeared in the direction of the stable, and it was only then that I was able to take a deep and natural breath. I felt as if I'd been under some spell. Well, I admitted to myself, you'll have to stay clear of that man if you don't want to end up under a doctor's care for heart palpitations. John Rock Davis was definitely not the type of man Blessing was accustomed to hosting, which was a good thing for my peace of mind. I didn't think I could get used to that peculiar sensation of my heart racing at the base of my throat, cutting off my air supply. Too unsettling by half.

I was putting a plaster on the cut under Billy's eye when Jim Killian came to see me.

"So I missed a newsworthy event, eh, girl?" He pulled up a chair and sat down next to me with his ever-present pad of paper. An Irishman from the streets of Boston, Jim had wandered into Blessing intending to write dime novels about cowboys and had stayed on as the editor of the town newspaper. With his thinning red hair, oversized ears, bowed legs, and perpetual air of mischief, he looked like a leprechaun with glasses.

"I don't want to find myself on the front page of *The Banner*, Jim."

"This is news, Lou, and I report the news. You'd best tell me what happened, or I'll just go making something up that'll be worse than the truth."

I laughed because he would do exactly that. "Some newsman you are. Whatever happened to integrity in journalism?"

"Oh, it's still there, girl, only sometimes you've got to dig deep to find it. If I promise you a bit of anonymity, will you tell me what happened to this young man here?"

"Bad men hit me," explained Billy. "I didn't like them. Miss Lou and a man made them stop. I had to lie on the ground. Then they went away." He went over to examine his patch in the mirror.

"Billy, go change your shirt like I told you, and then sweep the porch for me. I want to talk to Mr. Killian." After he left I said, "Billy pretty much told you the whole story, but I suppose you want details."

Jim scribbled while I talked, pausing when Harper's name came up. "Paul Harper's making me nervous," he commented. "He's too smooth for his own good. I've met his kind before, out for a quick profit and never mind what he has to do to get it. What's he need with ruffians like you're describing if he isn't up to no good? I have some questions for him he's not going to like."

When I said the name John Davis, Jim paused again. "John Rock Davis," he repeated slowly, stressing the middle name. "Now there's a name I should know. Something from Wyoming, maybe, or Colorado." He paused, trying to remember, then gave up, tucked his pen behind his ear and the notepad into his pocket, and rose to go. "Your Mr. Davis is right, Lou. You best watch your step now. I've told Katie the same thing. There's an element in Blessing that we aren't used to, and it would pay for you to be more careful."

I knew Jim was right, but his advice made me cross. My town, my friends, my store, my living, my life—no one had a right to barge in and disrupt any of it. But there was no use taking my bad temper out on a leprechaun.

"I know," I said meekly, then added with a touch of asperity as he headed for the door, "and he's not *my* Mr. Davis."

We were long spoiled in Blessing, a small Kansas town that always lived up to the promise of its name, an orderly and peace-loving community mantled under the rule of law. My sister Lily and I were born and raised on the southern edge of Blessing in what was for Blessing a mansion, a big stone house with a pristine white fence around the front yard and a welcoming crescent window of wine-colored glass over the elegant front door. Father had ordered that distinctive window from New York to surprise my mother, his dark-eyed Kansas belle with cameo skin and lustrous auburn hair. The window didn't match the color of her hair exactly, Father told us with apology, but I could tell the pleased smile on Mother's beautiful face made the effort worthwhile. Caldecott's General Store and Dry Goods, our family's flourishing business, sat solitary and successful on the eastern side of the street, directly across from the house. That small Kansas town was a wonderful place for two loved little girls to grow up.

"Not boom or bust," Father would often say, pleased with the play on words, "just Blessing."

By the spring of 1880, Blessing's prosperous balloon was

in danger of bursting. Fear, worry, and desperation were so tangible, they carried a presence all their own. The winter had been bitterly cold but snowless, and spring continued the unnaturally dry conditions with the addition of early and unrelenting heat. Farmers leaned against the counter in my store, and in low voices asked for enough credit to buy supplies and food for their families. "I'm good for it, Lou. You know I am. A good rain and we'll be all right."

That much anticipated "good rain" never came, though, and newcomers saw their dreams literally turn to dust, the first crop that poked forlornly above the thirsty soil destined to fail. If anything green managed to survive in defiance to the heat, it eventually turned into dinner for ravenous hordes of locust that would not be deterred.

Ranchers felt the heat, too, as their grazing land browned and blistered, natural watering holes dried to dust, and the river's boundaries shrank ever smaller.

When I think back to that early summer, John Davis's blue eyes are what first come to mind although the dreaded combination of drought and locust had us all on edge long before I met John. Already by late spring, the rippling waves of heat rose with the golden intensity of midsummer as if the prairies had been set on fire. Even for the old-timers, 1880 was turning into the hottest year in memory. By June the ground had started to dry out and crack, the corn stood stunted, the wheat too brittle, the yellowing grass sharp like pins.

Father, dead almost six years by then, was spared all the pain of that time. Had it been otherwise, I know the summer's terrible events would have killed that good and principled man. Augustus Caldecott, my father and the only man I can name who successfully combined ambition and principle, carried two passions with him to his grave. One, the memory of Rebecca, the woman with the cameo face who became my mother, and the other her perfect image, my sister Lily. The affairs of that summer would have struck so mortal a blow to those passions that Father would not have recovered. I never thought to say

"Thank God" for his quick and sudden passing, but with time and circumstance the words come more easily.

When my father died, he left me the store free and clear, and since I'd worked there with him practically my whole life and had a man's head for business, the bequest made good sense. My sister certainly had no reason to begrudge me the store. Except for a locket my father knew I cherished, he had bequeathed all our mother's jewelry to Lily as well as our family home on the edge of town; and she seemed more than satisfied with Father's decision.

Although he bequeathed Lily the big house, Father's will allowed me to live there as long as I chose; but when Lily married, I moved into more modest lodgings over the store. They suited me as the elegant mansion suited Lily. She needed cordial rooms and comfortable space to be happy. Even as a little girl she was never still, so much energy and sparkle, with gold-flecked hazel eyes and the same tumble of auburn hair that must have been our mother's. My charming, quick-tempered sister was mischievous to the edge of malice and beautiful enough to break hearts, doing so with careless abandon.

Lily was eleven months older than I, but I was always the caretaker. Holding my father in my arms as he lay dying, I saw the pain in his eyes as he gasped the words.

"Lou, promise. Care for Lily. Promise."

"Yes," I answered, unsurprised and unoffended that his last thought was of my sister, "I will. I promise." I knew my widowed father had feared losing Lily, for him a replay of the loss of my mother and more heartbreak than he could have borne. Caring for Lily was as much a part of me as breathing and that final promise no sacrifice. Father had willed Lily the house and the jewelry, but he had given me the store and, more importantly, he had left Lily in my keeping. I always knew I got the better of the deal.

Besides the store I inherited my father's height, his gray eyes, and his business sense. I could balance the store's books in my sleep, buy goods low and sell them for a fair profit, and track everything I bought—from spices to saddles—in my head. Under my direction the store continued to be good business for Blessing and for me. Owning Caldecott's guaranteed me the luxury of independence and the necessity of income, twin requirements to a happy life that other spinsters might find hard to come by. How else could I have survived so contentedly? Dependent on Lily and her husband for the rest of my life? Such an arrangement was unthinkable. So as the store thrived, I did as well.

The first hint I had, the first unsettling inner whisper that something besides the weather was not right, came one late spring day when Roy Winkelman and his family pulled up outside the store, all their belongings piled into their wagon. When the thin, humorless, dark-haired Roy entered the store, his wife and three children sat expressionless behind him in the wagon, not one of them turning to look in as he did so. The whole family appeared burdened and defeated. Roy threw a wad of bills onto the counter.

"That should cover what I owe you," he announced defiantly, but I noticed that his hands shook a little.

"I never asked for this money," I responded, not touching it. "You know your credit's good here." Roy looked ashamed then.

"I know, Lou. You're like your pa that way. A man's word was always good enough for him, and I never knew him to let a fellow starve, but I've sold out. Sold the land. Sold it all. Anything that grew got ate by the grasshoppers. The wife's tired. Hell, so am I. We're going back east to her folks. Her pa owns land and I can work for him."

"Sold out? Who did you sell to?"

"A man named Harper over at the hotel. I heard he was looking for land, and he bought my place for cash. Two bits on the dollar for what I paid for it, but we'll take the cash and be gone."

I walked with Roy outside and reached a hand up to his

wife's arm. "Barbara," I said, "God speed to you. We'll miss you." She looked at me with tired eyes, a woman not yet thirty who looked twice that age.

Who was Harper, I remember asking myself as I watched the Winkelmans pull out, and why would he want to buy their burned out homestead? The house was in need of work and the fields dry as powder. It didn't make sense. I decided to check with Steven and Eliza, who owned the hotel, and see what they could tell me about the man named Harper staying there. Something came up, though—I don't remember what—and I didn't do it, but I should have paid more attention to that inner whisper at the time.

By early June, the Winkelmans weren't the only ones who had left. At least four other families had pulled up stakes, too, and the name Harper was no longer unknown. He continued to buy up any land he could get his hands on, and no one knew why. Rumors flew.

I met the man unexpectedly in the dining room of the Hansen House, Steven and Eliza Hansen's hotel and boarding house. Late one evening I had gone looking for my ward Billy, who helped out at the store and slept in the back room. He hadn't come home for supper but I was only a little worried. Billy had a terrible crush on Sally, the Hansen's kitchen girl, and sometimes he just wanted to be around her. He thought she was the prettiest thing he'd ever seen.

"Liza, is Billy here?" I called, coming into what I thought was the hotel's empty dining room. It wasn't empty. Eliza Hansen was standing next to a lone man seated at one of the tables, finishing his supper.

"In the kitchen, Lou," Eliza answered, "helping Sally clean up, which is where I should be." At her words the man at the table stood.

"Louisa Caldecott," he said, more of a statement than a question.

"I'm sorry. I thought you two would have met." Eliza turned back from her way to the kitchen. "Lou, this is Paul

Harper. Mr. Harper, this is—"

He put out his hand to me. "Miss Louisa Caldecott. I've heard so much about you that I've been meaning to come and meet you."

I shook his hand and met his gaze, taking his measure. Sharp green eyes, fair hair, smooth hands, and a firm, hearty grip. Not much taller than I, but then, I'm a tall woman. At my quizzical look, he laughed and let go of my hand. He had a deep, confident laugh that invited you to join in the joke.

"You're the town heroine, I'd say. Always ready to lend a helping hand. Lots of folks in your debt tell me how you're filling the shoes of your educated and virtuous father, the famous Augustus Caldecott. It must be a sign of the times that Blessing's new patron saint is a woman." His tone was not as complimentary as his words, an easy mockery in it that could have been offensive.

"Well, I've heard about you, too, Mr. Harper. Ready cash and apparently a fervent love for the land, else why would you be so intent on loading up with dry Kansas farmland?" I think my response surprised him, for he gave me a second look with less smile and more attention.

"There could be lots of reasons," he responded easily. "Maybe an Indian School like the First Baptist Mission over in Furrow. Maybe just to help our red brethren."

He didn't look like the kind of man who would be interested in the well being of anyone but himself, but that was hardly a fair pronouncement based on one meeting. I had a lamentable habit of making quick judgments and regretting them at leisure afterwards. Maybe he really was intent on some charitable venture. But he was a smooth, good-looking man with a smile that somehow did not reach his sharp, green eyes; and I'd have bet money it wasn't the education of the Shawnee that brought him to Blessing or the Baptists that were funding him. Something else was going on here.

Billy came to the door of the kitchen. "Miss Lou, I'm comin'." He looked over his shoulder with a sloppy grin of puppy love on his face. "Bye, Sally." He came up to me and I tousled his hair. "You worried about me?" he asked with a little scowl.

"Not any more. I just wondered where you were, is all. It's getting late." I called good night to Eliza and then added, "And good luck with that school, Mr. Harper."

"Paul," he said, meeting my eyes with a look that seemed to be challenging me and laughing at me at the same time. "Call me Paul. We might as well get right to a first name basis since I'm sure we'll be seeing more of each other."

"You plan on being in Blessing a while, then, do you?" I asked.

"Oh, it takes time to build a school. Like Rome. It's not built in a day."

"No," I agreed mildly, "if it's built at all, I'm sure it will take longer than a day." I gave him another appraising look and went out into the cool evening with Billy. Paul Harper was a smart and attractive man—no fool—and something was afoot. He was no more going to build a charity school than an opera house, and he would bear watching.

When Fred Schmidt came in to settle his accounts and say good-bye, I was shocked. The Schmidts seemed to be making a go of it and I hadn't expected them to sell out. Young, industrious, and smart, Fred had worked the land with his father until the older man's death. He'd recently brought over a wife from Germany, and the two of them seemed well-suited to life in western Kansas.

"I can't believe it, Fred," I told him, dismayed. "I know it's tough right now, but I didn't think the grasshoppers ate your flax. I thought they were leaving that alone." Fred looked uncomfortable and nervous, even frightened.

"Ya," he said, in accented English, "that's true, but we're going south. I hear there may be land opening up in Oklahoma territory. Emma and I need to go someplace else."

"I thought you liked Kansas."

"Ya, we like it well enough, but it's time to go someplace

else."

"But why?" I persisted. "Your father's buried here, Fred. I thought Blessing was your home."

He leaned toward me and whispered, "We are afraid, Lou. I am afraid for Emma. Some men came and told us to go."

I couldn't believe what I had heard. "What men?!"

"Three men on horses. Bad men. They come in about three weeks ago. They ride up in the evening. I am washing up for supper. The one man he gets off and comes up to me. I ask him what can I do for him. He tells me lots of folks are selling their places, times are hard, was I going to do the same? I say no. We are all right. We are not selling. He says I am making a serious mistake. I should be thinking of my wife. It's not safe for her out here, he says, not a place a woman should be by herself. He had a gun, Lou. He was a bad man. He says there is a man in town who will buy my land and give me a fair price. I should consider it. Then they go away."

"Just drifters," I told him. "Troublemakers. You know there are always some around. Maybe we should get the sheriff from Scott City." Fred shook his head.

"No, they came back two days later and said the same thing. The next night somebody shot our dog. I found its body laid out on the porch. Somebody shot it and put its body where I would find it." I thought how it must have been for Fred and his wife, just the two of them there on the prairie, feeling threatened and watched and not knowing what—or who—would end up dead next. "Emma is frightened. I am, too. And she is going to have a baby now. I'm just a farmer, Lou. I don't know about those bad men. No sheriff can protect us from them. So I sold out. Better that than what might happen if I don't."

I couldn't speak, couldn't believe what he was telling me, but there was no denying the truth of fear and anger on his face. I pressed his money back into his hand.

"You keep it," I said. "Use it to stake yourself wherever you settle. I don't want it. You don't have any bill here." He protested, but I insisted, "You can get something for the little one." His face brightened a little at the thought of the baby.

"Ya. It's hard to go, but it's not just me now. We need to be someplace where we can live in peace. I am no fighter."

After Fred left, I called to Billy to keep an eye on the counter and went to find my friend Kate Wilhelm, best hand with a needle west of the Mississippi and owner of the dressmaker's and milliner's shop. She stopped working, her mouth full of pins and a tape measure around her neck, as I told her Fred's story. Kate was at least twenty years my senior, widowed, with two grown sons who both lived in Topeka. One son was a lawyer and the other a prosperous cattleman, and both wanted her closer to them. Kate said she stayed in Blessing because it was her home although I thought it had more to do with Jim Killian's Irish charm. I could tease her about Jim most of the time but wasn't in the mood that day.

Kate didn't look surprised at what I told her. "Well," she said, and then was silent. We looked across the table at each other, something fearful but unspoken between us. "There's been talk, Lou."

"What kind of talk?"

"About Paul Harper and his ready money. About why the D'Angelines left in such a hurry. About Gordon."

"Gordon? What about him?"

"He and Paul Harper are thick as thieves, Lou. Honestly, where have you been?"

I shook my head. "Not paying attention I guess. I didn't realize Gordon and Paul Harper even knew each other, let alone that they're conspirators. Of course, it's not as if Gordon and I are close, so I guess there's no reason I would know that. If he weren't married to my sister, I'd cross the street when I saw him coming. You know there's no love lost between us." I added with a small smile, "And I appreciate not having to pretend otherwise with you." Then, serious again, I asked, "What does it all mean, Kate?"

She shrugged. "I don't know, but I don't like it. Jim's

going to write an editorial in this week's *Banner* about the situation. Maybe he can upset the apple cart a little." We talked a bit longer, and then we both went back to work.

On the way out Kate asked, "When are you going to let me make you up a party dress, Lou? I have a bolt of raspberry rose silk that would look wonderful on you."

"What would I do with a silk party dress, Kate? Wear it to count cans of peas? Not quite the color for old maids, I don't think."

Instead of laughing, Kate replied sternly, "Louisa Caldecott, you are not an old maid. You're a beautiful woman who prefers to act like an old maid. The Fourth of July dance is coming up, and you ought to plan on dancing the night away. I know just how your dress should look, off the shoulder with a sweeping skirt. My, oh my! Those cowboys would take a look then with that long neck and those smooth shoulders of yours. Ooh la la!"

I blushed in spite of myself. "You are a tormenting woman."

"No, I'm your dear friend who thinks you spend too much time thinking about the man who got away and not enough time planning to catch the next one."

"I'm putting my fingers in my ears and singing *Yankee Doodle* until you're done," I called and slammed out the door, Kate laughing behind me.

Truth was I really didn't spend much time thinking about the man who got away any more. I had for a long time, it was true, but he was gone; and so was most of the memory of the whole sordid, hurtful time. I'd been five years younger then, more starry-eyed, not happier exactly, but certainly more innocent. Charlie McKinney, blonde and handsome and fun to be with, had not been the man for me after all. So if once in a while I spent a moment wondering how the years would have passed or what our children would have looked like, it didn't mean I was spending too much time thinking about him. I hardly did that at all any more, just a moment here and there.

Billy was waiting for me behind the counter when I got back, his apron on and his hair combed.

"I did just what you told me, Miss Lou. I waited here. I watched folks. I said, 'May I help you?' If they wanted something I got it for them, and I asked them to write down what they took. Here." He pushed the list toward me, his face a little flushed and obviously very proud of himself.

"You did a good job, Billy, a very good job." He grinned at me, pleased.

"I did, didn't I? I'm doing exactly what you tell me. I'm making you proud and not causing any trouble, just like Ma said." His words and his tone touched my heart.

His mother, a widow and the local laundress, had grown ill; and during that illness she must have said to him a hundred times, "Make me proud, Billy, and don't cause any trouble." To me she had poured out her heart. "What will happen to my Billy when I'm gone? Poor, simple boy. He'll go to some home. They'll send him away to the asylum at Osawatomie with all those crazy people. He doesn't belong there," weeping in a way that was painful to hear and see.

So I answered without thinking, just as I'm often accused of doing. "He can stay with me, Flo. I'll have work for him at the store. I'll take care of him, I promise." Hearing that, she relaxed for the first time in many days, slept through the night, and died not long after.

Once given, I could never have withdrawn the promise, and Billy had been working for me for the last eighteen months, doing fine. Truth be told, I liked having the company and knowing the boy was nearby. Billy helped with the heavy lifting, and he always had a cheerful way about him. Besides, he could play the fiddle. He couldn't read anything except his name, and he could hardly add two and two, but Billy could make his fiddle sing. It was a miracle, I told Kate, as if God, keeping so much from the boy, had decided to bestow one precious gift on him. So I had music on request and private concerts whenever I wanted them.

Paul Harper first visited the store the same week I met him. I had my back to the door, mentally measuring shelf space, so deep in thought that I must have missed the bell. When I turned around he was just standing there, watching me with that look of secret laughter I had noticed the first time we met.

"Mr. Harper, I didn't hear you come in."

"No, you were lost in thought. You made too pretty a picture to disturb with the streak of light through the window catching the gold in your hair."

He's flirting with me, I thought, surprised. I didn't understand why because I instinctively knew he didn't favor me, and I surely had no preference for him.

"Well, you've got my attention now," I remarked, ignoring the compliment. "How can I help you?"

"I'll be taking up residence out at the D'Angelines' place, and I'll need some supplies." He handed me a list. "I'll send someone to pick this up tomorrow if that will do. If you could set me up a tab, I'd appreciate it, and I'll pay you the first of every month."

"All right." I busied myself for a moment before adding, "The D'Angelines had a nice place. You should be comfortable there. Lots of room for that school." I looked at him innocently enough, both of us well aware that whatever his plans were, they didn't include a mission school. From the appreciative response I saw in his eyes, it seemed he enjoyed sparring with me.

"You'll be the first to know when the bell goes in."

He made no move to leave, and for just a moment I judged the space to the door and wondered whether I could get by him and out of his reach fast enough. It was a brief, unbidden thought. I caught his gaze again and knew that he had understood what I was thinking and had enjoyed my moment of discomfiture. I considered him dangerous the way a snake is dangerous, one moment coiled in repose and then a sudden strike.

"You'll have to come out and visit sometime, Miss Lou."
He spoke the word *Miss* with a little mocking twist to his
voice.

"I appreciate the offer, but I can't leave the store
unattended for very long."

"Too bad. You're wasted behind that counter."

After he left, I tried to decide what it was about the
conversation that made me shiver at the memory. At face value
it seemed a casual flirtation and an innocent exchange of
words, but I felt again, just as I had at our first meeting, that
Paul Harper was dangerous. I wasn't sure how or why or even
who was threatened. I knew only that he was a man who would
not tolerate opposition and who would be deadly to cross.

The next morning Paul Harper sent two bullies to pick up
his supplies, and because he did so, John Rock Davis stepped
into my life. Serendipity or fate or the hand of God. I know
what I believe.

CHAPTER 2

The store sat right across the street from the big house, both unattached and solitary, and that close, I suppose I should have seen Lily more often than I did. We lived in different worlds, though, and ever since her wedding, it seemed the only thing we had in common was our parents.

When five years earlier Lily had married Gordon Fairchild, the owner of Blessing's bank, she moved into a life that didn't have a lot of room or time for me. I didn't hold that against either her or Gordon. How could I? Lily's husband was becoming more prominent in state politics, with talk about his running for office, maybe even for governor, so she often traveled with him for political or business reasons. They went east for pleasure, too. The railroad's recent arrival in Kansas made the trip more convenient for them. Lily came back from her travels with fine, new, stylish dresses and hats, jewelry that made Mother's look crude, and furnishings for the house no one in Blessing could ever have imagined—oriental rugs and velvet chairs, porcelain and china and colored glass. I always thought Lily loved beautiful things same way Gordon loved her, loving the pleasure of the acquisition and the pride of the display. If either of them regretted that they remained childless, I never noticed it.

I enjoyed a rare visit from my sister the same afternoon Billy was accosted in the alley. She swept into the store with a force of energy that lit the whole place and saturated every corner with her sparkle and an almost visible vitality.

"What do you think?" she asked, swirling before me. The skirt of the dress that was so pleasing her billowed out around her. "Kate just finished it with fabric I ordered from St. Louis. Isn't it beautiful?" The dress *was* beautiful, a shimmery dark green silk that enflamed her deep red hair. I thought that Lily herself looked especially happy and satisfied.

"Yes, it looks wonderful on you, Lily. What's the occasion?" She sat down on a stool across from me and smiled.

"We're hosting some visiting dignitaries tomorrow. Gordon hasn't said who, only that I should look ravishing." She laughed, clearly pleased with herself. "I'm sure this dress will do." Then, abruptly changing the subject, Lily asked, "How's business, Louisa?"

My eyes narrowed at that double warning. My sister never asked about the store because she found the topic boring and she only called me Louisa when something out of the ordinary was occurring.

"Business is fine. The drought and the grasshoppers aren't making it easy for a lot of folks, but we're holding our own. Why do you ask?"

"Can't I ask my own sister how our family business is doing without having a reason?" But of course she had one. "Gordon thinks you're too ready with credit, Lou. He's said a few things that make me worry. Maybe he's right. Maybe you shouldn't be so helpful to some of these folks who are hanging on by a thread. Maybe you should call in their markers to be sure you don't take a loss."

"Gordon said that?" I asked, surprised. My brother-in-law and I would never be close, but he was as aware as I that I had a financially sound business, in the black every month.

Admittedly, I had known blacker months than the past few, but as Blessing's banker, Gordon knew better than anyone that the store was in no fiscal danger. "You can tell your dear husband that I'm fine, the store is fine, and he should mind his own business."

"In a way the store is his business, Lou. He holds the note for the room you added on and he approves all your credit orders. Maybe you should listen to him." The bell on the door rang as a customer entered and Lily stood. "I've got to go. Gordon wants me to put together a special menu for his guests. This is something exceptional for him and he wants everything just right." She absently greeted the woman who had entered and turned to say over her shoulder, "You should listen to Gordon, Lou. You really should. He's just looking out for your best interests."

In a pig's eye, I thought. Gordon Fairchild doesn't like me now, has never liked me, and he'd love to see Caldecott's fail so he could buy the place out from under me. And if for no other reason than that, just to spite my brother-in-law, I was determined to make the store a flourishing and lasting success.

My sister's anticipated guests arrived the next day. I saw Gordon leave early with the buckboard on his way to Hays to meet the train. Lily stopped in later that morning, excited about the company. She followed me about the store as I worked, quiet only when I was with a customer.

"I don't think I've seen you this excited since your wedding day," I told her. "Who exactly are these guests?"

"There's a banker friend of Gordon's from Wichita and an important man from the railroad. Gordon says he's got an opportunity to get in on a business venture that could make us rich."

"Lily, you already are rich."

"I don't think you can ever be too rich," she said soberly. "There's always that wolf at the door." Such a serious remark was totally unlike her, and I stopped what I was doing.

"*Is* there a wolf at your door, Sister? Is something wrong?"

She was gay again, the brief, sober moment past. "What could be wrong, Lou? What in my life could possibly be wrong?" On her way out she stopped, one hand on the door handle, to add casually, "Lou, Gordon and I would like you to come to supper this evening. Come around seven, meet the guests, spend a little time with us. Would you do that?"

I was astonished. Lily would have had me over more often, I believed, except Gordon didn't approve of me. Now as she asked, she had a look on her face I couldn't read, secretive but gleeful, too. My sister at her most enigmatic.

"Gordon aside, do *you* want me to come?"

"Yes."

"Then of course I'll be there."

Later I changed into a dove-gray dress, simply cut with a plain white collar, pulled my hair back with tortoise combs and put on my mother's locket. Billy was over at the Hansens' for supper and Steven had said he could sleep there that night, so I was free for the evening. Throwing a shawl around my shoulders more for appearance than warmth, I crossed the street to our house.

It didn't matter that Lily and Gordon had lived there for nearly five years. It would always be the home of my childhood, our—Lily's and my—house. I knew every room, every squeaky board on every step, the crack in the banister, the complaining pump in the kitchen, the tear in the wallpaper Lily and I had tried to hide from our father by moving the sideboard in front of it. I knew everything about that house and loved it. Father had built it for Mother, had the stone brought in from east Kansas and each rock laid lovingly for her, and so it was precious to me. Yet I had to knock on the front door and await a response as if I were a trespasser and didn't belong there at all.

Gordon answered the door, outlined against the many bright lamps lit behind him. I could hear the low murmur of conversation.

"Louisa," he said, "I'm happy you could join us." He spoke every word stiffly, even my name, always Louisa and never

Lou. That night he and I both knew he wasn't happy I was there, regardless of the spoken amenities. Gordon had never liked me, even from the start, and to be fair, it may simply have been a reciprocal reaction because he knew I didn't like him. Through the years for Lily's sake, I had tried more than once to convince Gordon to admit and discuss our mutual antipathy. Such openness might have helped the relationship, but it wasn't Gordon's style. He had a highly developed sense of propriety and maintained rigid rules about how people ought to act, and I definitely didn't fit into his correct world. For him there was no need for discussion. Women should not be unmarried, live alone, or run a business, and I was guilty on all three counts. His tone always carried a little sense of outrage whenever we spoke as if he resented both my independence and my solvency.

On my part I conceded that I never thought Gordon good enough for Lily. It wasn't because of his receding chin and parsimonious, thin-lipped mouth. Those could be forgiven. How was it his fault that he resembled the picture of Silas Marner in one of my books? He was certainly a sound banker, besides. During the financial panic of 1873, Gordon did not suspend his bank but kept the doors open for the entire alarming time. I couldn't fault his professional acumen.

No, it was instead that I believed Gordon had married my sister, purchased her more accurately, mainly because she would look good on his arm. Perhaps he loved her, but greater than any love he may have felt was the practical and cold-blooded realization that she could be a tremendous asset to him both politically and socially. My faulting Gordon for that suspicion, knowing as I did that Lily had her own agenda for the marriage, was illogical and unfair to him, but I couldn't stand the smug way he showed her off as if she were some prized doll to be exhibited to friends, eliciting their envy or gaining their admiration and support. Still, Lily didn't appear to be bothered by her husband's attitude. Gordon was not miserly with her, and she had not yet grown tired of all the fine things his money could buy. Perhaps behind closed doors he became a tender and loving husband, but looking at that humorless face with its disapproving expression, I doubted it.

I could be as well behaved as he. "Thank you for inviting me, Gordon. It was very kind of you and Lily."

He lifted my shawl from my shoulders and led me into the parlor. "Let me introduce you to our guests."

Lily came toward me, saying, "Lou, my dear sister, we're so glad you're here," and kissed me on the cheek. In my ear she hissed fiercely "Stop gawking, Lou," and then drew back. She may as well have greeted me with a three-headed calf at the door: I was so flabbergasted by her welcome. I could not recall in our history that Lily had ever called me "dear sister," and I was surprised that she could say the words so effortlessly and so shamelessly as if they were second nature and not practically a foreign language. Besides that a sisterly kiss upon greeting was unheard of. I could only stare at her as if she had lost her senses. Then she dropped me a quick wink and a quicker grin, and I knew she was reading my mind and enjoying herself. Her Lady of the Manor role, I realized. When Lily was like that, full of mischief, she really was irresistible.

The two visiting men were impressive, and even as I was introduced, I was mentally trying to put all the pieces together and figure out what type of business venture might link them with Gordon. Josiah Batchelor, owner of the Leavenworth Bank and Trust, and Cy Peterman of the Kansas Pacific Railroad were both wealthy men of statewide, even national, reputation. I had heard stories about Peterman's commanding personality but didn't find him at all daunting in person. I'd recently read that he had outfitted one of his rail cars inside and out with pink brocade and satin for his daughter's wedding party, and I mentioned that anecdote to him when I met him.

He responded with a great, hearty laugh. "An overly reported incident, I assure you, and as reporters usually do, they got it wrong. It was brocade and *silk.*" His obvious sense of delight at confounding the newspapers made me laugh, too.

"I believe I speak for all Kansans, Mr. Peterman, when I say that I am relieved to hear that the level of affectation did not sink to the greater depth."

For just a moment he was stern, surprised even, and then he gave another great roar of laughter. "If your eyes had not been twinkling at me, Miss Caldecott, I would have considered myself properly chastised."

Behind me, someone said, "You must let us all in on the joke, Miss Lou. Something to make Cy Peterman laugh like that should be shared." Paul Harper had quietly entered the parlor as I was speaking to Peterman.

I half-turned toward him. "I don't think so, Mr. Harper. I can't imagine you'd find it humorous."

"I have a well-developed sense of humor."

"I hope it's more developed than your ability to pick your hired help."

Harper didn't pretend ignorance. "Cobb told me about that unfortunate incident. Allow me to apologize for what occurred, but it's my understanding the boy wasn't hurt, and he should be used to being teased by now."

"You may call it teasing, Mr. Harper, if that salves your conscience, but in a civilized community it's viewed as threatening, bullying, and unacceptable behavior. I'll notify the county sheriff if it happens again." As if we had never been interrupted, I turned my back squarely to Harper and spoke again to Cy Peterman, who had been watching the exchange with interest. "Mr. Peterman, I assure you I would never dream of chastening a man who had the good taste to combine brocade and silk."

At dinner, the men kept the conversation purposefully light, avoiding any mention of business or banking, and although I remained curious about what drew Gordon and his guests together, my curiosity was not to be satisfied that evening.

Lily excelled as hostess, flirtatious, charming, with an uncanny ability to say the right thing, encourage a conversation, ask the timely question, flatter and admire. I'd never seen her more beautiful or in finer form, with that deep blaze of hair piled high on her head, her hazel eyes catching the lamplight and sparking gold. Over her breast, she wore a small feminine timepiece of gold-flecked amber that matched her eyes and dangled daintily from a graceful pin formed in the shape of a lily, an ornament as unique and memorable as she. If my sister's gown was cut a little low for my provincial taste, it displayed with just the right combination of style and propriety her beautiful figure. She should be a governor's wife, I thought proudly. She would be perfect.

Gordon sat at one end of the table and Lily at the other with Paul Harper to her right. I could watch her from where I sat, and as the evening progressed, I began to feel a nagging sense of unease with the currents of conversation in the room. I couldn't identify what, but for me something seemed very wrong. When we rose from the table to follow Gordon back into the parlor, my dress caught under the chair leg. I turned to dislodge it and surprised the source of my disquiet. Paul Harper, who had stepped behind Lily to pull out her chair, rested his hands on her bare shoulders and then very lightly caressed them. As Lily stood, Harper murmured something against her cheek that caused her to give him a surreptitious look of delight and satisfaction, a look of cat in the cream. Then she was up and walking to catch up with the others as if nothing had happened.

I stood there immobile, unwilling to believe what that brief exchange indicated but understanding now why my sister's contacts with that man throughout the evening had troubled me. On an intuitive level I must have sensed something furtive and erotic between Lily and Paul Harper. What was she thinking?! If Gordon were to become suspicious, there would be hell to pay. He had a punitive, vindictive streak that would only be exacerbated by such a humiliation. He would divorce Lily without a second thought, and she would be left with nothing.

Lily said from the doorway, "Lou, are you coming?"

"Yes, my skirt was caught."

She linked arms with me and we joined the men in the parlor. I was mistaken, I told myself—I misread the episode—but deep in my heart I knew that was not the case.

Before the men headed for the smoking room to indulge in cigars and brandy, I wished the visitors a good night. "Gordon frowns on a woman engaging in commerce," I told Cy Peterman, "but I'm afraid that's exactly what I am and what I do, so tomorrow's an early morning for me and a full day. I really enjoyed meeting you." I had, too. For an important man whose railroad was changing the face not only of Kansas but of the whole country, he was remarkably down-to-earth and unaffected. I had little regard and less tolerance for people who put on airs.

He raised my hand to his lips. "The pleasure, Miss Caldecott, was all mine." I'm sure I blushed at the courtliness of the gesture, unaccustomed to such gallantries.

As I stepped down off the porch, I was surprised to find that I had enjoyed the evening much more than I'd expected. I would just push that unsettling little exchange between Lily and Harper to the back of my mind and by tomorrow hope it had receded entirely.

I crossed the main, and only, street in Blessing slowly, enjoying the pleasantly warm evening with its light breeze, brilliant white moon, and huge, black, seemingly endless night sky full of stars. Kansas at its finest. As I stepped up onto the boardwalk on the other side, I felt a slight movement and turned to see a figure separate from the shadows at the front of the store. I gave a startled gasp.

"I beg your pardon," said John Davis. "I didn't mean to frighten you."

"Well, you did. What are you doing here?" I asked sharply. The words came out more acerbic than I intended but it was fear that spoke. I suppose the incident with Billy had affected me more than I realized.

"Just out for a walk. It's a nice evening for it. You must be doing the same."

He was hatless, and the clear moonlight turned a streak of his hair to silver. I motioned across the street, where the open windows of the big house spilled lamplight onto the lawn and Lily's laughter into the night air.

"I was at my sister's," I explained.

Davis frowned. "I thought that was where the banker, Gordon Fairchild, lived."

"It is. Gordon's my brother-in-law. He's married to my sister Lily."

"I see."

We shared an awkward pause, I uncertain what to do. I knew I could say good night and go up the side steps to my rooms above the store easily enough, but I found I was reluctant to do so.

Then, as if he too wanted to prolong the evening, John Davis asked, "Does your town of Blessing always quiet down like this?"

"No, not always. I admit it's not exactly Dodge City, but we have our share of activities. Sometimes it's a report from the Ladies Literary Society on the latest novel or the debate club might keep us up with some current controversial topic. We might have a poetry recitation in the Methodist Church or a Farm Bureau band concert of patriotic music. Hard to sleep after any of that kind of excitement, you know."

John Davis had a nice low laugh. "I imagine so." He moved out of the shadows and leaned against the porch railing, giving me a serious look. "People say nice things about you, Miss Caldecott. They say you help hold the town together with your generosity."

"I don't know about that, but I admit that Gordon thinks I'm literally generous to a fault. I just consider well-placed credit to be good business. It was my father who had a truly generous nature. He loved Blessing, and I don't believe there was ever a person he wouldn't help or lend to. Good thing he wasn't a banker, I suppose, but we didn't suffer for all that. I guess if you cast your bread on the waters, it really does come back."

"Have you lived here all your life?"

"Yes. I left to go to Baker University for two years, but that doesn't count because I came back to Blessing."

"Your father held with educating women?"

"He most certainly did." I responded indignantly to the question in his tone, then caught him smiling in the moonlight and laughed. "I'm only sensitive because I must have been asked that exact same question at least a hundred times."

"Did you learn how to run a store at Baker?"

"No, I learned how to be a teacher, but when I got home, Father needed help with the store and I liked that, too. I was good at it, and I wouldn't have to leave Blessing, so that's what I ended up doing. And don't say that all that education was wasted on me. I can recite half a dozen of Shakespeare's sonnets and name all the continents of the world. Not many storekeepers can say that." I quoted softly:

"They that have power to hurt and will do none,
That do not do the thing they most do show,
Who, moving others, are themselves as stone,
Unmoved, cold, and to temptation slow;
They rightly do inherit heaven's graces
And husband nature's riches from expense;
They are the lords and owners of their faces,
Others but stewards of their excellence."

My companion finished easily:

"The summer's flower is to the summer sweet
Though to itself it only live and die,
But if that flower with base infection meet,
The basest weed outbraves his dignity:
For sweetest things turn sourest by their deeds;
Lilies that fester smell far worse than weeds."

The words evoked a brief, distasteful picture that disappeared when Davis continued, "But not the sonnet I would have chosen tonight," then began, "'Shall I compare thee to a summer's day? Thou art more lovely and more temperate.'"

I was startled and flustered and so said, too quickly, "The poet may have wished for eternal summer, but the prospect is more than I can contemplate this year. We haven't had rain in weeks."

He didn't respond, and I wished I would have let him finish. John Davis had the disconcerting habit of making me feel and act gawky and girlish when I was neither. For whatever reason I was not at all surprised that this cool-eyed, dark, lean man could speak a sonnet into the night air. I thought I could have stood on that moonlit porch—that little island of a porch—with that man all night as if we were the only two people alive on the planet. That unlikely notion snapped me back to reality. This must be what moonstruck really means, I told myself, and I was much too old and too practical for that particular malady. John Davis turned to look at me, his own face in shadow with the moon behind him, so I couldn't read his expression.

"You're a man of many talents and some surprises, Mr. Davis. It's late and I need to go in, but I want to say thank you again. I don't know how I can properly express my gratitude for what you did for Billy and me yesterday. I'm deeply indebted to you."

"I'm not the least interested in your gratitude, Miss Caldecott," Davis responded but not unkindly. "Good night." He turned away, lounging against the railing and looking out over the street as if he had dismissed me from his memory.

Still slightly bemused, I climbed the steps to my rooms and after quietly closing the door behind me went to my front window. Without lighting a lamp, I barely pulled back the curtain, standing to the side and careful not to be seen. He hadn't moved, continuing to observe the big house across the street with focused attention. Although I knew it couldn't be so, for an oddly intimate moment I had the distinct feeling that John Davis was as conscious of my presence at the window above as I was of his on the boardwalk below. At last he straightened and gave a slight shrug as if shaking off an unwelcome touch. Then, for the second time in that many days, I watched John Rock Davis disappear down Blessing's broad main street.

CHAPTER 3

In the morning as Billy and I made room for an order of pharmaceutical supplies that had finally arrived, I teased him about being sweet on young Sally.

"Did you see Sally last night?" I asked. He flushed pink and didn't look at me.

"Yeah."

"So what did you do? Did you walk her home?"

"No."

"Billy, that's what gentlemen do. They make sure a lady gets home safely. Did you ask her if you could?" By all rights Sally, at fifteen, would have had cause to be a little annoyed by his obvious adoration, but she was a kind girl generally and especially kind to Billy.

"Didn't think to do it."

"Next time, then, you just say, 'Miss Sally, I'd be honored if I could walk you home.' If she says yes, then you let her take your arm like I'm doing," I tucked my hand under his arm, "and don't rush like you're on the way to some emergency. Walk slowly like this."

I was giggling at Billy's serious examination of my feet

when Kate appeared. We must have made a funny sight with me so tall and thin and Billy not even coming up to my chin.

"No use laughing at us, Kate. I'm giving Billy advice on the proper way to walk Miss Sally home."

"I'm not sure you're the best teacher for that," retorted my best friend, "since you don't let anyone walk *you* home."

"Who asks me?" I demanded.

"Well, I recall Harley Johnson asked after the Methodist social last April."

"Oh, Harley Johnson," I replied scornfully. "I suppose he's nice enough, but he's seventy-five if he's a day, and he walks so slow that if we had started out last April, we still wouldn't be home."

"Harley is *not* seventy-five. He isn't even fifty, I'd guess, and he doesn't walk slow. You just have to do everything so fast. You really try my patience, Louisa," but she smiled when she said it. I knew from experience that I could abide anyone's anger but hers. Lily might be my sister, but I was closer to Kate in temperament and affection.

"Well, for my money it's Jim Killian who isn't moving fast enough. You spend entirely too much time concerned about my connubial prospects when there's a certain Irishman who's been dangling after you for longer than I can remember." Instead of rising to the bait, she changed the subject.

"Jim's editorial about Paul Harper and his suspicious land grabbing comes out on Monday. We'll see what the general reaction is to that."

"Paul Harper was at Gordon and Lily's last night, so you were right about there being some kind of connection between him and Gordon." I told Kate about the evening but omitted the troubling exchange I had witnessed between Harper and Lily. In the practical light of a Kansas June morning, I thought I must surely have misread or imagined the incident.

"So what do you think is going on, Lou?"

"I wish I knew. By all appearances, it was sweetness and light, but I sensed something more complicated below the surface. I suppose it could be a perfectly innocent venture." At her expression I added, "You're right. Probably not so innocent."

Then the bell on the door rang and Harley Johnson himself came in. At least fifty, I assessed, and a master of stating the obvious.

"Hot day," he said by way of introduction. Harley was a slow man and so still a bachelor. I knew that if I had to spend more than thirty minutes in his methodical and plodding company, I'd go crazy.

Kate met my eyes with a smile. "Got to go, Lou," and with a nod to Harley, she disappeared. What a matchmaking and deceptive friend, I fumed inwardly, but I talked to the man easily enough and sent Billy to the back room to fetch Harley's order.

After he left, I thought that Harley was probably as disenchanted with me as I was with him. What do you say to a tall old maid with dusty hands and a pencil stuck in her hair, who spends her time tallying accounts and stocking shelves? Reciting poetry, too, when time allowed. Then I wondered why I hadn't told Kate about my brief interlude with John Davis. The conversation seemed too negligible and yet too private to mention. Maybe some other time. I needed to be sure I didn't turn last night into more than it was, exchanged conversation with a man who was little more than a stranger. Who was John Rock Davis anyway, and why was he in Blessing asking questions? Why had he been standing across the street watching Gordon and Lily's house from the shadows? He must somehow be part of the larger puzzle that included Paul Harper and his thugs, Lily and Gordon, the Kansas Pacific Railroad, and the Leavenworth Bank and Trust. All together too much mystery for my plain tastes.

Saturdays always stayed busy with a steady stream of customers. The farmers, ranchers, and their families rode in early for supplies or to pick up their mail. Cowboys came off the ranches in the evening with money in their pockets, all cleaned up and feeling sociable, ready to enjoy the amenities of the saloon, the beer garden, or the pool hall, or primed for a good home-cooked meal over at the Hansen House.

Although the grasshoppers had passed, the intense June heat and the absence of rain continued to cause everyone problems. Crops weren't growing and cattle were weakening from lack of good grazing land. I had never given it much thought, but I suppose I did offer more credit, take more people on their word, than I should. That practice was more noticeable to me on a busy Saturday. But how to say no? If they weren't newcomers to the area who needed help getting established in their first few years, they were older acquaintances going through hard times. How could I look at them and say, No, I can't help you, can't give you something to feed your children, don't care that your stock's dying? I couldn't do that. I knew we'd eventually get rain, we always did, and things would turn green and grow again, and I would get paid. That's how it had worked with Father, and I saw no reason why the future shouldn't look just like the past. Not boom or bust, just Blessing.

Paul Harper came in just before closing that Saturday. He counted out bills from a wad of cash. "Miss Lou." He never said my name without making me think he was laughing at me. "This should be enough. I'll take those supplies I ordered." I told Billy to load the boxes onto Harper's wagon. With Billy gone and the store empty, the man's tone changed, became smooth and secretive.

"You were pretty as a picture last night. I believe Cy Peterman was taken with you." I said nothing, waiting for Harper to leave, my distaste for him apparently showing on my face. He added quietly, this time with no laughter in his tone, "There may come a time you'll wish you'd been nicer to me. Someday sides may be drawn, and it would be unfortunate if you found yourself with the losers."

Someone came in behind him, and he left without

saying more, but he had been less cryptic, more direct, and thus more worrisome than usual. For me, the summer portended nothing but heat, dust, and trouble.

Ever since he'd moved into the store, I had insisted Billy accompany me to services every Sunday. Not knowing what he really understood, I thought it could only benefit him to come to church on a regular basis on the theory that something might eventually sink in. Many wives appeared to drag their husbands there with the same hope. Billy had surprised me from the beginning, though, by looking forward to attending and actually enjoying the experience. It didn't take long to figure out that he was fascinated by the pump organ and thrilled by the songs. The boy had a strong, resonant voice and a pronounced musical sense, evidenced by his ability to play the fiddle. If the words of the hymns escaped him now and then and he substituted his own, no one seemed to care.

Pastor Smith reminded me that it was what was in Billy's heart that mattered, and then he patted Billy's head as if he were a puppy. "He's a good boy. Let him sing out."

After services, I always fixed Sunday dinner with some special treat for Billy and then enjoyed the afternoon as my own personal time. I might go for a walk or take the buggy out to visit someone I didn't get to see on a regular basis. Sometimes Billy got out his fiddle and played, and the muted melodies entertained me from below as I read or wrote in my rooms upstairs.

That particular Sunday I asked Caleb, who ran the stable and smithy, to hitch up the buggy for me. I planned a visit to the Sullivans to see the new baby in their household, a little girl named Marie, so new she had yet to be taken out and shown off.

Despite the heat that Sunday was beautiful with a broad, blue sky and enough clouds to offer some relief from the sun's warmth. Might be rain there, I thought at first, looking at the clouds, but then decided I was much too optimistic. As soon as I crested Pattycake Ridge, Blessing was out of sight behind me, and all that lay ahead was Kansas countryside. I could look out at the horizon across vast fields and an infrequent oasis of trees and sunflowers and spot only an occasional house in the distance. Several homes were empty and their owners gone—like the Winkelmans and the Schmidts—but some families were still hanging on. Someday, I thought, a hundred years from now someone will ride down the same road and see a settled, hospitable landscape, unaware of the sacrifice and spirit it had taken to settle this demanding, unsympathetic, yet beautiful, land.

Kansas homesteaders lived a harsh and grueling life, especially the women. Isolation from other women, bearing children on an annual basis, caring for home and family with little assistance or encouragement, helping out with the farm work all aged women before their time. Barbara Winkelman's worn face presented the rule, not the exception. Still, the women I knew seemed able to construct a satisfying life with just a few building blocks: faith in God, a rich and wry sense of humor, and an extraordinary devotion to their families. Enduring incredible hardships, they turned Kansas dust into a home. I never came back to town from an afternoon visit without feeling an inordinate pride in the people of Kansas and a little bit of shame at the relative ease and luxuries of my own life.

That day I found myself daydreaming to the steady rhythm of the horse's hooves as I traveled down the road. If I had married Charlie McKinney, we'd have been homesteaders ourselves, and I might already have had children of my own. We would have settled on nearby land, and who knows what course our life together would have taken? Charlie was the first—and last—man I'd ever pictured as my husband, certainly the handsomest man I'd ever seen, and it didn't take me long to fall for him head over heels.

His thick, fair hair caught my attention first. When he rode into Blessing, the early spring sunlight glinted it to gold, and I was lost from that moment. When Charlie McKinney came into the store for the first time, I stared at him in awe, a twenty-year-old woman, educated, confident, with a certain natural poise, suddenly blushing and stumbling over my words at the mere sight of his fair good looks. What he must have thought! Like me Charlie was accustomed to being on his own, and so started out a little shy, but he was full of dreams it didn't take him long to share. I was young, too, so his dreams all made sense to me. In hindsight, even knowing what I know, I think we could have made a go of it. I never wanted for backbone and I loved him so much I would have walked on hot coals if he'd have asked.

I remembered how it felt to step into the shadowed doorway of the stable and see Lily in Charlie's arms, as if someone had suddenly struck me in the chest knocking all the air out of me. He was holding her, crushing her really, saying her name over and over in a tone I had never heard him use before. Certainly he had never held me like that or said my name with such longing or kissed me with the same intense passion. Charlie's back was to me, so Lily saw me first. Her gaze met mine over his shoulder, eyes languidly half-closed but still very aware, content, and unashamed. I could have killed her. When Charlie, sensing my presence, turned and saw me, I could see his color fade even in the dark interior. I don't recall what any of us said at the time. What was there to say after all? Do you choose the one you love or does love choose you? Even then, along with the sharp hurt, I felt an odd pity for Charlie. I knew Lily had no intention of marrying him, not for her the hand-roughening work of the farm or the demanding and unending labor of a rancher's wife, so what would become of all his dreams then?

In the days and weeks that followed Lily said nothing as if the incident had never happened. We lived in the same house then but like silent strangers, not sisters. I couldn't trust myself to talk to her and found it easier to pretend she wasn't there.

Charlie came to see me, his hat in his hands, warm brown eyes pleading for understanding. "I didn't mean to love her,

Lou. It just happened. I can't explain why. I always wanted it to be you but she—" His voice trailed off, but he didn't have to finish his sentence. I understood exactly. When Lily wanted to be irresistible, she was possessed of an extraordinary inner power to make it happen.

What could I say to such a bewildered confession? "You should have told me" was all. He nodded dumbly, poor man, knowing I was right but made helpless by the power of his passion for Lily.

Not long after that exchange, when it became clear to Charlie that Lily didn't love him and he would never have her, he went back alone to the land he'd bought, the land of his dreams. That didn't last, though, and soon Charlie came into the store to tell me he was leaving. By then everyone knew Lily was engaged to marry Gordon.

"I just came to say good-bye, Lou. I'm selling out and going west to Colorado or Wyoming Territory, maybe even to California. I always wanted to see the ocean, and it's not working for me here." I thought that Lily had wounded him as deeply as he had me, but on his way out he paused with his hand on the door. "I was a fool," he said, looking right at me, his voice rough with emotion. "I was blinded for a while, I guess, or under a spell maybe, but it was always you. I wouldn't have hurt you for the world, Lou, and I wish you could give me another chance." At my look, he held up a hand. "No, I can see that's not possible. I've lost my chance then, but you should know there's not a woman who can hold a candle to you. It was always you and I was a fool." That goodbye was the last I ever saw or heard of Charlie McKinney. If his words were any comfort, they were cold comfort at best.

But even when you can't believe it, or you just don't want to believe it because emotion runs too deeply, time really does have a way of healing old hurts. Now I could think of Charlie, of what we planned and how those plans had changed, without that lingering and profound feeling of betrayal. And Father had died in my arms begging me to take care of Lily, so how could

I keep my sister at arm's length, holding that betrayal against her, and still fulfill my father's dying wish? How could I fault someone whose charm and vivacity seemed spontaneous and unplanned, as natural to her as breathing? Lily didn't seduce with intent any more than the flame intended to incinerate the moth.

Francie Sullivan, coming to the door at my knock, was clearly glad to see me. She and Lloyd had three other children and all of them gave me an excited welcome. The vastness of the prairie isolated people, so visitors were an occasion for celebration.

"She's a beautiful baby," I exclaimed, taking little Marie in my arms and talking to her in that silly baby voice adults tend to use with infants. Truth to tell, she was rather a bald, plain child, but in those situations honesty is neither practiced nor expected.

Francie, perhaps two years my senior, laughed. "Lou, she's a homely little thing, but we love her. Marie sleeps through the night and I admit that that and good health are the only attributes I need in a newborn. Besides, the others all started out bald with jug ears and grew into their faces, so I expect she'll do the same. Will you stay for tea?"

I had brought something for the baby and a little basket of treats for the other children, stick candy and raisins and a play ball. As the three older Sullivan children tossed the ball to one another out in the yard, Francie, Lloyd, and I sat under the sparse trees outside their sod house and sipped tepid tea. Marie, making little baby snores, slept in a cradle next to us.

"We heard there's someone on the D'Angelines' place now."

I answered Francie cautiously. "Yes. A man from town bought it. You haven't been tempted to sell out, have you?"

Lloyd said, "God knows there've been enough mornings lately when I'd have paid someone to take the place off my hands, but no, we're not going anywhere. We're too far south, I guess. From what I hear, it's only the places on the east side of Blessing that anyone's interested in buying."

I was struck by his observation and annoyed with myself that I hadn't seen the pattern. It was true, the Schmidts, in fact all the families who had left, had lived in a defined corridor that stretched east of Blessing. The eastern location must mean something, but I hadn't a clue what.

I stayed longer at the Sullivans than I had planned, and even with the long days of summer, the day began to grow dark before I reached home. A stunning sunset streaked red across the sky, and the sun dropped gracefully behind the horizon, leaving behind a mellow June twilight. When I pulled up to the stable, Caleb came out, wiping his hands on his pants.

"I was just saying to John here that you was later than you said you'd be, and I was getting worried about you, Lou." John Rock Davis followed Caleb out of the stable. From the dust on his hat and boots, it looked as if he had been out riding as well.

"You know women, Caleb. Francie and I were just talking too much." I handed him the reins and hopped down. "Were you out yourself, Mr. Davis? Looks like you carry a little Kansas dust on you."

"Enjoying the countryside, yes Ma'am."

As I lifted the empty basket from the buggy, Caleb started to lead the horse inside and I called after him, "Sullivans have number four, Caleb. Perhaps not the prettiest baby but good-natured."

"I believe that's called damning with faint praise," Davis remarked. His dry tone made me laugh.

"I believe you're right although there's something to be said for preferring temperament over beauty."

Davis regarded me seriously before responding. "Yes, I think that's true." Then, after a pause that made me suppose he wasn't thinking about babies at all, he commented, "You only brought an empty basket home with you, Miss Caldecott, so it appears you went out without taking something to protect yourself with."

"You mean a clear conscience isn't enough?" When I saw he

wasn't going to take the matter lightly, I added, "I suppose you're right. I didn't think about it. I've made Sunday calls for years, and I've never felt the need to take a weapon along with me." Davis stepped closer.

"Miss Caldecott, you're not an unintelligent woman, so you must see that your town has changed in the last few weeks and not for the good. It would be a wise idea for you to take protection with you when you're out and about. It can't hurt, and you may have cause to be glad you did." In the twilight I wouldn't have thought he could see my expression, but he must have because he added gently, "I'm sorry. I know you've enjoyed peace and safety here and it troubles you to consider that Blessing is changing, but you're not a child, and you need to stop living in a child's world."

I should have been offended at his words, I suppose, but his tone was kind, not patronizing, and I found it difficult to work up any pique when I had to admit that he only spoke the obvious.

"Yes. You're right. I am being foolish. I'll be more careful in the future. Good night."

After supper, I asked Billy if he'd play his fiddle for a while. He was happy I asked, loving music and always pleased and willing to do anything for me besides. Sometimes it seemed that Billy's true self showed most clearly when he was making music, that the lame gait and thick speech weren't really Billy at all. Instead, the Billy that God intended was this lithe and bright-faced young man, the fiddle tucked under his chin and the bow in his hand as supple and graceful as a willow branch. He stopped abruptly in the middle of a tune.

"You crying?"

"A little," I admitted, "but they're fiddle tears, so that's all right."

"Fiddle tears," he repeated, the look on his face troubled and confused.

I don't know why I was sad that night, whether for the Billy that would never be or for Blessing because I sensed something was coming that would change it forever or because thoughts of Charlie McKinney and my visit with the Sullivans had made me unwillingly conscious of what I did not have in my life.

Fortunately, I am not maudlin by nature, so I brushed the tears away and said briskly, "It's late, Billy, and time for bed. Don't forget your prayers. I'll see you in the morning."

CHAPTER 4

*T*he *Blessing Banner* did not get its due acclaim, unfairly but consistently outshone by the bigger and more colorful papers such as Leavenworth's *Conservative* or the *Kansas Weekly Herald.* I couldn't understand why that should be since there was no denying that "James Killian, Ed." wrote with an Irishman's distinctive and literary flair. I found the front-page article of the next edition so impressive that I cut it out and kept it for future reference.

"MYSTERY MAN! MYSTERY PLAN!" read the bold *Banner* headline out that Monday afternoon. Jim's commentary continued:

When Paul Harper first set foot in Blessing, who could have imagined that his entrance would be the cause of so many exits? What spell does he cast, what power possess, that like the famous Piper of Hamlin, he can pipe so many of our friends and neighbors out of Blessing? Is it for a reason more ominous than simple homesteading? While we who make our living and raise our families in Blessing well understand the appeal of our quiet little community, how is it that a newcomer should feel that attraction so immediately and so compellingly that he continues to buy all the land along the eastern corridor of our fair city? What use can one man have for so much land? How can one man and his disreputable crew of ne'er-do-wells hope to compensate for the loss of so many fine bedrock families? Blessing has always cherished its children, and it is with distress that we see the dust kicked up by the departing wagons filled with the dear little faces of those who should have been the next generation of Blessing's citizens.

I read the names of the departed families with interest and dismay, more than I had remembered certainly. Jim was right, what would one man want with all that land, and where was he getting the money necessary to buy so much acreage? The article concluded:

Surely, we who have long made Blessing our home and revel in its peaceful simplicity can only be alarmed by Mr. Harper's actions and the influx of the unregenerate and menacing band of ruffians who do his bidding. This week a certain prominent female business owner was accosted by two of his disreputable hooligans on the premises of her own establishment. Had not a helpful citizen intervened, we are persuaded that her safety and well-being would have been compromised. Is this the environment in which we wish to raise our families, where our women cannot walk the streets of Blessing in broad daylight without fear and misgiving? We can only appeal to Mr. Harper: 'Step forward and declare your intentions.' What lies behind the increasing camaraderie between Mr. Harper and our own redoubtable citizen, banker Gordon Fairchild? Again we request, 'Mr. Harper, step forward and declare your intentions.' We citizens of Blessing are ever ready to welcome into our midst all who, with hard work and honest industry, wish to become part of our proud Kansas heritage. But how can we be sure that represents your wish, Mr. Harper? We challenge you now, today, to step forward and publicly declare your plans for our blessed community.

I folded the paper thoughtfully, certain Jim Killian had just put the fox among the chickens and equally as certain there would be repercussions. Paul Harper did not strike me as a man who would ignore so public a challenge.

At the end of the day, having overheard a number of store conversations about the headline article, I walked down to the *Banner* office. "Well done, Jim," I told him. He sat with his feet propped up on his desk, reading through the recently published edition. Kate stood beside him, looking troubled.

Jim looked up long enough to remark, "That's not what Katie's saying."

She sent me a quick frown. "Don't encourage him, Lou." Then to him, "These men are not farmers, Jim, and Paul Harper isn't some stolid German immigrant whose chief concerns are grasshoppers and the wheat crop. These are men to be wary of and you've stepped out too far."

"Perhaps you're right, Kate. I can't say I didn't think twice before publishing, but how else to get to the truth?" Jim brought his feet down hard against the floor and stood up. "There's something happening around us and my Irish nose says it isn't something we should welcome. Harper has a bad smell about him. He isn't a man of much delicacy, so it would hardly suit for me to beat around the bush and hint at what I think. If I read him right, he'll respond only to the obvious." He put both hands on Kate's shoulders. "I'm a newspaperman, Katie. It's what I do."

"I know." She gave a weak smile.

"Ah Kate, you needn't look like that. No doubt you're overrating the effect of our little paper and my talents as a writer. What do you think, Lou?"

I saw Kate's furrowed and worried brow and knew I had to agree, regardless of my true feelings. "Really Kate, Jim just did what newspapers are supposed to do. Everyone knows they exaggerate issues to sell more papers."

"A bit too cold-hearted, Lou," protested Jim as I went on.

"Paul Harper seems a man of the world. He knows that's what the press does, and I predict he'll hardly give the article a thought. Freedom of the press is a hundred years old and the law of the land. And even if he is upset, what could he do? Storm in and demand a retraction? Well, on second thought, I suppose he could do that, but there's no scurrilous libel in Jim's editorial. All he did was ask a few intelligent and searching questions that Harper can choose either to answer or ignore. I don't think you have any cause to worry."

"You are my dear friend, Louisa," Kate answered, "but sometimes I could shake you. You only see what you want to see and that's both endearing and dangerous. Mark my words—we have not heard the end of this."

She and I left together with the sunset behind us. I tucked her hand under my arm.

"It was a brave thing Jim did, Kate, and I really don't think anything will come of it. But I know you're worried, and I am too, in a way. You said I see only what I want to see, and John Davis told me that I live in a child's world. Maybe it's just that I don't want things ever to change."

Kate looked at me curiously. "I suppose I should be honored that Mr. Davis and I agree on something. Your tone when you mention him tells me you hold him in high and perhaps affectionate regard."

"Neither high nor affectionate, but he stepped in and spared both Billy and me from humiliation if not injury, so you shouldn't be surprised if my tone expresses my gratitude."

Kate opened the door to her shop and turned to examine my expression. "I don't think it's gratitude I'm hearing, Lou," she said gravely, "but I suppose I could be wrong. I haven't had the pleasure of meeting your knight-errant yet, so I won't say any more until I do. I can't help but wonder, though, if this isn't another of those times that you're wearing blinders. No, no." She put up a hand. "Don't look at me like that. I didn't mean anything by it. Anyway, thank you for trying to make me feel better. I hope you're right about Jim and that I truly am creating a mountain from a molehill. I must say it's burdensome to care for a man so obstinate and mulish."

"Maybe, but I'm guessing the good outweighs the bad for all his obstinacy."

Kate responded to my observation with a little secret

smile I had noticed before in women in love. "Yes. Yes, it does."

I finished the walk home, lost in thought. In my heart of hearts, I thought Kate was right to be alarmed, and Jim Killian should watch his back. Paul Harper's recent remarks to me about being on the side of the losers had sent the ominous message he had intended, of a contest of some kind, one with both winners and losers in the end—and pity the losers.

Once home, I went in search of Father's rifle. As a girl I had been taught how to shoot, and although never especially good and now very out of practice, I could still handle it with some assurance. In the back room I took the weapon apart, oiled and cleaned what needed attention, then loaded it.

"Billy, you are never to touch this gun," I ordered sternly. "Never. Do you understand?" He had surely seen firearms before, even gone hunting with men who carried rifles like this, but I was not confident that he understood the deadly seriousness of a loaded weapon.

"Yes Ma'am." Billy was a child in so many ways and I felt I had to repeat myself to him even more firmly. He looked at me with a surprisingly mature expression. "I know. A gun can kill you. I won't fuss with it. I promise. What you gonna do with it?" I laid the rifle on the shelf under the counter so it was out of sight and only I would know it was there.

"Nothing," I answered. "I sincerely hope not one thing."

That evening after dark, Lily came to visit me. I couldn't recall the last time she had made the effort to climb the stairs and visit me in my rooms. Many months at least. Her knock came late enough that I was ready for bed, in my nightgown and my hair down.

"Who is it?" When I heard her voice, I threw on a wrapper and opened the door. "Lily, is something wrong?" The moonlight behind her formed a kind of halo around her head. How deceptive, I thought, for Lily was anything but angelic.

"Nothing's wrong. Is it that late?" She gave a cursory glance at the reading lamp and the book turned upside down to keep my place.

"It's past nine, Lily. Your company must be gone."

"Gordon drove them over to Hays to meet the afternoon train. He's not back yet." I watched her move restlessly about the room.

"Anna did a wonderful job in the kitchen. Her special recipe chocolate cake is always perfect."

Ignoring my culinary small talk, Lily picked up our mother's picture from the end table. "Am I that much like her, do you think, Lou? As much as people say?" I came up behind Lily to look over her shoulder at the photograph.

"You're a mirror image. The hair, the face, the eyes."

"She was so beautiful, wasn't she? I wonder how different our life would have been if she had lived." The two of us gazed at the picture for a quiet moment and then Lily sat down, still holding the photograph in its heavy gilt frame. "Lou, do you ever think about leaving Blessing?"

"Never. Blessing is home. Where would I go?"

"New York, San Francisco, Chicago, Boston, Philadelphia. How can you think you're happy here when there's so much in the world you haven't heard and seen?"

"You forget I was at Baldwin for two years when I went to Baker University."

Lily looked at me scornfully. "Oh fuss. Baldwin is just another Blessing. You don't know what wonderful places there are, what sights and stores, what music and theater. Really, Lou, you've buried yourself in this little backwater. Why don't you think about moving where there are bright lights and glorious activities?"

I motioned to the book that lay on the arm of the chair. "I don't need to leave Blessing to appreciate and enjoy other places. I can read about them."

"What's that worth? What can words on a page tell you about how New York's streetlamps light up the sidewalks after a rain or how an orchestra's sound fills a concert hall? You've never heard a Mozart opera performed surrounded by velvet hangings and padded seats and women dripping with diamonds that catch the glint of the chandeliers, so you don't really *know*. Have you ever seen the ocean or heard the waves pounding against the shore so strong that you think it's your own heartbeat? Lou, you have no idea what you're missing." Her voice and expression were so animated and passionate, I thought I was appreciating something about my sister I had never fully understood before.

"Lily, that's you. My dear, those are your loves, not mine. I'm small town. I'm a single reading lamp and a well-worn book and sunflowers and wheat fields. I'm Blessing, Kansas. San Francisco and New York hold no attraction for me."

There was an enigmatic urgency in her look, and she slid down to sit on the floor by my feet, resting her cheek against my leg.

"Oh Lou, you should think about going. You're buried in the store just like Father was. You spend your days thinking about molasses and undershirts when there is so much more to life. You should sell the store and move to where there are bright lights and maybe some man right for you."

"Sell the store," I repeated incredulously. "Lily, you're talking foolishly." I stroked her soft hair. "What would I do? Sell the store and then what? Spend the money and then what would I do? That's just not sensible."

She lifted her head and looked up at me, gave me a disdainful glance. "You're always so sensible, aren't you, Lou?" Her mocking tone stung.

"And if I am? Should I discard everything that gives my life purpose? Why should I leave this town where our parents are buried, where I have friends and activities, a life and a livelihood, all to take in bright lights and dripping diamonds? Those are meaningless things that have no real worth."

Lily rose gracefully. "You're so superior, Lou, so proud of being good and doing the right thing. How scornfully you dispose of the things I love. Why don't you just come out and say that I am a vain and superficial woman? God knows you've thought it often enough."

I was ashamed because some of what she said was true. "Lily, I didn't mean that the way it sounded. Please forgive me. But can't you see that I'm not you? Blessing is my home. I don't think I could live anywhere else, even if I wanted to. I love it here."

"You should think about leaving, Lou," she repeated, as if I hadn't spoken. "I know Gordon would buy the store from you, and he'd give you a fair price, more than fair. I know he would. You're my sister, after all."

I stood, taking her firmly by the shoulders and looking her in the eyes. "Lily, I am not going to sell the store, not to Gordon, not to anyone, not now, not ever. I'll never leave Blessing." I said every word firmly and distinctly so there was no chance of being misunderstood.

When I finished, she only stared at me. Some emotion crossed her face, anger maybe, or frustration, or even something close to despair.

"Then you'll die in Blessing an old maid, an unloved and unwanted old maid. Who'd have you here? Gordon's right. Your plain speaking drives away anyone who might be interested in you. No man wants a woman with ink on her hands, dust in her hair, and a receipt book for a heart." That was the Lily I knew best, the one who could wound so deeply, using words like darts, always aiming for the heart and seldom missing. She flung herself out of the room, leaving the door open behind her. I heard her feet clattering on the wooden steps, and then she was down the stairs and onto the boardwalk.

I closed the door and, turning down the lamp, went to watch her through the front window as she crossed the street and stepped onto her own porch. The front door opened before she could reach the knob, and Gordon stood silhouetted against the light behind him. Without a word Lily slid past him to enter, and I thought as I watched her that she kept a distance between them as she did so as if she could not bear to brush against him or touch him in any way.

That unsettling exchange with my sister occurred the same week I lost Billy, literally lost him. The morning started innocently enough with the arrival of an overdue shipment of leather goods.

"Billy, go and tell Caleb his order's in and then come straight back home." Billy, always glad to get out of the dim confines of the store, took off his apron and left. Some considerable time later, Caleb came to collect his goods.

"Did you bring Billy along with you?" I asked as I pulled his wooden box from the back room. Caleb hoisted the crate onto his shoulder.

"No. He come down to give me the word my order was in, and we talked a while about the weather and such. I ain't seen him since." Caleb saw my frown. "Now, he's fine, Lou. Playing hooky, like as not, just like a regular boy. Boys is all the same in here," he pointed to his chest, "even if he's a little lacking up here." He motioned to his head.

"I suppose."

But Caleb didn't really understand. Billy interpreted everything so literally that it wasn't like him not to come straight back if that's what I told him to do. As people came in and out of the store, I asked after Billy but no one had seen him. The initial small disquiet I had felt was turning into a real, full-blown worry. If we hadn't had that run in with Harper's bullies, I probably wouldn't have been picturing such frightening scenes in my head, but I couldn't help myself. What could have happened to him between the stable on one end of town and the store on the other without someone noticing? At closing, I turned the sign on the door and went out to look myself, checking every alley as I went, asking people that I passed if they'd seen Billy. By now it was a gnawing concern that I couldn't ignore.

Even little Sally over in the Hansens' hotel kitchen could tell I was worried. She shook her head in response to my query.

"No, Miss Lou. I ain't seen him for a couple of days now and sure not today."

I could see on her face that my mood was affecting her, so I found myself saying in comfort, "Straw-haired, thirteen-year-old boys don't disappear into the air. I'm sure he's somewhere safe and just forgot about the time. Will you send him home if you see him, Sally?" I just wished I could believe my own words.

By then it was dusk but a June dusk that still held a lot of daylight. I hoped that by the time I got back to the store, Billy would be sitting on the steps waiting for me or sprawled asleep on the bench by the door, but his stocky figure was nowhere to be seen. I went inside to get a hat, determined to go out on horseback looking for him. I could ride well, had learned to ride astride for safety and speed's sake, and that's what I planned to do to find my missing boy. Billy wasn't in Blessing anywhere, so by elimination he must be outside of town, I had no idea where or why.

I stepped out of the store, hat in hand, pulling the door shut behind me, when I saw a horse and rider plodding slowly up the street. Riders, really, a broad-shouldered man on a large bay horse with a shorter passenger in front of him, who was holding on to the saddle horn with both hands for dear life. Once they reached where I stood, John Davis slid the boy off to the ground.

"I believe this young fellow belongs to you."

"William Philip Stringer, where have you been?"

Billy was a pitiful sight, grimy with sweat and dust, his hair plastered to his head, and his face sunburned. When he came toward me, his slight limp looked more pronounced than usual. He sat down heavily on the steps and pulled off his boots and then his socks. Even from where I stood, I could see one big toe was sporting a large, soft blister.

"Hurts," he said, probing the blister with a forefinger.

When I looked at Davis, I'm sure my expression reflected my bewilderment. "I must be missing something important here. Where on earth did you find him?"

John Davis dismounted and threw the reins over the rail. "A good mile and a half outside of town, heading west. The only way I could persuade him to come back with me was telling him how worried you'd be. He was a young man on a mission."

I sat down next to Billy, who was still fascinated by the blister and poking it with his finger. "You worried, Miss Lou?" He looked up at me sheepishly. "Was you worried about me?"

"Of course I was. You didn't tell anyone you were going away, Billy. I looked everywhere for you, but I couldn't find you. You were supposed to come straight home from Caleb's, remember? What were you doing out in the countryside?"

He mumbled a single word that sounded like *surprise*. Davis had come up to rest one foot on the step, meeting my puzzled glance with a shrug and a look that held more than a little laughter.

I turned back to the bedraggled boy, who had shifted his attention to his other big toe and seemed to be scrutinizing it for a matching blister.

"Billy, I am sometimes slow about things, and I admit that I don't always understand you, but what in the world are you talking about?"

At my exasperated question, Billy finally stopped examining his feet. "I went to find the rain. Caleb said there was rain in the next county. I asked him where that was exactly, and he said down the road a piece, so I went to bring you home some rain. I heard you say a little rain would solve a lot of problems. I never did find any, though, and I guess that was a good thing, 'cause I forgot to take a bucket along."

The relief set me off, and once I started giggling, I couldn't stop. I put a hand over my mouth, afraid of hurting the boy's feelings, but I just couldn't stop. There he sat, streaks of dirt across his forehead, sitting on the porch with his bare feet dangling and an expression of self-disgust on his face as if the only thing that had kept him from bringing rain to Blessing was lack of a good pail.

Finally I caught my breath enough to say, "You must never leave town without telling me. Never. Do you promise?"

Billy nodded. "Yes, Ma'am."

"Now you stay right there. I have fresh lemonade and cookies for you." I leaned over, hugged him, and repeated, "You're never to leave town without telling me. I was that worried." I stood. "Mr. Davis, please join us. I don't know what your business is, and whatever it is, it's none of mine, but I can't imagine how you find time to get anything done when you're so busy rescuing us. We must seem like the most inept pair you've ever met."

"I agree the two of you are quite a pair, but inept isn't the word I'd choose."

He sat down on the bench next to the door. I went up the side stairs, then came back down precariously balancing cookies and a pitcher of lemonade on a tray. After handing Billy his treat, I sat down next to John Davis on the bench.

Billy, his mouth full of cookie, saw the gun at Davis's side. "Miss Lou's got a gun under the counter. I ain't allowed to touch it, though."

"I do listen," I admitted to Davis's inquiring look. "I don't like to admit being wrong, but I was and you were right. I have been living in a child's world."

"That's not always a bad thing," he responded. I couldn't read his expression.

"No, I suppose not. If you're a child. But those days are long gone for me."

"Not that long gone."

"I won't see twenty-five again. My sister says I'm hopeless, just a bookish, plain spinster with ink on my hands and dust in my hair." I said it flatly without emotion. "And I think she's right, just like you were right."

He turned and took my chin in his hand, tilting my face up so he could look at me with those blue, those sky blue, eyes. "Your sister is not right at all," he said very distinctly, looking straight at me. "I was right but just barely. You live in a child's world because like Billy, you shine with a child's honesty. But make no mistake, you are a grown woman, and there's no way a man could miss that."

For a moment I thought he would kiss me, right there on that bench in clear view of anyone who happened to pass by, and I found that I didn't care, that I wished he would, and anyone who saw it could go to the devil.

"Can I have another cookie, Miss Lou?" asked Billy with his mouth full, looking over at us from his seat on the steps.

The moment dissolved. Davis took his hand away, and I turned to Billy. "No, it will spoil your supper." When I stood, John Davis did the same. I rested my hand briefly on his arm and smiled. "I wish rain was so easy to come by that all you had to do was send someone out to fetch it in a bucket. But since it's not, I appreciate your bringing Billy home."

"Even without the rain?" he asked with the ghost of a smile.

"It will rain sooner or later. It always does. Good always follows bad. It's just a matter of holding on and not giving up while you wait. You took good care of Billy. I don't know why you took the time to do that, Mr. Davis, but thank you."

"No trouble." He swung himself into the saddle, then sat looking down at me from atop his large bay mount. "And someday I'll tell you why I took the time."

CHAPTER 5

The following Monday Jim ran another lead article about Paul Harper in *The Banner* that again questioned the man's intentions and asked where he got the cash he used to buy land. At the end of the day, I had my elbows propped on the counter, reading the newspaper spread out before me, when Harper himself entered. He handed me a list of supplies, then flicked a thumb at the paper.

"I would think a busy woman like you could find more to do with her time than spend it with a two-bit rag like that."

"It's always an interesting read. Jim Killian has a way with words."

"He should be more careful about how he uses them." His voice held barely concealed disgust and a more obvious threat.

I took the list from him and began taking items from the shelves and putting them in a box on the counter. "Does the truth make you uncomfortable, Mr. Harper?"

"Not as uncomfortable as Mr. Killian will be if he doesn't exercise more restraint in his editorial duties."

I heard the anger in his tone and responded, "He has the constitutional right of freedom of the press."

"This is western Kansas, not Boston. The only rights I know of go to the one with the best aim and the most money."

"The war has been over for fifteen years and guns no longer decide the issues. We have the rule of law now."

"The rule of law is only as strong as the man of law you have to enforce it, and I haven't noticed anyone up to that particular task in Blessing."

"We have a county sheriff just a few towns over if we need him, but we've managed to exist through some very troubled times without resorting to guns or bloodshed." I moved from behind the safety of the counter to get some items from a side shelf, and he followed behind me as I did so.

"I can't imagine that as an intelligent and perceptive business woman you honestly believe the pen is mightier than the sword."

"I believe there's no reason people can't get along with one another as long as they don't get greedy. That way we won't need the sword at all." I turned my back to reach up for something, and he put both his hands on my waist, then moved them down my skirt in a caressing, suggestive manner. I turned around to face him, closer than was comfortable for me but determined not to retreat.

"You forget yourself, Mr. Harper, and I find your conduct offensive."

He removed his hands but did not back away. Instead he brushed my cheek lightly with the tips of his fingers. "Has anyone ever told you that when you're angry, you flush a becoming shade of pink? You're a beautiful woman." His previous tone of annoyance with the newspaper was gone, replaced by something evocative and unpleasant.

Behind him the door opened and Kate entered the store, calling too brightly, "Lou, I saw the Fargo delivery wagon come through earlier. Is that bolt of blue muslin I ordered in? I'll need it for Wilma Marks's Fourth of July dress."

I slipped back behind the counter as Harper stepped away with a relaxed indolence, then turned to touch the brim of his hat to Kate.

"Ma'am." He put money down on the counter and picked up the box of supplies. "Always a pleasure, Miss Lou. Always a pleasure."

After he left, Kate asked, "What did I interrupt?"

"I don't know. I honestly don't know. The man doesn't like me, but for some reason known only to him, he's pretending to be quite taken with me. I don't know what to make of it unless he's just doing it because he knows his attentions are unwanted and he enjoys my discomfort."

"It could be he does find you attractive, Lou."

"I realize there are stranger things in heaven and on earth than some man being interested in me, but I'm certain that's not the case with Mr. Harper. He has another motive for making me feel uncomfortable. I just don't know what it is."

"He had a little talk with Jim earlier this afternoon."

"About the *Banner* articles?"

Kate nodded, taking a seat by the unfired stove. "Jim says he felt it was a veiled threat. Harper said he was not going to stand by and allow these attacks on his name to continue, and Jim said he was only asking questions, not making attacks. I'd guess Harper understood that as Jim saying, 'If the shoe fits, wear it.' Harper said if Jim was smart and valued his enterprise, he'd highlight some other topic in the next edition. And Jim, because he cannot keep that Irish mouth of his shut, said something like, 'We'll have to wait until the next edition to see, won't we?' Then Harper told him he hoped that Jim understood how very upset he would be if he saw his name on the front page again."

"Paul Harper is not a man to be trifled with," I said. "When he wants something, I think he intends to get it, and heaven help anyone who gets in his way. I just wish I knew what it was he wants."

As I started to pull the shade on the door for closing, John

Davis entered. He took off his hat and stopped just inside the doorway.

"You're closed."

"No, not yet. Just in the process." He saw Kate, who had risen from her seat by the stove. "Kate, this is John Rock Davis. I believe I've mentioned his name to you and how helpful he's been on a couple of occasions. Mr. Davis, this is my friend, Kate Wilhelm. She owns the dressmaking establishment down the street."

"Mr. Davis, I've heard a great deal about you, all of it good. Those of us who hold Lou dear are very appreciative of the services you've offered." I thought he colored a little as she spoke, but that may have been the result of late afternoon shadows inside the store and nothing more.

"I was glad to be of some help."

"You've been in Blessing how long now?"

"Two weeks."

"Staying at the Hansen House, I imagine." A question, not a statement. At Davis's brief nod Kate put out her hand, and when he took it, she used the gesture as a pretext to step closer and examine his face thoughtfully. Then, with a tone that indicated she was satisfied with what she saw there, Kate said briskly, "I'm glad to finally meet you, Mr. Davis." To me she added, "Lou, I was serious about that blue muslin. You know how we all look forward to the big Independence Day dance, and Wilma Marks has her heart set on wearing blue with red ribbons. So patriotic. Will you be coming to the dance, Mr. Davis?"

"I haven't given it any thought, Mrs. Wilhelm. Would you recommend it?" They seemed to understand each other in an immediate and suspiciously amiable way as if they shared a common bond from which I was excluded.

"I believe I would," she answered slowly. "I think you might enjoy it, although, of course, that depends on the company you keep. We look forward to the celebration all year long. Wonderful food and lively music. This year we'll celebrate it on the Saturday before, since dancing and drinking on the Sabbath doesn't settle well in Blessing. What a pity it's too dry for our usual fireworks show."

"When the blue muslin comes in, Kate, you'll be the first to know." I interrupted her nostalgic reminiscences without compunction. Kate's prosing on to John Davis about food and fireworks was definitely suspect.

Oblivious to my tart tone or perhaps just accustomed to it, Kate only smiled. "Good. Such a pleasure to meet you, Mr. Davis." Then, as if an afterthought, she added, "Lou, I still have that raspberry silk waiting for you."

After she left, John Davis raised his eyebrows in a question. "Raspberry silk?"

I opened my mouth to explain and then stopped. Kate had been purposefully matchmaking, and I wasn't sure I wanted or needed her assistance. I sidestepped his comment by asking, "May I help you with something, Mr. Davis?"

He gave his little half-smile. "First, you might call me John, and then I wondered what you knew about the Schmidts, the family I heard left town suddenly a few weeks ago."

"Fred Schmidt and his father lived here about seven years," I answered promptly. "Still during my father's lifetime, so maybe even longer. Both of the Schmidts were hard-working men. After his father died, Fred brought his sweetheart over from Germany and they got married. He and Emma seemed to be doing really well. Fred had some progressive ideas about using river water for irrigation, and he'd heard about this wheat called Turkey Red that you planted in the fall. Everyone got pretty excited about a second wheat crop and as far as I knew held Fred in high regard. I couldn't believe it when he came to say they were leaving." I told him the story Fred had told me, about the men who had threatened them and the death of his dog. "I believe it was those men in the alley, the ones picking on Billy, who scared the Schmidts away. Maybe they threatened others, too."

"Why would they do that, do you think?"

"I don't know, but I'm sure there's something afoot. You'd have to be blind and deaf not to realize that somebody has a plan of some kind, but I don't know who or why. None of it makes sense to me. When the Winkelmans left, I thought it was just hard times and this dry, hot summer. I hoped my offering credit would convince people to stay. Now I believe there may have been more of a story behind all those others who sold out. I guess I should have done something then or should do something now, but I don't know what. Why are you so interested in Blessing?" As I talked, John Davis had pulled up the chair Kate had vacated and sat with his hat balanced on his knee, listening intently.

"Curious, is all. Blessing seems like a peaceful place where folks would want to settle and stay. It's an established town with good land and good neighbors. Some may have left because of the drought, but it seems like an awful lot of folks in just one area pulled up stakes about the same time."

"I don't know who you are," I told him honestly, not fooled by his innocent tone, "but I don't think you were just passing through Blessing, and I don't think you're a man who walked over here to ask me some questions just because you're curious."

"What do you think?"

"I think that somehow you're part of what's going on in Blessing, but from what I've seen, you're a good man and not here to hurt anybody. I guess if I'm going to trust anyone, it might as well be you. Maybe there will come a time when you'll return the favor and trust me enough to let me in on the secret."

"It's not a matter of trust, Lou." He slipped easily into using my first name.

"What then?"

"Necessity. Obligation."

"I don't know what that means, John. Everyone's been speaking in riddles lately, and I'm finding it more bothersome than I can say."

"I can tell. You get high color in your cheeks when you're annoyed."

That observation coming from John Davis didn't cause the same revulsion Paul Harper's similar remark had generated. Far from it. I didn't take the time to consider the disparity in my reactions, however, just responded bluntly, "And you're changing the subject. Fine with me, but don't underestimate me. I know you didn't come here to ask questions about the Schmidts out of idle curiosity."

"Could be I came here just to see you."

"Could be, but I'd say that was unlikely," I retorted, but inwardly I wished it were so. No use being too honest with him, though. Too early for that.

"Then it was tobacco." He wasn't a smooth talker like Paul Harper, and his expression was harder to read, so although I thought he might be teasing, I couldn't be sure. I set some tobacco out on the counter.

"On the house."

He stood and deliberately counted out some coins. "It wouldn't be right to take advantage of your good nature." As he dropped the tobacco into his vest pocket, he added, "I know there's no reason for you to credit anything I say, and I know I have no right to say it, but you need to be careful, Lou. I want you to be careful." I hadn't thought six words could be so warming and so alarming at the same time.

"What is it you know, John?" He laughed a little at that. "I know you will look fine in raspberry silk. Will you be at that Fourth of July dance?"

"I imagine so. I've gone every year I can remember."

"Then I expect I'll be there as well." On his way out he stopped to grin back at me. "I'd never make the mistake of underestimating you, Lou. I've seen what you can do with a broom."

CHAPTER 6

The Blessing Bank and Trust was set up by Gordon's father Clarence, who in some respects had been everything Gordon was not. Clarence Fairchild and his wife Lizbet had been friends of my parents, and I remembered Fairchild Senior as a large man distinguished by unruly hair and thick muttonchops, with nothing parsimonious about him. I don't recall him as a particularly charitable man either for that matter, but he was expansive in his gestures and hearty in his speech and people took to him. Gordon, to his misfortune, favored his mother. Lizbet Fairchild outlived her husband, but as soon as she died, Gordon proposed to my sister. I always suspected that Gordon's mother had not liked or approved of Lily, forcing Gordon to bide his time until his mother's death. Perhaps as the mother of a sole son, she would never have thought any woman good enough for him, but I found it telling that Lizbet Fairchild was hardly cold in her grave when Lily came to me with the news.

"Lou, I'm getting married." I was still recovering from the sight of my sister in Charlie McKinney's arms, so naturally I thought she was talking about the two of them.

"I hope you and Charlie will be happy," I responded stiffly, not hoping that at all.

Lily gave a small, artificial laugh. "Oh, I'm not marrying Charlie McKinney," she explained with a touch of defiance. "I'm marrying Gordon Fairchild." She wore a serious, almost calculating, expression as she spoke.

"You love Gordon Fairchild?" I asked, incredulous.

"Oh, love," she said scornfully and then at my shocked look added, "I care for Gordon, Lou. Of course I do. And he certainly wants to marry me. It's an arrangement that will suit both of us."

"An arrangement? Is that what it is? You make it sound like a business deal."

Lily gave my comment serious thought before she spoke. "That's what marriage is, Lou, a business deal. That's all it's ever been. A woman is a commodity, and in your business you should understand what that means. She has something the man wants, and she makes sure she gets something in return for it—something generous. They make an agreement to trade services. That's all marriage is."

"That's not much different from the ladies who live upstairs at the Palace Saloon," I remarked dryly.

"You're right, little sister. It's not much different from that at all. You're just a romantic, which Gordon says comes from too much book learning. He says those two years at Baker ruined you for any man."

I knew then that there would be no love lost between my future brother-in-law and me, a prophecy that quickly proved true.

Gordon's was the only bank in town, and it galled me that he had clear access to my finances and an unencumbered knowledge of my financial situation, that I had to go to him for permission to do what I knew was the right thing for my business. The addition to the store was a good example. As newcomers arrived to settle the land, the store's business naturally grew as well. Space became cramped, filled with everything from pickle barrels to boots, and I stacked things out in the alley for lack of storage space inside. Obviously I needed more room, but when I requested a loan to add on to the store, Gordon at first refused even to consider it. He had the nerve to tell me in that patronizingly pretentious voice he used whenever we talked business that it was something he—he!—needed to think about first. Only when I threatened—and Gordon knew it was no idle threat—to take my banking business to Hays did he ungraciously capitulate. He realized that both the store and I had a good reputation, that I was financially solvent, and that the Hays bank would have agreed to my loan request in a moment, especially with the store as collateral. What had they to lose after all? Even when Gordon finally told me he would arrange the loan, he had to do so with a condescending warning about the risks involved.

Now every time I had to go to the bank, I purposefully went around noon, hoping my brother-in-law would be home for lunch, and I could slide in and out without having to interact with him. No such luck that week, though.

Gordon saw me from his office and stepped out long enough to say, "Louisa, come and see me, please."

"I've been summoned," I said with an expression that made Mr. Cuthbert, the teller, smile. Since Gordon was my sister's husband, I tried not to speak disrespectfully about him to others, especially to his own employees. I'm a terrible poker player, though, and it became quickly evident to the bank's staff that Gordon and I shared a mutual antipathy.

He sat behind his desk, leaning back in his chair with his fingers tented together in front of him.

"Gordon," I said by way of greeting. "How are you this afternoon?"

He only spent amenities on people who could bring in some return on the investment, so without prelude he began, "Lily and I have been giving a great deal of thought to your future, Louisa."

"So kind," I murmured, "but so unnecessary."

He frowned at my tone but went on, "We feel, Lily and I, that it's time you considered your future realistically. The work you do is demanding, both physically and mentally, and hardly suitable for you in the long term. What expectation have you for your future other than long days in a dimly lit store and a set of modest rooms above it? That can hardly be what you wish for your life, and certainly it is not to my or Lily's advantage to have such an eccentric in the family."

"You talk a great deal of nonsense, Gordon. It's not as if I've become a bull whacker or taken up dancing in a hurdy-gurdy house. I run a store, a perfectly respectable if unexciting venture for a woman, and I expect to do that for a great many years to come, God willing. You really shouldn't upset yourself on my account. I don't think it's good for your digestion."

Whenever I refused to take his advice seriously and responded with a soothing tone usually reserved for crying babies and barking dogs, Gordon invariably flushed deep red with annoyance and anger. To be truthful, I suppose I used that tone for the perverse satisfaction his obvious irritation always gave me.

"Louisa, Lily and I have your best interests at heart. I'm willing to extend an offer to buy your store, a generous offer that would allow you to live comfortably for some time." He mentioned a figure that was indeed generous.

"What do you suggest I do when the money runs out?"

"A woman with money will not be alone long."

"Ah, I see. I should purchase a husband with the proceeds of the sale. Now I understand the plan, but, Gordon, have you priced husbands lately? Even with the figure you mentioned, I'd be hard pressed to afford the latest model although now that I think about it, I might be able to get a discontinued version at a discount. Maybe there's even bulk pricing." I gave an unladylike snort and stood up. "Do you ever listen to yourself, Gordon? Sometimes I swear you are possessed by a disagreeable demon whose only purpose in life is to aggravate me."

"You are prone to an unbecoming levity that gets in the way of good judgment, Louisa," he countered, rising also. "You would be wise to set aside any personal dislike you feel for me and consider my proposal objectively. I don't believe you'll ever receive a fairer or more generous one." I saw that he was very serious about the offer he had made and so responded in a similar tone.

"You misunderstand me, Gordon. I didn't mean to imply that the offer was not fair or generous, only that you're wasting your time. I'm not in the market to sell the store. Not now. Not ever."

I winked at Mr. Cuthbert on my way out, poor man, who must come to work every day under the unrepentantly critical eye of Gordon Fairchild. Over the past years I had begun to think, "Poor Lily" as well. She had contrived a business bargain with Gordon years ago, and I wondered whether she was now using Paul Harper to repent of that decision. I was afraid she would only be exchanging one evil for another, and who could guarantee that it would not go from bad to worse?

When I delivered Kate's blue muslin later that week, she took the fabric from me and examined it closely. "It is pretty, although with Wilma's coloring it may not be the best choice. But she *will* have this particular shade of blue, and she has her heart set on this style." Kate pointed to one of the fashion plates in a magazine that lay open in front of us. I met my friend's look over the page and both of us giggled. The thought of stout Wilma Marks shoe-horned into that hourglass dress was too much. "I don't mean to be unkind," Kate went on. "Wilma's a very nice lady, but I couldn't for the life of me talk her out of it. We can only hope it doesn't completely cut off her breathing during the dances, otherwise she's likely to keel right over."

"There's something so appealing about theme dressing," I commented cattily. "I'm not sure we'll be able to dance, we'll be so busy saluting her." Then, feeling guilty about my uncharitable remark, I added, "I'm sorry. I didn't mean that.

You're right. Wilma is a nice lady and she deserves exactly what she wants, so if that's red, white, and blue, God bless her."

Kate turned a page in the magazine. "Now this is what I see for you, Lou. A square neckline and only a little sleeve. See how plain the bodice is cut? It's just a straight line down to the skirt, which would show off your little waist perfectly."

"Too much skin showing for me, Kate."

For a moment we contemplated the picture wordlessly. The dress on the page was beautiful, less embellished than current fashion and so would suit me better. With my height I looked and felt ungainly and school-girlish in flounces and flourishes.

"Maybe." Kate gave me a cool, examining look and turned to eye the illustration quietly, mentally rearranging the parts of the dress to fit me. Then she reached for a pencil and with a few sketches redid the pattern so the design was exactly right. "Yes. That's it. That's you, Lou." She put the pencil down, pleased with herself, and added casually, "I liked your Mr. Davis."

I started to say, Not *mine,* but we had known each other a long time, and it would be useless to pretend with Kate. "I like him, too. At least I think I do. Problem is, I don't know anything about him, and he's not volunteering any information. John Rock Davis is as much a mystery as Paul Harper."

"John Davis is not like Paul Harper at all, Lou, as you know if you have the sense I think you have. There's something there, for sure, something deep, but I would say Mr. Davis is as straight a man as I've ever met."

"Straighter even than Jim?"

"Oh, Jim," Kate said, laughing. "There's nothing straight about an Irishman, especially Jim Killian, God help me." She brought out the bolt of raspberry silk she had mentioned earlier and spread it out on her worktable. "Look, Lou. Isn't it beautiful? When's the last time you got a new dress for yourself?" The stunning material, a deep raspberry rose color, shone lilac purple where it caught the light. I couldn't help but stroke the smooth, cool fabric.

"It has been a long time. Over a year at least and that was that gray dress with the white collar I wore to Lily's the other evening. I've never had the nerve or the occasion to consider anything as grand as this." I examined the bolt of radiant silk soberly. "You don't think it's too much?"

"Too much money? Lou, I'll give you a deal you can afford, believe me. This is between friends."

"No, no, I meant too much for me to wear, too splendid for a plain woman. You can tell me the truth."

"You're a goose, Louisa. Sometimes I could just shake you. Honestly, for a woman who can run a business at an enviable profit, raise a child not her own, make time to visit new babies, recite Shakespeare, and ride astride, there are times you don't have the sense God gave rocks. Just trust me. This will be perfect for the Independence Day dance. I can't wait to get started, and when I'm done, you'll understand."

At the Hansen House, business seemed to be flourishing. A steady stream of traffic kept Steven and Eliza busy, drummers passing through, cowboys off the trail who wanted a bath and a soft bed, passengers from the stage who spent the night and picked up their journey on the succeeding day, speculators, ranchers on their way home with their pockets full of cash, even traveling theatrical entertainers and performers.

Lately Billy had found watching the hotel's parade of guests mesmerizing. Sometimes after supper he disappeared, and I would eventually find him sitting on the porch of the hotel, clearly enthralled by the variety of humanity passing by. He was full of questions, too. What's a corset? Where's Ohio? Is a stage like a stagecoach? Had I ever seen an opera house? Since he also asked about "soiled doves"—he guessed a whole flock of them nested over the Palace Saloon—I wasn't sure it was exactly the kind of education he should be getting.

"Liza, your place is booming. I don't believe you've had a vacancy for weeks." I had come to retrieve Billy after supper and take him home. Eliza Hansen, heavy with her third child, smiled wearily.

"I know. Steven chides me for my ingratitude because I have the audacity to complain. All those years when we scraped along and didn't know if we could stick it out, borrowing from Peter to pay Paul, borrowing from *you*, Lou, and grateful for your patience with us. Now that we're doing well I'm not allowed to complain that my back hurts and my feet are so swollen I need Steven to pull off my shoes in the evening."

"After the baby comes you'll feel more yourself, and this dreadfully hot summer will be behind us, too. Just be sure you don't overdo it and cause some harm either to you or the baby."

"I won't. Steven's ambitious, but he comes from a line of Free-Staters who didn't hold with slavery, so he allows me to sit down when I feel the need. My problem is getting up again. Pretty soon someone will have to tie a rope around my middle and pull me up like a heifer from a mud hole." Liza was by nature a plump, round-faced woman, so the extra weight of her pregnancy had to be hard on her, and with five-year-old Jeffy and Arnie, just turned two, she had her hands full. "Billy went to walk Sally home, Lou. They left about ten minutes ago, I'd say."

"He's not a bother to you or her, is he?"

"No, Billy's a good boy and good sized for his age, so I think Sally feels a little safer with him on her way home. There's been an element around town that's made her uneasy."

"Yes, I've noticed that, too. Not your run-of-the-mill cowboys. It's a little worrisome."

After I said good night, I went out onto the broad hotel porch that wound around three sides of the building. The porch was so large that when the hotel was full, men simply spread their rolls on the porch and slept there. That night a few people relaxed in rocking chairs, fanning themselves, enjoying the quiet evening and the welcome cooler breeze that blew faintly off the prairie. John Davis, sitting on the front steps, rose when I came out.

"Hello, John. I thought you said you were staying here."

He nodded. "Mrs. Hansen sets a good table."

"Liza's famous for her fried chicken," I agreed. "Sometimes she lets it be known that she's planning on chicken for a Sunday, and people skip church just to line up early so they can get a seat. I suspect the parson spends some time the night before praying for Sunday pork chops."

"Speaking of Sunday, I wondered if you were free this Sunday afternoon."

"I am," I answered cautiously.

"I thought you might be willing to take me on a tour of the area, point out the places that went vacant as people moved out, and show me who's left. I'd be obliged."

"That curiosity again?"

"Yes, Ma'am."

"You know what it did to the cat, John, so I'd suggest you be a little careful, but if you really are interested in those eastside homesteads, I can show them to you. Sunday would be fine. Besides, I'm in your debt, so how could I say no?"

I was sorry as soon as I spoke because he got cool and formal, losing the open friendliness that had been in both his tone and his eyes. For a hot summer night, the temperature on that porch dropped considerably.

"You don't owe me a thing, and you don't need to do anything you don't want to do." Clearly he was a proud man, surprisingly sensitive, and I'd made a tactical error in judgment if I wanted to get to know him better. I'd have to be more careful in the future. If there was a future for us, and I was beginning to hope there would be.

"Forgive me. I didn't mean that the way it sounded. It was my poor attempt at a joke. Gordon says I'm prone to an unbecoming levity, and as much as it pains me to admit he's right about anything, there's probably some truth to that. Even if you'd never been kind to Billy and me, John, I would still be pleased to spend time in your company and show you Blessing."

He caught and held my look of apology and after a pause, his engaging and completely unnerving smile slowly appeared. I wondered whether I would ever get used to the breathless, slightly disoriented reaction I had to that combination of smile and eyes.

"You have a way of taking the wind right out of a man's sails, Lou. I'll look forward to Sunday then."

Walking home, I admitted to myself that it was doubtful this was any kind of a courtship. At least not any kind I was used to, no plodding conversation or painful compliments, such as Harley Johnson employed, and nothing like the wild, exuberant rush of emotion I had felt with Charlie. There were compliments, I supposed, although I didn't think that "taking the wind right out of a man's sails" was the type of pretty phrase that usually made a girl's heart beat faster. Fortunately, I was past girlhood and had never been prone to rosy-colored imaginings, even in my younger years. I knew that John Davis was here for some purpose known only to himself and that he might well be using me to accomplish it. Still, a number of years had passed since Charlie McKinney, and I thought I would do Harley Johnson some physical hurt if I had to hear him prose on about the weather one more time, so I guessed I would take my chances with John Davis and see where they led. It didn't hurt that once in a while I saw an appreciative gleam in his eyes when he looked at me or that I felt uncompromisingly safe when I was with him.

Sunday dawned another clear, hot, dry, blue-skied day like so many days before. I put on a light blouse, a practical skirt, and a hat to protect me from the sun. I had tried the homesteading woman's slat bonnet, but it was too much like blinders for me and too confining, so instead I pushed my hair up into a soft, wide-brimmed hat and pulled the cord tightly under my chin. John got off the buggy to help me up, but without thinking I pulled myself up into the seat before he had the chance even to extend a hand. At his glance I must have flushed.

"I'm sorry. I didn't mean to be rude. I'm just used to doing things on my own and taking care of myself."

He climbed up next to me and took the reins. "Nothing wrong with a strong-minded woman" was all he said.

Riding out of town, I was momentarily caught up in memory. "When Lily and I were little girls, Father took us out riding in a buggy exactly like this. We were so small that our feet didn't reach the floor from the high spring seat, so every time we'd hit a hole or go over a rock, up we'd fly. We had the best time, all three of us giggling out loud at each bump, Lily hanging onto Father and me hanging onto Lily. Our bottoms were sore for days afterwards. Lily held onto Father so tightly he had a bruise on his arm in the exact shape of her little hand."

"You look like you reach the floor all right now."

I laughed a little ruefully. "I didn't stop growing when Lily did, so I definitely reach the floor and then some."

As we got farther out of town, the great vacancy of territory began to sink in. Before then I had not really appreciated how much land Paul Harper had purchased and how many families had left. But after we passed the Millers' and the Winkelmans' quarters, and then stopped at the Schmidts' empty place, I could only stand, staring, my hand at the base of my throat.

"What is it?" he asked, standing next to me, seeing what I saw but with a stranger's eyes.

"So many families gone, John, so much empty land. What is Harper going to do with all of it?" Paul Harper owned everything as far as I could see: dried fields, islands of sunflowers, stands of trees, and vacant homesteads. "I guess it didn't really register until right now. Why does he want this corridor of land, do you think? What will he do with it?" Davis didn't answer and when I looked over at him, I thought, He knows. He knows exactly what Paul Harper is up to. But he said nothing, and I didn't pursue the matter. John Davis wasn't a man to be cajoled or bribed into indiscretion, and I wasn't going to waste my time or dignity trying. Instead, once more in the buggy, I changed the subject.

"What do you think of Kansas, John?"

"I think it's flat," he answered with a laugh in his voice.

"It's not that flat," I protested. "We have some hills. Look north. There's one over there."

"Lou, that is a pitiful excuse for a hill. I wouldn't even call it a hill—it's more like a pile." His tone made me laugh, too. "Have you ever seen real mountains?"

"Pictures in books, is all. Have you?"

"I've seen the Rockies in person more than once, and I own a little place along the Laramie Mountains in Wyoming Territory."

"Is Wyoming where you're from then?"

"No. A man named Calvin Lockhart left me that land."

"That was generous of him."

"I did Calvin a favor during the war, and he invited me out to Wyoming to see his place. I was young and didn't have any ties, so I went. It was as pretty a place as I've ever seen. Plenty of green grazing land, clean cold water, dark forests wherever you looked, and surrounded by mountains. I never breathed air like that in my life." I hadn't heard him talk so freely before, and there was a new enthusiasm in his voice that I liked the sound of. "Cal's gone now, and I've got the papers saying he passed the place on to me, but I haven't been back there since." Something in his tone made me turn to look at him as he drove, his strong, almost harsh profile with the wisp of silver at his temples appearing more severe than before.

"Since what?"

"We had an argument about a pretty woman."

"Oh, that."

At my remark he turned to me with a quick, quizzical grin. "I imagine you know about that, don't you?"

"I know that the sanest men of the greatest equanimity can turn into irrational and blithering idiots when it comes to a pretty woman. I've seen it happen often enough with my sister Lily."

"I've seen your sister." I felt a brief and ignoble pang of dismay. Well, it was to be expected. He couldn't be in Blessing any amount of time without seeing Lily about town, her dazzling hair and face and that striking figure immediately noticeable.

"Then you can understand what I mean. Father was always advising young men away from our house. I can't tell you the cow eyes and the serenades and the fist fights that followed her around. You men and a pretty face! It's awfully predictable behavior. At least women have figured out there's more to a man than what meets the eye."

"Yes, there's the bank account."

"Because of your apparently unfortunate experience and your broken heart, I'll forgive that remark and its slur against my sex."

"I don't think my heart was broken," he said contemplatively. "More like wounded pride."

"Most of the time it's one and the same, isn't it?" I recalled Charlie McKinney. "What happened to the woman?"

He followed my change in conversation. "She decided she didn't want me, and last I heard she decided she didn't want old Cal either. She turned us both down, married a whiskey drummer, and left for Sacramento."

"A whiskey drummer. What a letdown for her and aren't you fortunate you escaped?" I thought that woman must have been either intellectually impaired or addicted to the bottle to turn down the young man that John Davis must have been for a prosaic whiskey salesman. As if I'd known him then, I saw clearly what he would have looked like, understood how he would have spoken and acted. I patted his arm. "If it's any consolation, I'm sure the alcohol and the travel have taken a toll on her, and she's aged ten years to every five of yours. She could probably pass for your grandmother now."

He laughed out loud, which I guessed was rare for him. "Thank you."

"I understand that young men's hearts can be sensitive objects and easily damaged, but why haven't you gone back to Wyoming? Don't tell me the place has too many love-struck memories for you?"

"No, not that. Time, I guess. Other things got in the way like earning my keep and making a living."

"What do you do, John? How do you make a living?" He didn't answer for such a long time I wondered if I had stepped over an invisible line and asked something unacceptable.

Finally, in an expressionless voice, he replied, "I'm a shootist, Lou. I sell my expertise with a weapon to those who can afford it. I offer protection for a price. I've done work for the Cattlemen's Association and the Pinkertons to name some."

John sat quietly intent on the road ahead as I sorted through that information. Then I asked, "Who are you working for now?" When he didn't reply, I answered my own question. "I know. Necessity and obligation." When he still said nothing, I added, "You aren't wanted by the authorities, are you?"

"No, Ma'am. I've managed to stay on the right side of the law."

I considered his comment seriously before responding, "Well, that's something, I suppose. I'm relieved to know your picture isn't hanging over in Sheriff Badger's office." "Yes, so am I." I looked at him quickly, suspicious of his tone, but he was looking straight ahead with not even a twitch of a smile. His sober expression notwithstanding, I suspected he found me amusing and was enjoying the conversation at my expense.

Thinking back on what he told me, I commented, "I can't believe you were old enough to have fought in the war."

"We joined up in the last eighteen months."

"We?"

"My brother Tom and me. I was just of age and he was too young, but by then no one was asking volunteers a lot of questions."

"Which side did you fight on?" Sometimes I thought I detected a slight Southern drawl and wouldn't have been surprised to find he had fought for the Confederacy.

John turned to look at me. "Does that matter to you?"

My father's daughter still, I gave sober thought to his question before I answered. "I don't think so, not any more, but it mattered ten years ago."

"Blue or gray, north or south, all those bodies scattered across the fields were just as dead. It didn't matter what side they were fighting on."

"I think what we believe and how we live is important. Shouldn't what we're willing to die for count for something good?"

"I don't know that a man's thinking about that as he's dying. Someone smarter than me will have to figure it all out. I don't have the answers."

Something in his bleak tone caused me to ask, "Where's your brother now, John?"

"Tom's gone. He died at Five Forks, outside Petersburg, Virginia. We spent nine months of bloody hell around that city, and he died eight days before the surrender and the end of the whole damned war."

"How terrible. I'm sorry."

"We got separated. When it was all over, I didn't know where he was. It took me over a day, body by body, to find him. I guess I should be grateful he died right off and didn't lie there wounded and bleeding, cursing, weeping, begging for water like so many did. Those voices are a sound I'll never forget. We were just eight days away from peace, but Tom was gone."

I knew intuitively that he hadn't shared that memory with many people, realized there were depths to him I hadn't expected and private feelings he kept to himself. That he trusted me enough to give me a glimpse of those feelings made me want to say the right thing but, a rarity for me, I couldn't find the words.

"Did you go home after the war, then?" was what I finally

said because I felt the conversation had veered onto a course that was difficult for him and wanted to spare him the pain.

"My mother's brother and his wife raised Tom and me after our parents died. They got free farm labor, and we got two meals a day and beds in the barn in exchange. We joined up to get away from the farm. I wasn't going back there." I was silent for so long that he turned to look at me. "This is too serious a conversation if it makes you that quiet."

"'Too sad for mirth, too rough for rhymes,'" I quoted softly, then took a breath and said, "I was wishing that you would have come to Blessing. I was just a girl right after the war, but I remember a lot of soldiers passing through on their way west. Some of them were missing limbs, some still wearing their uniforms, and some of them looked ill and haunted. Most, though, just seemed excited about being mustered out and on their way to a new life. Dr. French came here after the war and George Marks, too. Have you met George? He's the barber. George was passing through, met Wilma, and just stayed on. Sometimes he goes a little crazy, not dangerous or anything, but you can tell he's not himself. Wilma just takes him home, and he's back to normal in a day or two. Blessing has been good for him. I know you'd have liked it here, so sane and peaceful. Blessing would have been good comfort for you." I thought to myself that there might never have been a Charlie McKinney in my life if John Rock Davis had been part of my growing up years.

"I never settled any place, Lou, and I don't know much about comfort. No place ever seemed right. Something was always missing. I've been on the move a lot of years."

"I can't imagine not having a home, a place that you love that's yours, a place to come back to."

"Like Blessing." A statement, not a question.

"Yes," I said, "just like Blessing."

As we passed two neighboring homesteads still inhabited, I pointed out, "Jess McGruder and his boys live there. The McGruders are a pretty tight-lipped family, but I saw them just last week, and they didn't say a word about leaving. And the Palmers' quarter section is next to the McGruders behind that stand of hickories and maples. I haven't heard that they're planning to leave. Maybe Harper just hasn't gotten around to them yet." When we were on our way back to Blessing, I motioned to a set of dusty wagon tracks that veered off to the right. "The D'Angelines' place is just up ahead. It sets way back so you can't see it from the road. That's where Harper settled."

"So I heard."

Ahead, coming toward us from town over Pattycake Ridge, I saw three riders. As they neared, I identified Paul Harper along with the man from the alley, the one who wore the seaman's cap, and a young, handsome man with a small mustache and dark hair curling down to his collar. The three spread out in front of us so that John had to pull the buggy to a halt.

"Miss Lou, you should have told me you were coming. I'd have put out the good china." Harper turned his attention to John. "I don't believe I've had the pleasure of meeting your escort."

Behind him the man in the cap said, "He's the one," and Harper's eyes lit with interest.

"So you're the man with the Colt Peacemaker. You made quite an impression. I hoped we might meet."

John said, mildly, "Your hopes are realized, then," but he didn't introduce himself.

Harper turned his attention back to me. "Now don't tell me, Miss Lou, that you were just going to pass by without stopping in to say hello. You've hurt my feelings."

"We're just out for an afternoon ride." I explained and then stopped speaking as the two men with Harper pulled away from him and moved over to my side of the buggy. The younger one sat so close he could have reached out and touched me. I found my voice. "I believe it's later than I realized. We need to be on our way."

John must have felt me shift closer to him on the seat because without comment he gave the reins a gentle shake. Before we could move, however, the long-haired young man next to me put a hand out lightly to my shoulder. "Maybe we ain't done talking yet."

I pulled back as if his touch were red hot and sat stiffly, pressed against John's muscled shoulder for support, furious at the young man's effrontery.

John's words were directed to the man John's words were directed to the man with his hand on my shoulder, but he looked right at Harper as he spoke. "I would take my hand away if I were you." Something unspoken passed between the two men that caused Harper to stop smiling. He still sat loosely in the saddle, still appeared relaxed, and was still lazy in his speech, but I knew something intangible had changed. I could feel it. Harper studied John seriously for a moment. A knot had formed in my stomach, but beside me John seemed unperturbed and casual about the situation.

Finally Paul Harper spoke. "Oba, what are you thinking of? That's not how you act around a lady." Harper gave me an insincere smile. "I apologize for Oba's behavior. He's spent too much time in saloons and not enough in church."

Oba found the remark funny and hooted with laughter before he finally pulled away from me. "Now that is true. No offense meant, Ma'am." But of course offense was meant and was taken as well. John and I rode away in silence, leaving the three men behind us, and it was a while before I drew a deep breath.

"I believe they are bad men," I stated simply.

"They are that." He looked over at me. "You all right?"

"Yes, but the notion that we can't ride our own roads without being accosted by ruffians and desperadoes infuriates me. If I were a man I'd be a sheriff and spend my life putting those kinds of men behind bars where they belong."

"It's been obvious to me for some time that you're not a man, for which I'm grateful."

"Are you complimenting me, John?"

"That was my intention."

"I find it hard to tell sometimes, is all."

"I'm not much given to flowery language, Lou, and I'm a fairly formal man, but I'll try to be clearer next time."

"No, that's all right. You don't need to do anything you don't want to do." He smiled faintly, recognizing his own words. "I'll just ask if I'm not sure. I get my fill with Harley Johnson, who comes calling periodically and is fond of flowery speech when he's not declaring that it's sure been hot and dry." I flattened out my voice at the last words and gently mimicked Harley's slow, unemotional tone.

"I wouldn't think that you'd easily tolerate dullness in a companion."

"Oh, Harley's not a bad man, and I should be ashamed of myself for making fun of him. He's kind enough and a hard worker. He's just very boring through no fault of his own. I try to be tolerant, but after thirty minutes in his company, I find myself creating outrageous excuses just to get away."

We came into Blessing, flanked by Lily's big house on one side and the store on the other. John pulled up to the boardwalk at the front of the store and came around to help me down. This time I waited for him. He swung me down with both hands around my waist and did not let go immediately, which I did not protest.

"You can tell me if you find me boring, Lou, without feeling you have to make up stories to escape."

I looked up at John with deliberate thoughtfulness before saying, "I think it would be unlikely, if not impossible, for me to be bored in your company. If anyone gets disinterested, it will most likely be you with my small town chatter. Couldn't we just agree always to speak the truth to each other? Then neither of us would have to bother with excuses at all." I pushed away from him and held out my hand. "Deal?"

He didn't hesitate but took my hand firmly in his. "Deal."

Later it occurred to me that he never had told me what side of the war he'd fought on, but by then it no longer mattered.

CHAPTER 7

Jim Killian's third *Banner* editorial was nothing short of inspired:

We will soon celebrate the auspicious commemoration of our country's birth. From this great land, watered with the blood and tears of our heroic forefathers, have grown the freedoms of which we are so proud and on which we stake our future, those freedoms of speech, religion, and not least, the press. How can it be, then, that a man new to our community would dare attempt to curtail that precious freedom of the press? How can it be that a man whose roots do not go deep into Blessing's soil and soul, who is in fact a stranger to us, would attempt both to threaten and intimidate this humble editor, whose only objective is the preservation of our beloved community? Yet it is so! I ask you, reader, would a man who has nothing to hide so fear attention that he would demand his name no longer appear in any articles in this humble paper? Would one whose intentions toward Blessing are honorable terrorize its citizens? Surely we must look with repugnance on one who attempts to use brute force on a civilized population.

Jim waited until the second column to come out and

actually name Paul Harper, but his was an outraged and fervent article. Clearly, Jim Killian felt that Paul Harper posed a threat to Blessing. I could imagine the newspaperman hunched forward over his desk scribbling away, his glasses low on his nose and the tips of his ears turning red as he became more impassioned.

Regardless of Jim's sincerity, I felt an uneasy foreboding as I read. I could recall Paul Harper's earlier expression as he spoke of the newspaper's unwelcome attention to his business dealings. For a few moments the smooth-talking man with the pretense of civilization was briefly replaced by the true Harper, a ruthless and determined man who recognized only the power of money and violence. I was proud that Jim had shown such courage of conviction, but at the same time I knew a very real apprehension for him and for Blessing. Novels often portrayed the fight against oppression with a certain noble and fearless rectitude, but in real life it felt much less gallant and far more frightening.

I was awakened two nights after the paper came out by the sound of gunshots, accompanied by a great deal of hooting and shouting. Cowboys "cleaning out a town" as folks called it, I thought with disgust, and got up to look out the window. Too much liquor after too many hot and dusty days on the cattle trail sometimes fueled high spirits and caused a noisy disruption. Such a display was annoying and only a little frightening, since no real harm had ever been done, but every time it happened, I felt an increased charity for the local Temperance Society. In the moonlight I could see only the dust kicked up by the departing horses, counting three or four riders hellbent out of town. Then as I saw doors along the street open one by one, Billy pounded on my door, calling my name.

He stood with his nightshirt shoved into his jeans, wide-eyed and excited. "Mr. Jim's got trouble," he said. He pulled at my sleeve. "You should come."

"What kind of trouble?"

"Bad men made a lot of noise. I think they broke stuff. You

should come."

"All right. Wait right there for me."

I went in to pull a skirt over my nightdress and tie back my hair with a ribbon. By the time Billy and I reached the *Banner* office, a number of people were already there, milling around in a curiously helpless way. The cloudless moonlit night and the lamps several people carried illumined the destruction of what had once been the newspaper office. As I approached I saw a chair lying on the street and the window through which it had been thrown shattered. The door was hanging crookedly off its hinges. Even the sign over the door, proudly stating *The Blessing Banner,* had been pulled down and lay in the street, broken in pieces.

"See," Billy said excitedly, "trouble for Jim."

I pressed past a small group of men that included Caleb and Steven Hansen and pushed inside. Even in the dim interior, the office was a terrible sight. Nothing remained whole. The furniture seemed to have been chopped into kindling, and the press was smashed beyond repair. As I walked, pieces of type skittered around my feet. All Jim's books had been ripped apart, and I could see through the door into his sleeping quarters in the back where feathers still flew from his slashed mattress. Lamp oil had been splashed about the room and its acrid smell was overpowering.

Once inside, I heard Jim Killian before I saw him. He was muttering a string of very profane and colorful oaths under his breath as he stood in the center of the room observing the destruction around him. Kate clung to his arm.

I went up to Kate and put my arm around her shoulders. "What happened? Who did this?" My voice came out a whisper.

Jim said fiercely, "I'll give ya three guesses, and we won't count the first two. Who do y'think? Who's been threatenin' to keep me from writin' any more articles about him?" Emotion always intensified his Irish brogue, and tonight the accent was as thick as I'd ever heard it.

I didn't follow his words at first, still caught up in the idea of rowdy cowboys under the influence of too much alcohol. Then, finally realizing his meaning, I protested, "No, Jim, you must be mistaken. Do you really believe Paul Harper is responsible for this?"

"Oh, darlin', I'd stake my life on it." Jim moved away to step into the back room. Behind me some of the men were going through what was scattered about, trying to find anything that could be salvaged. Caleb brought in the chair from the street and set it in the office, one small, undamaged item in so much destruction.

I turned to my friend. "Kate, I'm so sorry."

She was afraid but angry, too. "Thank God Jim was with me," she said without shame. "What if he'd been here when they came? What would they have done to him? Oh Lou, he'd be dead. He's such a cantankerous man—he'd never have stood by and just let this happen. They'd have killed him for sure."

As I looked around, I didn't see as much anger at work as meanness and a calculating, arrogant bad temper intended to teach Jim a lesson, maybe to teach all of us.

Steven Hansen said to Jim, "We'll finish cleaning up in the morning, Jim. Why don't you come over to the hotel? We've got a room for you, no charge."

"This is my place. I'll sleep here."

When Steven would have protested, Kate took over, shooing everyone out. "Come back in the morning. Please. We'll need help then. It's too late for anything now. Thank you, thank you."

After everyone else left, I still hovered around Jim and Kate while Billy prowled the room, fingering what recognizable items he could find. I think the hubbub was puzzling yet somehow exciting to him, and he didn't know what to make of it all. In a voice that was unfairly sharp I sent the boy home, then said, "We need to involve the county sheriff, Jim."

"What do you think he can do, Lou? Did you see who did this? Did anyone? Clever bastards snuck in and out without witnesses. How would we prove who was responsible? Harper's a smooth man and he'll deny everything, but he's worse than a fool if he thinks this will stop me."

"Lou, you go home. Jim and I will be all right. They've done their damage for the time being. I'll stay here with him." Kate's voice trembled as she looked around the room. Then she put an arm around Jim's waist as if she were protecting him, her expression a mix of sadness, anger, pride, and love. To me, her constancy made her beautiful.

Because they were my friends, I felt angry, too, and annoyed because of my helplessness, and although I hated to admit it, afraid as well. What if the store were the target of such malice?

"Billy and I will come back in the morning to help clean up. We can order new furniture tomorrow, Jim, and if you need a loan to replace the press, I'll talk to Gordon. We'll make it right again." Despite my words as I left, I didn't think life really would be right again, not for a long time, maybe not ever.

As I stepped outside, John Davis separated from the moon shadows in the street. "Is he all right?" He motioned with his head toward the *Banner* office.

"Yes, thank God, but his livelihood, everything that was his, the press, his books, all the tools of the pen that he used to bring civilization to Blessing are ruined. It was a mindless, senseless, malicious act." Moonlight glinted off the gun at his side and I couldn't help but drop my gaze to it before I looked back at his face. He'd probably been awakened like the rest of us, since his shirt was partly open and stuffed unevenly into his trousers. What kind of man straps on a gun before he buttons his shirt?

"I'll take you home, Lou."

I stretched out my hand palm forward as if to ward him off and keep him at a distance. Although part of me knew better, at that moment I considered John Rock Davis to be part of a package of uninvited and violent men who had invaded all that was familiar and safe in my world.

Unjustly, my voice conveyed blame, scorn, and anger. "No. I don't need you. I'll be fine." As an afterthought and so obviously insincere he could have considered the words either mockery or insult, I added, "Thank you," my tone too abrupt and accusing for him to misread my feelings. I turned from him without a backward glance and hurried home.

At daylight I headed back to the newspaper office with brooms and a pail of paint as Billy carried a mattress awkwardly over his head. Others were there before us and had already made progress in the clean up. Kate was busy scrubbing floors, her graying blond hair held off her neck by a scarf. All the debris had been dragged out into the street where Caleb was shoveling it into a wagon he had backed up to the pile. We all worked steadily, hardly speaking, so that by midmorning the *Banner* office was empty but clean and the smell of lamp oil almost gone. Someone had screened over the window until we could reorder a pane of glass for it. I set to work repainting the sign and when I was done, Jim himself got onto a ladder and carefully pounded it over the door in its old spot.

"This is still a newspaper office," he muttered grimly, perched on the ladder and staring at the words *The Blessing Banner* that I had painted in bold letters. Then he got down and the four of us, Jim, Kate, Billy, and I, stood in the middle of that empty office.

"I'll be making a trip to Hays this afternoon and spending the night," Jim volunteered. "I sent a telegram this morning to my old rival Pete Keating, and he says he may be able to help me put my hand on a new press. He's meeting me there."

"I'll talk to Gordon," I volunteered. "If he won't loan you what you need to get started again, I'll take it from my own account. You know you're welcome to whatever you need."

Jim raised my hand to his lips and a bit of the old twinkle reappeared in his eyes. "You are a darlin' girl."

Gordon would have none of my request. Looking at me over the top of his reading glasses, he seemed annoyed by the interruption. "Jim Killian loses money with every paper he publishes, Louisa. I have neither the inclination nor the intention of loaning the man a penny." He sounded prissier than ever.

"Very well." I stood up and immediately went out to Mr. Cuthbert at the teller window, Gordon right behind me. "Mr. Cuthbert, I would like to withdraw three-hundred dollars from my account."

Behind me Gordon said, "I forbid you to use your money to help reestablish a newspaper that has never made and will never make one cent of profit."

"Mr. Cuthbert, I am waiting."

"Cuthbert, you are not to give Miss Caldecott so much as a nickel from her account."

Poor Mr. Cuthbert's face was a study in irresolution, and taking pity on him, I turned to Gordon. "Gordon, you can't keep me from accessing my own money held in my own name in my own account. That would be fraudulent and illegal. I'll file a complaint with the state and you'll be investigated. Consider the unpleasant repercussions. You won't like the notoriety, especially when the headlines blare that we're family. And you know how difficult it is for me to let sleeping dogs lie. The whole tawdry affair will be the topic of tasteless gossip for several weeks. Someone is bound to ask how a man who can't manage his own family could be competent enough to run the state of Kansas."

Gordon paused at my words, killed me with a look, and then stomped—there's no other word for it—into his office, closing the door with unnecessary force.

"Mr. Cuthbert, three-hundred dollars." I tucked the bills into a small wallet I carried and took them to Jim, pressing them into his hand. "Don't protest. If this helps you get a new press, use every penny. You'll need something to live on besides, so use it for that, too. If you need more, just ask. You and Kate are my best friends and I want to help. We need the power of the press here. How else can we hold our little town together? Just be careful, Jim. I have a bad feeling this is not the end of it."

I couldn't have been more right. Two nights later I was again awakened in the early morning, this time by the clanging of the emergency bell by the stable. The last time it had been rung was two years ago at the sighting of a distant funnel cloud. I stumbled down the steps and looked east, where the reason for the bell's alarm was clearly visible. Against the early morning horizon glowed the bright orange haze of fire, a sight to terrify. With the dry summer and the wind blowing toward town, we were all at risk. Just a few years ago during a summer not nearly as dry as this one, a prairie fire had partially destroyed the neighboring town of Butler, and the community still hadn't completely recovered from the effects of the catastrophe.

Already several men on horseback were headed toward the blaze. I shouted at Billy to get all the blankets off the shelves, then rushed back upstairs to change into a pair of men's trousers and an old shirt of my father's. I was pulling back my hair with a kerchief as I waved down Frank Monroe in his wagon.

"Frank, I've got blankets and buckets." Together we threw everything into the back of his wagon. Billy jumped in, too. I clambered up on the seat next to Frank, who had been a colleague of my father's for many years and was currently Blessing's mayor. "Where do you think?" I asked, referring to the fire. Frank knew exactly what I was asking.

"Looks like the Palmer place or thereabouts. Good thing there's not a stronger wind."

Frank was right about the Palmers. By the time we got there, the barn was fully aflame and two outbuildings had caught fire as well. Billy and I tossed brand new blankets out to the fire-fighting men, who seized them to beat out the embers that flew from the burning buildings. Other men had loaded up a wagon with washtubs and pails and were headed down to the river to fill the containers. Despite the best of efforts, though, I knew that all we could hope for was to contain the flames. The buildings already on fire would be a total loss.

The scene, filled with the voracious crackling of the flames and dense black smoke shooting skyward, was made more horrible by a terrible stench. Apparently not all the barn animals had been rescued, I thought, then stopped with a blanket mid-swing, filled with an inexpressible, sickening fear that I was not just smelling the odor of burning animal flesh. Where was the Palmer family?

I turned toward the house and saw with relief that Mrs. Palmer was standing on the porch with two little girls huddled against her. I hurried over to where they stood.

"Mary, are you and the children all right? Where's Matthew?"

The Palmers were a black family who had been lured to Kansas from Kentucky by the promise of land of their own. They had arrived with little in the way of material goods and had worked without complaint to turn their land into one of the most progressive farms in the county. The losses from the fire would be devastating to their plans and future.

A woman of dignity, Mary Palmer responded calmly, "Matthew's fine, Lou. I lost track of him with all the other men here, but I know he's safe." She and I stood shoulder to shoulder, wordlessly watching the men beat down the flames and douse them with river water, like a dance of sorts, a terrible dance of purposeful steps shown in the outline of the men's figures against the fire behind them.

After a while we contained the flames and eventually beat them out entirely. The house had been preserved, but the barn's skeleton stood completely charred, and what was left of the granary would have to be razed and rebuilt. By full daylight the frantic, synchronized performance was over, and all I saw was a bedraggled group of dirty-faced, tired, and sweaty men.

Matthew Palmer handled himself with great poise, going

KAREN J. HASLEY

from man to man to shake each hand and offer a personal thank you. As everyone began to head home, he came up to the porch where I sat with Mary.

"Lou, I am much obliged for your help." Matthew was a quiet man with dark, intelligent eyes, now reddened and watering from the smoke.

"I'm so sorry this happened, Matthew. Besides the buildings, what else did you lose?"

"One milk cow and the mule, all my seed corn, and the Turkey Red winter wheat I was going to plant this fall."

"We'll order new. Your credit's good."

He and his wife looked at each other. Mary Palmer said, "I don't believe we'll be staying," speaking to me but looking at her husband. "This wasn't no accident. There's been men telling us to go, wanting us to go, and trying to scare us off. I told Matthew, No. This is our land, I said, the first land we've ever owned, and we won't be scared off it. I buried a baby here, and I wasn't willing to leave him behind." Matthew remained wordless, his eyes fixed on her dark, expressive face as she continued. "But we'll go now. I won't bury any more of my children here. I won't bury my husband over a piece of land."

Matthew Palmer got a mulish, stubborn look on his face. I saw that he wanted to speak but was hesitating because I was there. They had things to say to each other but not in front of an outsider like me.

"I need to find Billy and get home," I told them, rising quickly, "but if you decide to stay, you've got a line of credit at my store for whatever you need." They heard me but didn't respond, only looked at each other, too many unspoken words between them that still needed to be said. As I left, I saw Matthew sink exhausted to the porch steps. Mary sat down next to him and pulled his head to her shoulder, her arm resting along his back. Behind them the two children sat wide-eyed and quiet. Then it seemed too personal for me to see more and I turned away.

~ 94 ~

Frank Monroe, stripped down to undershirt and suspendered pants, leaned against the wagon. Billy lay asleep in the back, his face grimy with soot and smoke. Frank straightened as I approached.

"I thought I lost you."

"No. I was talking to Matthew and Mary. They think someone set the fire on purpose."

"More likely someone forgot a lantern and the mule kicked it over."

"No, I don't think so. I believe them."

For the first time that I could remember in all the years I had known Frank Monroe, he seemed reluctant to talk to me. He looked away, pretended to brush a cinder off his shirt, then said, "Well, let's get back. Too hot to spend time out here talking under this morning sun. Looks like another scorcher." He remained uncharacteristically silent all the way back to town.

Billy slept soundly despite the bouncing he took in the back of the wagon. Sleep of the innocent, I thought wryly, and had to shake him awake. "You need a bath, Billy."

He grinned at me. "You, too. Your face is dirty." I supposed it was. I was dead tired, grieved to the heart in an inexpressible way for the Palmers, and filled with a terrible dread. It seemed there was no end to the alarming things that were happening around me. I had wanted to talk to Frank Monroe about the situation, but it was clear he didn't want to talk to me. My friends were becoming strangers, my world was suddenly out of control, and I felt helpless to do anything about it. The knowledge humbled me. All my life, and especially since Father's death, I had lived in security and freedom, making my own decisions to control and affect my own future. No one kept me from doing anything I chose and whatever I thought was right. I had my own way, independent to a fault. Now I was caught like a stick in a rushing river, powerless to do anything, pushed along by a current of fear and anxiety that threatened to drown everything I held dear. I decided to contact the county sheriff the first chance I had. The rule of law governed us, I had told Paul Harper, not violence and not fear, and while Blessing's particular rule of law made his home several towns over, I knew where to find him.

When we got home, Billy and I dragged the old washtub behind the store and filled it with several pails of water from the pump, then let it sit in the morning sun for a while. Not like the lengthy process of a winter bath, where I had to heat the water first, and even then it cooled so much by the time I got into it that the bath was a hurried and chilly experience. In summer the sun did the heating for me. I opened the store, then sat on the bench outside the front door and waited for Billy to finish. Next it would be my turn, and it had become a matter of personal urgency that I get out of my grimy, sweaty clothes and remove the smell of smoke that clung to me.

Before I could do so, however, Lily crossed the street to examine me critically. I thought wryly that the contrast between us as sisters had never been more obvious. Here I sprawled in men's clothes, my face streaked and dirty, my hair unbound and snarled and smelling of smoke. There she stood, her glorious hair pulled back into a chignon, her complexion like ivory, wearing a high-necked dress of dark green chintz with a ruffle of alabaster lace at the neckline that framed her beautiful face exactly right.

"Louisa, Mother is spinning in her grave. You have men's pants on. Do you think you could at least sit inside instead of out on the street for everyone to see?"

"I am a mess, aren't I?" I admitted, looking down at my soiled shirt and dirty hands. Then, for no special reason the scene struck me as funny, and I looked back at Lily with a grin. At that moment we were little girls again, caught in some forbidden mischief, and all the years between rolled back with that look.

"Your face," Lily observed, "is like an Indian's on the warpath. Really, Lou." A gurgle of laughter came from us both at the same time. She clamped her hand over her mouth to try to control the sound but ended up laughing so hard she had to clutch the porch rail for support. I was wiping tears from my eyes, trying not to picture how they must be streaking the smudges of soot on my face. I hadn't heard real laughter from Lily in a long time. Too often it was an artificial and forced sound that told me she was pretending.

"Yes, dear sister, I can go inside. I'm sorry I'm embarrassing you."

She followed me into the store, trying not to get too close to me and wrinkling her nose when she did. "Gordon said it was the Palmer place. Was anyone hurt?"

"No. They lost some livestock and some outbuildings, but the family's unharmed."

"What happened?"

Because I knew Lily very well, I thought her tone too innocent and turned to examine her expression. "Matthew thinks someone set the fire deliberately."

She moved around the store's interior, casually brushing her hand over the bolts of fabric on the shelves. "That's terrible. Who would do such a thing?"

"I don't know, Lily, although I could make a good guess. Who do you think might be responsible for such a callous act?"

At my words she stopped abruptly and turned to face me, her voice unnaturally defiant and loud as if I had accused her of the arson.

"I don't think the fire was set at all. I think someone was careless and doesn't want to admit it."

"Ah, I see. So perhaps what happened to the *Banner* office was carelessness as well."

"Those were rowdy cowboys off the trail. Gordon said there were some in town, drinking at the saloon all afternoon and that they'd gone over to the billiards hall in the evening. That's happened before, Lou."

"Odd, though, don't you think, that they picked only the newspaper office to ransack? It's not like it's a prominent building or especially noticeable in any way. The *Banner* office is small and nearly hidden, but it was the only target, almost as if they'd gone looking for it." Despite myself I could hear a preachy tone creeping into my voice. "If Jim had been there, he could have been hurt, Lily! And it's only by the grace of God that the fire didn't spread to the Palmers' house. What if the family had been sleeping and not awakened in time? The two children could have been killed along with their parents." The disbelieving, rebellious look on my sister's face made me add meanly, "Your face is going to freeze in that unflattering expression, Lily."

"Well, you—you—stink!" With that final parry she flounced out. For my money that was the only truthful thing she had said since she entered the store.

Billy joined me, scrubbed spotless, his straight, yellow hair plastered to his head. "Done," he said proudly, stretching out his hands for me to examine. I checked under his nails, inspected behind his ears, and pronounced him clean.

"My turn now," I told Billy with relief. Lily had been right about one thing. I did stink. We pulled the tub into the back room, refilled it with sun-warmed water, and I had a lovely bath, an unheard of luxury in daytime hours. On previous summer evenings we would head to the river for a quick swim. Recently, however, with the river low and men I neither liked nor trusted roaming the countryside, I didn't feel confident in such a vulnerable state.

After bathing, I spread my wet hair to dry in the sun, then plaited it into a large, loose braid. Mine wasn't a bad face, I thought objectively, checking in the mirror to be sure I'd removed all my smoky war paint. No moles or pockmarks roughened my skin, my eyebrows were arched and relatively uniform, and my nose nondescript. But my mouth was too large for my other features, my eyes a plain gray with no depth, and my dark brown hair unremarkable. More than that, I did not have whatever it was that made Lily sparkle from the inside, that set her eyes and skin glowing and attracted people to her like moths to flame.

"You're common," I told myself in the mirror, "but I suppose there are worse things."

The early morning fire caused a late start, and business consumed the rest of the day. I heard a great deal of shared talk and speculation about both the *Banner* office and the Palmer fire from my customers. As the weather cooled, the seats around the store's pot-bellied stove would fill up with a variety of folks who used the occasion of coming to town for supplies to get the latest news as well. That communal sharing of information, gossip, and jokes was one of the things I liked most about my business and my life. I liked feeling central to the goings-on in Blessing, liked knowing who was courting, when the next baby was due, who was adding on to their house or bringing family in from out of state. The knowledge made me part of Blessing in a special way. I had never examined why that was important to me, only knew that it was. Maybe I inherited the need from my father.

People were also spending a great deal of time in recollection and anticipation of the coming Independence Day festivities. Kansas had a reputation for the expansiveness of its Fourth of July celebrations that traditionally included speeches, poetry readings, music, fireworks, parades, races and contests, some of the best food in the country, and dances that continued well into the night. Blessing held its own with a number of bigger towns. People looked forward to the day as one of the few times they could stop working and enjoy themselves without guilt or worry about what they weren't getting done. The town would fill with people from mid-morning through the evening dance. Everything closed down except the Hansen House, where Eliza and Steven fried up platters and platters of their specialty fried chicken. The annual town party was always a topic of animated conversation weeks before and after the memorable event.

Toward closing time Kate stopped by. She looked at me gravely. "You look tired, Lou. I don't believe I've seen you with circles under your eyes like that before."

"At least I don't stink," I said, laughing at her expression, then told her about Lily's and my conversation. Because I had never shared my suspicions about Lily and Paul Harper, Kate could not know why I doubted the truthfulness of Lily's words. I wasn't convinced that Lily truly believed that either carelessness or serendipity had caused the incidents she and I had discussed that morning.

"You don't think it could be just coincidence or accident, do you, Lou? Jim's convinced that Harper is behind things, but I don't know if I believe that. Maybe I just don't want to, but what would be Harper's purpose? I can't talk about this with Jim, though. He dismisses any other alternative."

"I don't think anything that's happened is accidental, Kate. Remember the Schmidts? What did their dog do, accidentally shoot himself and then drag his own dying body up on the back porch? I believe there's some kind of conspiracy or plan at work, and Paul Harper and Gordon are right in the middle of it."

Kate looked as troubled as I felt, gave a brief, unconscious shudder, and changed the subject. "When can you come over for a fitting? The dance is only a week away now, and I've got the dress almost done. I'm excited for you to see it. Are you too tired to stop by after supper tonight?"

"Never too tired for raspberry silk, although—" I hesitated.

"Although what?"

"I don't know. Somehow it feels wrong to celebrate when things are so serious, and I don't know about John Davis, Kate. Who is he, anyway, why did he come to Blessing, and why is he staying on? He wears that long gun that makes me shiver every time I see it." I paused, then admitted, "I was a little rude to him the night the *Banner* office was vandalized. More than a little rude, I guess. He volunteered to make sure I got home safely, but I felt angry and threatened in a way, so I rushed off as if I were afraid of him. The skittish way I acted would be enough to make any man lose interest."

"First, make no mistake, John Rock Davis is not just any man. Everyone who sees him knows there's something about him that's just a little terrifying, and I'm not talking about the gun. It's all in the way he carries himself. I don't mean he's a bad man—that's pretty clear too—but he's not a man a person wants to get on the wrong side of. Besides, maybe you really are afraid of him, Lou."

"I am not afraid of John Davis," I retorted, surprised. "I spent several hours alone in his company and never felt threatened once. Just the contrary, in fact."

"There are threats and then there are threats."

"More riddles."

"Lou, couldn't it be that you don't want your self-sufficient, safe little world disrupted, and somewhere inside you realize that a man like John Davis has the potential to do exactly that?"

"Nonsense."

"Fine, don't listen to me, but that night after everyone left, John came in and talked to Jim and me for a while, asked some questions, told us if we needed him just to call. Hardly suspicious behavior. Jim has a lot of regard for him, and you know Jim is not easily deceived."

"Jim is a man of great sagacity and very good taste, hence his affection for you." I gave her arm a squeeze and she smiled.

"All right, I can take a hint. You don't want to talk about this subject any more, but come by later so I can put the finishing touches on your dress."

That night, back from Kate's, I thought I was tired enough to fall asleep immediately, but instead I lay awake thinking about what Kate had said about me. Was there truth to it, after all? And was there something wrong with loving Blessing and being comfortable in my life? Was it selfish to want what I wanted on my own terms? Had I really become such an unadventurous stick-in-the-mud that I tolerated only the familiar? I hadn't thought of myself like that before, and if it were true, I didn't like the woman I had become.

The next day I watched the Palmers pull up in front of the store with dismay. Another goodbye, I thought, coming to settle accounts, but at Matthew's words realized I was wrong.

"I'm driving Mary and the girls over to my brother's near Pratt, then I'll be back."

"Not selling out, Matthew?" I responded with pleased surprise. "I'm so glad. Blessing can't afford to lose any more good families."

Mary spoke. "We talked about it. I was firm for all of us leaving, but I married a stubborn man, and he won't go. I don't like the separation, though. We've never spent a night apart since the day we were married."

"My father never owned his own land or his father before him. I'm the first in my family to own property, to be free from birth, and owned by no one. I ain't giving it up." Matthew's jaw was set, and I could see he was determined to take a stand. I hoped that we would not one day have to send a telegram to Pratt with terrible news for his wife.

Paul Harper came into town that day, too. While his companions went on, he stopped at Lily's house. I knew Gordon was at the bank, so Harper's visit made me uncomfortable. I'm not the only person in Blessing who notices such things, but after a short while he left Lily's and walked farther down the street. On pretense of sweeping the porch, I watched him stop first at the barbershop and then the meat market. He made a final stop at the larger of our two saloons and went inside. I thought about going over to see Lily but what would I say? She had taken dangerous chances before and always managed to escape the consequences, but I thought this time she was in over her head with a man who could control her and not the other way around.

I was inside the store, now closed, balancing receipts for the day when someone banged on the door. When I opened it, Harper and the man in the seaman's hat came in past me without invitation. They both carried the reek of the saloon.

"We're closed." I remained by the door, still holding it open. Although I thought he must certainly have been drinking, Harper gave no indication of it. He spoke in the same lazy, almost insolent voice he always used with me.

"I saw the sign and I apologize. I'm a little later than I hoped to be. Do you think you could find it in your heart to fill this small list of supplies?" I didn't move from my spot by the door.

"That one," I indicated the other man, "is not welcome here. I told him never to set foot on my property again and I meant it."

"Cobb, I believe the lady wants you to wait outside." Cobb hesitated, obviously unwilling to leave until Harper gave a quick jerk of his head toward the door. Cobb walked past me as I still held the door open, purposefully coming too close and brushing against me. I willed myself not to back up. Then on his way out, very quickly and without warning, he brought his elbow back forcefully and smashed out one of the small panes of glass in the door. The window shattered, the pieces flying against me with such force that later I found small shards of glass in my pockets. Despite myself I jumped back from the door and the breaking pane.

"Sorry. Accident." Cobb went out and stood next to another man who waited in the street, both now wearing big grins on their faces.

"I am so sorry, Miss Lou." Paul Harper at his most mocking. "Put that on my tab. Cobb's a sailor from the Boston docks, and sometimes he can't find his land legs. Clumsy of him."

To keep Harper from seeing my trembling hands, I moved to the list he had placed next to the cashbox and stepping behind the counter, gathered the few items he wanted.

"I'm tempted to say it was more than clumsy, Mr. Harper. It seemed purposeful." I was frightened and angry with myself for feeling so.

"Purposeful?" His tone sounded hurt. "I can't imagine what I've done to make you feel that way. That was an accident, pure and simple. You must know that I would not purposefully do you any harm."

"I don't spend time speculating about your sensitivities, Mr. Harper."

"That's a pity, then because I have sensitivities about you, Miss Lou, that are not common to anyone else." He leaned over the counter, alcohol strong on his breath. "The problem is that I have a group of men I cannot always control. They're a clumsy and uncivilized bunch, and unfortunately I can't guarantee the peace when they're around. Lord knows I try." I pulled back from him to place his supplies in a small sack.

"I believe you could try harder, Mr. Harper."

He straightened. "You know, I think you're exactly right. Men like that can sometimes be reasoned with. For a price, I might be able to convince them to keep their distance and not disturb your peace, and I'd be willing to make the price very easy, maybe even enjoyable, for you to pay."

Disgusted, I pushed the sack of goods toward him, then pulled the rifle out from under the counter and placed it in front of me.

"Mr. Harper, any price you'd ask would be too high a cost. I will not be extorted. You will simply need to remind your men, forcefully and at regular intervals, not to bother me or my property."

He looked at the rifle and gave a little crow of laughter. "You are a constant source of surprise, Miss Lou." On his way out he lightly fingered the broken door pane. "Such a shame. There's just no telling how much damage a clumsy man can do."

Through the door I watched him tuck the few supplies into his saddlebags, then pull himself up onto his horse and ride slowly out of town with the other two. Whatever polite facade Paul Harper had tried to assume disappeared forever that afternoon, and the nastiness that I had always sensed just below his smiling surface had emerged for anyone to see. The fact that he no longer felt the need to dissimulate increased my worry. It didn't take a genius to realize that Harper's public and shameless confidence did not bode well for Blessing.

CHAPTER 8

Preparation for the Fourth of July began in earnest two days before the event. In the middle of Blessing's main street, several men constructed a small platform from which speeches would be made and then on the western edge of town, a large wooden dance floor. Several business owners, myself included, hung red, white, and blue banners and decorations from our storefronts. Billy grew more excited each day, giving me a detailed report of every new preparation.

"There's gonna be a race, Miss Lou. Can I be in it?"

"Of course you can, and there'll be games and other contests you'll want to be in, too. Maybe you'll get a chance to play the fiddle. There's always lots of music, a brass band for the speeches and a dance band at night. Mrs. Hansen is going to make her fried chicken and mashed potatoes. We'll have a wonderful day." Privately, I wasn't completely convinced that was true. I hadn't seen John Davis since the night we had spoken outside the *Banner* office, and his absence dimmed my anticipation of the festivities.

It was clear to me, although I wouldn't have told anyone else, not even Kate, that if John Davis wasn't there on the

Fourth of July, the raspberry silk dress would be a waste of Kate's time and my money. In fact for me, the thought of the whole day lost some of its promised luster without his presence. I wasn't sure how or when that had happened, but there was no use denying it. I might be able to fool others, but in the privacy of my own daydreams, John Davis was never far from my mind. My only salvation was that no one else could be aware of how often I thought of him and how scrupulously I pretended not to look for him when I was really scanning every alley and corner for his tall figure. It was ridiculous that I allowed such a girlish indulgence, but I hadn't yet learned how to control my too lively imagination.

That afternoon Billy and I were in the side alley, still discussing plans for the celebration as we moved some recently delivered boxes into the store.

"There will be a dance in the evening, Billy. Maybe you could ask Sally to dance with you."

"Can't dance," he muttered, not looking at me.

"Maybe you could learn."

"Can't. Too dumb."

"Who told you that?"

"People. Can't hardly write my name and can't remember all my letters. Too dumb. Can't dance."

"You don't need to be able to read to dance, Billy. Put that box down and come here." When he stood before me, I put my hand lightly on his shoulder. "This is how you hold a young lady to dance. Now of course I'm a foot taller than you so it won't be exactly like this, but I'm going to show you a waltz." I counted aloud, "*One,* two, three, *one,* two, three. See, it's easy. It's like playing the fiddle." He was watching his feet with great intensity and counting under his breath as I hummed a melody, and it didn't take long for him to catch on.

After a moment he looked up at me with a glowing look. "I'm dancing. Look at me." Then he stepped on my toe hard and the moment was gone.

"Billy, if you step on a lady's foot like that when you're

dancing, especially if she's wearing dancing slippers, you'll cripple her, so don't stomp so hard. Waltzing should be like floating."

Behind me John Davis said, "I'll keep that in mind. Is this where I sign up for dancing lessons?" I don't know how long he'd been standing there watching us.

Billy crowed, "Miss Lou is teaching me how to dance a—what is it again?"

"Waltz," I supplied.

"A waltz and I can do it. Did you see me? Miss Lou says I just have to do two things—count to three and not cripple the lady."

Davis laughed. "Billy, you've just learned the man's secret to dancing."

"You may laugh," I pointed out, "but I'd wager you've never been stepped on by some gangly, bow-legged cowboy with more enthusiasm than ability."

"You'd be right. I find that a lot of cowboys won't even ask me to dance." That brought a little choke of laughter from me.

"Then count your blessings. But I admit I'd pay real money to watch you swing some Texan just off the trail around the dance floor."

"I have no desire to swing anyone around the dance floor except you."

"Oh." His words took me by surprise, the wind out of *my* sails that time. "I imagine that can be arranged."

"Good. I'll do my best to float and not stomp."

"I'll take my chances. Will you be around for the whole day?"

"I may be gone in the morning, but I should be back in time for the fried chicken."

"Too bad. You'll miss the morning speeches and Gladys Blanchard reciting her annual patriotic poem."

"That's hard to pass up, but you can fill me in on the exciting parts."

"Frank Monroe always gives the same speech every year so I could probably recite the whole thing for you right now, and

I've heard that Gladys, who favors eagles, is going to perform Mr. Ware's poem, "He Who Has Lived in Kansas Though He Roam," the one that was published in Ft. Scott some years ago." I stood ramrod straight and with a dramatic gesture, placed my hand over my heart before I recited,

"Oh, grand old bird! O'er many a weary mile
They've made you sail in oratoric style
While fledgling speakers in refulgent prose,
Capped many a gorgeous climax as you rose.
Today our choicest colors are unfurled
Soar up, proud bird, and circle 'round the world
And we predict that nowhere will you find
A place like Kansas, that you left behind."

"Seems to me they've got the wrong woman doing the reciting." For a moment I caught something warmer than friendliness in those blue eyes.

A series of thuds interrupted the moment as Billy dragged the last box through the side door. I went around the corner to the front, speaking over my shoulder. "Oh, no. Gladys is very theatrical. I could never do the poem justice like she can."

John followed me inside, pausing to examine the broken door glass I had not yet repaired. "What happened here?"

"That depends on who you ask. The man named Cobb who works for Paul Harper stuck his elbow through it. Mr. Harper said it was an accident, apologized profusely, and paid full price for its repair. But if it was an accident, I'm the Queen of Sheba."

"What then?"

"Oh, I'd say it was an attempt to let me know who's boss or just to frighten me or maybe just to make mischief. I'm not exactly sure what. Anyway, it can be repaired. I suppose I should just be glad my place doesn't look like the inside of the *Banner* office." As I spoke, I knew he must be remembering how I'd acted that night, so I went on hurriedly. "I believe I was rude to you that night, John. I was upset, but it was wrong of me to act as if you held any fault in that incident. I was less than civil to you and I apologize."

"No offense taken. I knew you were upset."

Something in his tone, the same proprietary warmth I'd seen in his eyes earlier, made me suddenly conscious of my appearance. My hair had come loose from its pins in little curls that stuck to my neck, my blouse was damp from working out in the sun, and I had smudges of dust and dirt across my skirt, if not across my face. An unfortunately disheveled woman and not quite the picture I would have liked to present.

"Is there something special I can help you find, John?"

"I already found what I was looking for."

After an awkward little silence, he put on his hat and prepared to leave. "Do you keep that rifle near?"

I went behind the counter and lifted it to show him. "Right here."

He nodded. "Good. You never know when it might come in handy."

After he left, I thought that he didn't know how right he was. The ability to display the rifle had offered a small comfort when I had felt threatened, but I was nowhere as certain that I could actually use it against a person if I had to.

Independence Day morning dawned exactly like all the mornings of the preceding week with a clear blue sky and an early sun that foretold another hot, dry day. But what a difference in the town's activity level! From my front window I could see Blessing's broad main street already full of buggies, wagonloads of families, and riders on horseback. Through the window came a wonderful jumble of noise, too, shouts and conversation, creaking wood, jangling metal from the horses' harnesses, laughing children, and in the distance the sound of the brass band practicing. Billy was so excited he could hardly eat breakfast, and I felt just about the same.

Frank Monroe spoke first (too long, in the opinion of the impatient Billy) about the country's heritage of freedom, Kansas's "proud, unbowed, and bloody" history—a phrase Frank had favored for years—and Blessing's charmed life and flourishing prosperity. It was true that Frank gave the same speech every year, but he did it with aplomb. He carried an appropriate air of prosperity about him with a flourishing mustache and a full head of wavy hair despite his years. People felt good seeing him up on that podium, as if he were a living, breathing symbol of Blessing's success in the past and promise of future achievements. Frank had owned the meat market and the beer hall since before I was born, a peer of my father's in Blessing's early years. It would not be exactly true to say he was a friend of my father's, too many heated discussions and forceful disagreements between them over matters about which my father felt conscience-bound, issues like free-statehood and open education. Frank had come from Missouri and didn't have the same foundation of beliefs as Father, but I believe they worked side-by-side with respect for each other despite their differences. Frank spoke at Father's funeral, and I would always feel indebted to him for his heartfelt and moving tribute that day.

Following Frank's speech, Steven Hansen read the Declaration of Independence aloud, with a histrionic flare I hadn't known he possessed. Then the community brass band played several patriotic tunes with a great deal more enthusiasm than skill. Gladys Blanchard took the podium and did indeed recite "He Who Has Lived in Kansas Though He Roam," as rumor had predicted. She wore a flowing scarf draped around her neck and shoulders and at particularly dramatic moments broadly flung out both arms enwrapped in the scarf. The gesture gave her lean figure an uncanny resemblance to a large bird of prey so that I found her performance especially credible. Finally, although the Methodist circuit preacher had not arrived in time for the celebration, the Lutheran pastor had traveled through the night in order to give a last, stirring prayer and benediction. Altogether a very satisfying morning.

I went over to the Hansen Hotel to help in the kitchen because Eliza was by now so big she could hardly stand upright. While she directed from a chair, fanning her face that was turning an alarming red, young Sally, Lily's cook Anna, and I spent the better part of two hours dipping chicken parts into the Hansen's secret batter recipe, then coating and frying them to a splendid golden brown. We loaded the much-anticipated chicken onto platters and carried them out to the long tables set up in the street, placing them next to a bounty of food already waiting. Cured ham, brisket, potato salad, succotash, homemade egg noodles, sliced fresh tomatoes, cabbage salad, pickled eggs, late strawberries, sliced cucumbers and relishes, fresh bread, and enough pies and cakes to feed the whole state.

Eliza sat on the hotel porch, her head resting against the back of the rocker. "Lord, this baby is going to be the death of me."

I sat on the rocker next to her, just glad to be out of that hot kitchen. "Maybe you should go upstairs and put your feet up for a while, Liza. Sally and I cleaned up the kitchen, and folks are busy eating. No one will miss you."

"I can't move is the problem. I believe I'll be sitting right here when the baby finally comes, cobwebs strung from my head to the windowpane." I laughed at the picture as she examined her protruding stomach. "I didn't carry either of my other two out this far. This child always gets to a room before I do. I'm just going to sit here, Lou. Go get something to eat yourself." At my concerned look she shook her head. "It'll be heaven just to sit, and I honestly couldn't eat a thing right now. Don't worry about me."

I stood, trying ineffectively to push my hair into the net that held it at the back of my neck. "I believe I will. Billy's in some of the races this afternoon, and I promised to cheer him on. Are you sure you'll be all right?" At her nod I stepped into the crowd around the food tables, seeing more unrecognized faces than familiar. Where had all these strangers come from? Gone were the days when I knew everyone in town, their names and the names and birth dates of their children. I admitted to a certain excitement about the changing sea of faces, but I was more saddened than pleased. I had never thought of myself as resistant to change, so I was surprised at the vaguely resentful feelings I had toward these strangers who dared to upset my notion of what Blessing should be. Which made me think of Kate's words. She probably was right about the "self-sufficient, safe little world" I had constructed for myself and my reluctance to let anything or anyone change it.

"You're looking deep in serious thought for so fine a day," said John Davis next to me, and at the sight of him, hatless and blue-eyed in the sun, my heart lifted. Surely if the sight of this man could cause that little flutter in my stomach and brighten up my whole day, as the sight of him always seemed to do lately, I wasn't quite as unadventurous and staid as I feared.

"I'm overcome with indecision. Should it be Millie Taylor's pear pie or Johanna Swan's apple cobbler?" I laughed up at him, suddenly very happy. Later I would take time to consider what it meant that just having John Davis next to me put me in such high spirits. Right now I would just enjoy the sensation.

Together we loaded our plates and found two places across from each other at the end of a table.

"Were you able to catch any of the speeches?" I asked.

He shook his head. "I had to be away for a while. What did I miss?"

I couldn't help but wonder briefly where a man would have to go on an Independence Day morning, but he was not volunteering the information, and I was certainly not going to inquire. Between bites I described Gladys Blanchard's voluminous interpretation of an eagle in a way that made John nearly choke on his chicken.

"Not that I mean to be unkind. I'm not the one volunteering to get up in front of people, and I give Gladys a lot of credit for doing it. I just think she's wasted here in Blessing. We've never known exactly what to do with Gladys. I've always thought she should perform in one of those dramatic reviews in Denver or Carson City or San Francisco. I suppose her husband would miss her if she up and took to a career on the stage, but knowing her husband, I can't help but think Gladys would be a lot happier somewhere else."

John said my name with a touch of laughter and perhaps surprise. "Sometimes you have a very sharp tongue."

"Yes, I do," I agreed, "although I'm usually better at keeping it under control. I blame the occasion and not the company. Father often despaired of my lack of proper decorum, and I suppose it's one of the reasons I'm a spinster." I eyed him across the table. "If my manners bother you, John, I'll try to be on better behavior."

"Everything about you delights me." Startled, I flushed at the look in his eyes and the warmth in his tone, but he went on in his normal voice as if he hadn't taken my breath away. "So you said the boy has races this afternoon?"

"Yes. I promised to watch and cheer him on. I saw him by the biscuits just a minute ago, but I've lost him again. Billy's a little clumsy and I'm afraid he won't win anything, but his heart is set on those races. I'd hate it if he got his feelings hurt."

"He has to grow up, Lou. Didn't you say he's past thirteen? He's not a little boy, so you need to let him fall a few times and get up a few times. He'll find his way."

"I suppose. He's never going to be like other boys his age, though, and that's why I promised his mother I'd watch out for him."

Around us people were clearing things away, moving the remaining food onto the hotel's verandah and taking down the tables, clearing the street for the races. Foot races first, followed by a sack race for the children, and then I'd heard that some of the cowboys would be holding impromptu horse races.

When I look back at that afternoon, I can't recall many details. I know Billy didn't win any of the contests, but he was pleased with himself for making the effort, and when Frank Monroe pinned a special ribbon on Billy's shirt at my request, the boy grinned so widely it threatened to split his cheeks. There was a great deal of good-natured hooting and hollering for the horse races, and I'm sure money must have changed hands at the results. Over time, though, most of the details have faded. All that stands out in my mind from that afternoon is how happy, how blissfully happy, I was to be spending time with John Rock Davis, whoever he was and whatever his intentions were. None of that mattered for that Fourth of July afternoon. I was as happy as I had ever been.

Late in the afternoon the pace began to slow a little. Those living in town went home to put their feet up before the dancing started. Some who had come in from outlying homesteads drifted back to their farms. Cows could not wait to be milked, after all. Families who planned to stay for the dance pulled a short distance out of town under available trees and spread out blankets for a little rest before the evening's entertainment.

"I'll see you tonight then," John said, unexpectedly shy for so self-confident a man.

I walked home with my arm slung around Billy's shoulders, thinking the day could not be improved upon.

As Billy washed his hair and changed his shirt, I bathed too, sprinkling a little lavender water around my neck and shoulders before going to Kate's.

"Look how pretty you are!" I exclaimed, and it was true. Kate wore a pale green gown and had plaited her hair into two braids, then wound the braids on the top of her head like a crown.

"Never mind me. Come here and let's see how my masterpiece looks." The dress hanging there was beautiful, plain in design but of such a rich rose color that in the lamplight it seemed to glow.

"Kate, you've done wonders." I fingered the fabric. "It's so beautiful I don't feel I should be wearing it."

She clucked at me as I stepped out of the old dress I had on. "Wait until you see. I made this gown for you, and no one else but you should be wearing it." She slipped the cool silk over my shoulders, then turned me around so she could fasten the buttons down the back, all the while smoothing and stroking the fabric as she did so. I thought that a sculptor must act the same way when he had formed a work of art, caressing the stone with the same pleasure of creation.

' I sat as Kate pulled my hair out of its net, brushed it and piled it all on top of my head, using tortoiseshell combs the exact color of my hair to keep it in place. As the final touch she fastened a ribbon with my mother's locket on it around my neck. Then I stood nervously before her.

"Do I look all right? People won't laugh at me, will they, Kate, or think I'm acting sixteen again?"

She took me by the shoulders and turned me toward the long looking glass. "My dear Louisa, look at you. No one will laugh."

Because it was early evening and the room was growing dim and because I gave only a tentative glance at the mirror so my mind couldn't at first take in what I was seeing, for the briefest of moments, I thought Lily stood there. But I saw that the figure was too tall for Lily and not full-figured enough, and then I realized I was looking at my own reflection.

"Oh Kate, what have you done?" I felt a queer mixture of dismay and happiness.

My friend laughed, pleased with herself. "Won't we have fun tonight? Now stop fussing with the neckline—it's modest enough. There's nothing wrong with showing off those white shoulders once in a while." Then Kate put her arms around me and hugged me hard. "Haven't I told you, my dear friend, that you are beautiful in your own way? You always see yourself as a poor reflection of your sister, and you try to force other people to look at you that way, too, as if you're afraid someone will see you as the woman you really are. But tonight everyone will see exactly that. I hope you won't display ingratitude to me by hanging about in the shadows."

"I could never be ungrateful to you, Kate, never. If I do end up lurking in the shadows, it won't be because of a lack of gratitude. Maybe a lack of dancing partners but not gratitude."

"Your sitting out any dances tonight has as much chance of happening as a good rain shower."

With Billy gone on ahead, Kate and I walked slowly to the west end of town, mingling with the crowd of people on the street. From a distance I could hear the band already playing and see the faint glow of the lanterns hung around the dance floor. This was Blessing as I knew and loved it, a place of kinship and community, not boom or bust, just Blessing. If clouds of trouble and change hung over the horizon, if there was danger or fear anywhere, it could all be forgotten for tonight, long enough to enjoy one evening of music and dancing and friendship and the joys of home.

Frank Monroe asked me to dance first. He gave a courtly bow, saying, "Miss Louisa, would you do me the honor?" We moved around the floor in time to the music, conversing comfortably. "Until tonight, I didn't realize you favored your mother as much as you do."

"Lily favors Mother, Frank. I have Father's height and perhaps his eyes, but I don't think there's much of Mother in me."

"I remember your mother looking exactly as you look tonight even to the locket," he insisted.

I patted his arm affectionately. "Because I wish that were so, I'll choose to believe it, but I think your memory may be a little flawed."

Frank shook his head and then ended the dance with a flourish. "Not when it comes to your mother," was all he said, making me wonder if there was more of a story behind his remark. My mother had been a beauty, like Lily, and Frank Monroe remained a lifelong bachelor.

Everything about that night was wonderful. I was even in charity with Harley Johnson, who danced as methodically and unimaginatively as he did everything else. He posed only a minor threat to the well-being of my feet and was, in fact, more animated in his conversation than I could remember, but when John Davis tapped him on the shoulder and smoothly transferred me from Harley's to his own arms, it was as if Harley Johnson never existed.

"He doesn't know it, but I'm doing him a favor by sparing him from one of your outrageous excuses."

"I don't think you forget much, John."

"Only what I want to and lately not very successfully at that." He was a good dancer, not inspired, but then neither were most men, and neither was I, for that matter. After a while I adjusted to him and found myself quite content in his arms as if I'd been there all my life. The floor remained crowded all night, and I had a number of partners, but I was always glad to find myself back in his embrace.

Jim Killian danced with me, too, not at all put out by the fact that he had to look up at me. "Lou, I can't remember ever seeing you to better advantage."

"You should tell Kate that. It's her handiwork that's made the difference."

"I'm thinking there's something besides the dress that accounts for the glow on your face, but Kate can tell you I'm not a man of many sensibilities."

We stepped to the side to take a breath. "Did you have any luck finding another press, Jim?"

"Yes, as a matter of fact, I did. It will be at least a month before it gets here, but my old friend Keating over in Hays put me in touch with a man in St. Louis looking to sell one."

"A month! How can we be without a newspaper for an entire month? The whole state could collapse, the country even. The press is the bearer of civilization. It was a terrible thing that someone did to *The Banner,* Jim."

"Not just someone, Lou. That man right over there." As I followed Jim's gaze, Harper looked across the floor and made a small saluting motion toward me. I looked away quickly.

"Yes, you're probably right. He's a nasty piece of work and not one you should challenge unless you're sure you can take care of yourself, so please watch your step with him."

Jim gave a snort and would have answered with something

caustic, but John came up beside us and said, "This conversation is wasting the music." Another waltz began, and I wasn't sure whether I should be dancing with either or both of them, but as I made a teasing comment, my attention was distracted by the sight of Lily and Paul Harper on the dance floor. Others were there, too, of course, but everyone faded in Lily's presence. She wore a dress the color I thought the ocean must be, and with her splendid hair down and unrestrained, she was breathtakingly lovely. Lily and Harper danced with intimacy, her body pressed very close to his and his mouth against her ear saying something that caused her to smile against his shoulder. I looked quickly for Gordon and found him examining the couple as intently as I was. The relationship, so apparent to me from their embrace, must also have been apparent to him, but his expression was fixed and cool. Gordon stood for a moment watching them, and then purposefully turned away to engage the man next to him in conversation. On the floor Lily and Harper danced with such revealing closeness that I was embarrassed to watch them. I knew they were lovers and thought everyone else must certainly see it, too, although it didn't appear many took notice. Conversation and music and laughter swirled around me while I stood mesmerized by that couple swaying in the shadows.

"Lou." John said my name inquisitively then followed my gaze, and in that prescient way he had developed when he was with me commented, "So there's something going on there that troubles you."

"Lily has always played with fire without considering the consequences, and while she's left a trail of hurt behind her, it's never been her own. Now I'm afraid she's in over her head. She doesn't know what she's gotten herself into."

"I believe she knows exactly what she's doing."

"You don't know my sister, so don't judge her," I flared at him. "My father's dying request was that I take care of Lily because he knew that she would always need someone to protect her."

"Your sister is a full grown woman with a husband and a home of her own. Your father did not expect you to be her keeper all her—and your—life."

"You didn't know my father, and you don't know my sister, and you hardly know me, so don't presume to understand what my father expected. There's nothing that entitles you to do so."

John's voice lost its expression as did his eyes. "You're right. Forgive me."

After he walked away, the music stopped, and I watched Lily and Harper leave the floor, she holding onto his arm as if staking a claim. I couldn't believe that she didn't see him as I did or fear him as I, and others, had come to. And what of Gordon? What did he know or had he any suspicion at all? From the look on my sister's face, I thought she might really have come to love Paul Harper, but I knew there was no love in him to reciprocate. Lily was acting a fool and asking for heartache at the least, if not something more dangerous and long term, and I determined to speak to her about Harper the first chance I had. I doubted that she would listen to me, but how could I not try to talk some sense into her? Lily might have a husband and home, but I was the one who had been tasked with caring for her, and I had never taken that commission lightly.

Jim Killian had not missed any of my exchange with John. "Lou, you were wrong to speak to him that way. John wasn't saying anything that you haven't said yourself on occasion."

I was already regretting that I had not held my tongue. "You're right. I know I was rude, and I won't make excuses for myself." At his reproachful look, I added, "I don't know what's come over me lately, Jim. Worry, maybe, or fear."

He flicked my cheek with his finger. "You'll figure it out. I'll tell you one thing you can be sure of, Lou." He motioned to John's retreating back. "That's not a man who would do you any harm, not in word or deed."

Jim walked away, leaving me deservedly alone and

unhappy. How had I allowed this lovely day to degenerate to such a sorry state? Finding a chair on the sidelines, I sat down, declining offers to dance and wishing I could turn the evening back thirty minutes to what it had been before. I would defend Lily to my dying day, but in my heart I knew she could be selfish, defiant, thoughtless, hurtful, and petulant. Only there was another mischievous, funny, brave side of her, too, and that was the Lily I knew and loved. How could I expect John or Kate or Jim or anyone who was critical of her to know my sister the way I did? They saw only a superficial, even shallow woman, the person Lily allowed them to see. I knew better, recognized a bright, restless woman beneath the surface, and admired and loved that woman, the Lily of my childhood. I had been ashamed of her wanton conduct on the dance floor this evening, but now I was more ashamed of my own bad temper. For a moment earlier this evening I thought I had seen a physical resemblance to my sister in the mirror. Now I had displayed an unfortunate resemblance to her in temperament as well. It was becoming a night of sobering revelations.

The band stopped to take a break, and over the laughter and chatter of voices I heard Billy's fiddle start up. I knew it was he even without seeing him. No one else could make music like that, everything out of his head, sometimes the notes racing along almost faster than his fingers could follow and then suddenly becoming something plaintive and beautiful. Billy stood on a corner of the platform with his hair slicked down, dressed in a clean shirt and pants like any of the young men there that evening, playing his fiddle, eyes closed and just playing as though he were alone in the world despite the gathering crowd. I saw that Sally stood there, too, and I thought, He's playing for her, for Sally. The bittersweet realization touched me so that tears sprang to my eyes. Fiddle tears, I thought, in more ways than one. He was nearly fourteen with a terrible case of puppy love for that kind girl and no ability to tell her how he felt except through his music. When Billy finished, he opened his eyes and realized for the first time that it wasn't just Sally listening but practically the whole gathering, now giving him an enthusiastic round of applause. His face turned red right up to his hairline, and suddenly he was Billy again with his awkward stance and slightly slack-jawed expression. When he saw me, he grinned, and I did too, as proud and protective of him as if he'd been my own true child.

"You said he played, but I didn't understand what you meant."

I turned at the words, practically into John's arms he was so close, and thought to myself, I love this man. The words came unbidden and were gone as quickly as they came, but the realization was so authentic and so obvious that for one panicked moment I thought I had said the words aloud. What I felt was nothing like I remembered or expected, only a comfort at his presence and a vague, restless unhappiness when he was not around, certainly not that giddy, gay feeling I'd had with Charlie McKinney. This was a different emotion altogether, deep and quiet and true, not fireworks but definitely fire. All that went through my mind in a moment. I said quickly, "John, I'm—" but he didn't give me time to finish. Instead, with a gentle touch he brushed away one tear still on my cheek.

"I don't like to see you cry," he said quietly, not smiling, then added, "I think this is our dance," and without waiting for a reply, not even standing on the dance floor but right there on the hard-packed ground, he put his arms around me, and we began to dance. As the slow and dreamy waltz played, we moved together, our bodies hardly touching, his cheek against my hair and my hand lightly in his. I wanted to say, "I'm sorry I spoke in that scornful, condescending way. I didn't mean it. I wish I could take the words back," but I didn't say any of those things. Perhaps later I would apologize, or he would bring it up and we would talk about it, but now was not the time. The world had righted itself, and I would not risk upsetting it again.

Much later, as the band began to pack up and couples slowly faded into the night, Billy found me.

"I was gonna do what you said—make sure Sally got back to the hotel all right—but she went off with someone else."

I thought of the gift Billy had given Sally that night and how he'd put his heart on his sleeve for her, but I couldn't blame Sally for anything. She was a pretty girl, with her share of beaus, and no one could fault her for wanting to walk home with one of them instead of Billy.

"You played beautifully tonight, Billy. That was the finest music I've ever heard, and I was very proud of you. Your mama would've been proud, too. I wonder if she didn't hear you, even in heaven. Will you promise me to go straight home now? I'll be along in a while."

He held his fiddle in both hands and said without sentiment, "I ain't never gonna have no girl of my own, but I got this music in my head, and that's some company." Then he smiled his gap-toothed smile and said, yes, he'd go straight home.

John and I walked back slowly, my hand tucked against him under his arm.

"Has he always played like that?"

"All the years I've known him. His mother came to Blessing when he was about six. She said she was a widow and maybe she was—it never really mattered—but from the beginning he could play the fiddle as if he'd had years of lessons from the finest instructors. None of us had ever heard or seen anything like it, the way he could make up music in his head or play any song he heard after hearing it just one time. It's like a gift, John, like God gave Billy a gift. And it's only right since he's been cheated out of a normal life."

John rested his hand on mine, an unexpectedly intimate gesture. "You want life to be fair, Lou, but it's not."

"I know, but I can't help wanting it to be. I'm not willing to meekly accept the injustices of life as if there's nothing to be done about them. That trait runs in the family. My father didn't approve of John Brown's violent methods, but he was still a true abolitionist at heart. He believed that a civilized society has an obligation to do the right thing by others, especially others who are vulnerable or weak. Anyway, it seems to me you have similar inclinations. How many times have you come to Billy's aid when it was no fight of yours?"

"You shouldn't make me out what I'm not, Lou. I'm no knight in shining armor."

"Tarnished a little bit, maybe," I said, teasing.

The people in front of us had moved farther ahead, and it was only because there were just the two of us in that place at that moment and we were talking quietly that we heard a girl's voice, frightened and panicked. A small, high, young voice cried out a feeble "Help," then "You stop," and the word "No," more than once.

The sounds registered with John first, who ran in front of me, around the corner and into the alley that ran between the stable and the undertaker's. I picked up my skirts and ran after him. John disappeared down the other end of the alley into darkness as I paused next to the shaking, crying little figure who pressed herself against the wall of the undertaker's as if trying to make herself as small as possible. The alley was so dark that at first I couldn't see who it was, but as I came closer and put my hand on her shoulder, I recognized Sally.

At first, unable to tell who I was either, she jerked away from my hand, but when she finally saw that it was someone who wouldn't harm her, she threw herself into my arms and held onto me as if she were in danger of drowning and I the only thing keeping her head above water.

"It's all right, Sally. Sh-sh-sh. It's all right now." I murmured all the soothing, meaningless phrases that came to mind and patted her shoulder. "Sally, what happened?"

She pulled back from me, and I could see that her dress had been torn from the neck halfway down to her waist. I put an arm around her shoulders and moved her out of the shadows so I could see her more clearly. The moonlight revealed a little trickle of blood from a small cut on her lip, untidy hair, and wide, dark, frightened eyes. I thought, She's such a little thing, just a child after all. What pleasure would a man find taking liberties with her? She clung to me with one hand as she held up the bodice of her dress with the other.

"Sally, who did this?" I asked.

Behind us we heard a horse ridden hard down the main street and out of town, and I knew we would not catch her assailant, not tonight at any rate.

Sally answered in choppy, breathless sentences, interrupted by little hiccupy sobs. "He was at the dance and we danced together. He was real handsome and I liked him right off. He asked to walk me home. I didn't know he'd try something. We was walking and talking real nice like, and then he just pushed me into the alley. He said all's he wanted was a kiss, but he scared me and I told him to stop. I said I had to get back. He wouldn't stop. I told him to let me go but he wouldn't, so I slapped him, and then he got mad and slapped me back. The look on his face scared me, Miss Lou."

I blotted the corner of her mouth with my handkerchief and said calmly, "There's no need to be scared any more. You're safe now." Inwardly I was raging, but she had had enough to frighten her this evening without seeing me in a temper. John pounded down the boardwalk and turned the corner into the alley, breathing hard, and she pressed back into me, frightened again. I put both arms around her. "John won't harm you, Sally. You're safe with us now."

"I lost him in the darkness." John stopped next to us to catch his breath. "He must have had a horse tied up somewhere."

"We heard him go, the coward. Sally, who was he?"

"He said his name was Oba. I met him at the races this afternoon, and he seemed real nice. He said I should save a dance for him." She looked down at her dress and said with childish despair and another little sob, "What'll Ma say when she sees this? It was my best dress," and then she began to cry in earnest.

I sat on the edge of the boardwalk in front of the undertaker's with my arm around her shoulders and just let her cry. After a while the storm subsided, and she took a shaky breath.

"I'm not a forward girl, Miss Lou, and I never meant no harm."

"I know you didn't," I agreed, speaking as evenly as I could, although infuriated that she should blame herself for the assault. "You're a good, kind-hearted girl, and no one thinks anything but that. Are you able to stand up now? John and I will walk you to the hotel. I'll bet Eliza is that worried about you not being back yet. She knows your mother counts on her to take care of you." Sally held onto me with the grip of a wrestler, sniffing a little and clutching the neckline of her dress as we walked.

Despite the hour, the hotel still blazed with light to welcome the stragglers coming in late from the dance. John sat down on a porch bench to wait as I took Sally inside. A few people were still about but not many. The clock in the lobby said it was morning now, so most sensible people had undoubtedly turned in already. I tracked down Steven, who was still up, and asked him to get Eliza, and as much as I regretted it, requested that he wake her if necessary. He looked at Sally and did not argue.

When Sally saw Eliza lumbering down the stairs, she gave an apologetic sob. "Oh, Miz Hansen, I didn't mean to disturb you. I'm just trouble tonight."

"You didn't disturb me, Sally. It will be a long time before I'm able to sleep through the night again, believe me." Taking in the girl's disheveled appearance and torn dress, Eliza spoke in a purposefully unemotional voice. Over Sally's head Eliza's eyes met mine with an unspoken question.

"No," I told her quietly. "We interrupted it before it got that far."

"It's late, child," Liza said to Sally, "and you can tell me all about what happened while you change for bed. You've had a long day, and breakfast will come early, but my guess is everyone will want a late start tomorrow. It's Sunday after all, so we'll get our day of rest in the afternoon." She took Sally into her own capable hands, saying over her shoulder on her way out of the room, "Lou, Steven can walk you home."

"Thank you, but John's on the porch. He'll see me safely home." Liza raised her eyebrows slightly at that, but I noticed she didn't ask, John who. I stepped out onto the porch, and John stood quickly as if he'd been watching for me.

"How is she?"

"Sally got a scare, is all, thank God, but what if we hadn't come along?" We went down the porch steps. "You know who that was she was talking about, don't you? The young man who was with Harper the other Sunday, the one we met on the road."

"Yes."

I was agitated, the earlier pleasant mood gone. "The idea of that insolent pup frightening and striking a child!"

"I know. You can't abide bullying, and if you were a man, you'd be sheriff and out after him even as we speak." I don't think he quoted me with any mockery, and I took no offense.

We walked without speaking or touching, side by side down the length of the boardwalk toward the store, the bright moon ahead of us. Searching for a lighter topic, I said, "When Lily and I were little girls and Father wanted to surprise us with something very special or with something we'd been asking for, he'd say, "Come out and look at the moon, girls." At first we'd go out and stare up at the moon like two little coyotes, waiting for something to happen. Father would ask, "Did you see him?" We'd just look at him dumbly and shake our heads and then he'd say, "Well, I did. I just saw the man in the moon dancing." After a while we figured out that if the man in the moon was dancing, something wonderful was going to happen."

"Is he dancing now?"

"No, I don't think so. He's looking pretty serious, even a little angry. Definitely not in a dancing mood."

We reached the store and stopped at the foot of the steps that led to my upstairs rooms. When I turned to say good night, I smiled.

"I said earlier that you don't forget much, John, but I hope you'll be able to forget and forgive my bad temper tonight and not hold my words against me."

"I could never hold anything against a woman who looks like you do tonight. The promised raspberry silk was worth waiting for." He reached up very deliberately and pulled out the tortoiseshell combs so that my hair fell in loose waves all around my shoulders. "I have been wanting to do that all evening."

I could only look at him wordlessly, safe and content in his presence, sure that with this man at this time was the right place for me. I knew my heart must be in my eyes and didn't care that it was.

"When you look at me like that, Lou, you try my endurance. You have only yourself to blame for what happens." John dropped the combs to the ground, put a hand on either side of my face and kissed me, stepped back to look at me with some searching emotion I could not interpret, pulled me into his arms and kissed me again, intensely, passionately.

After a little while I laughed softly against him. "I'm not exactly sure what it was you'd been wanting to do all evening, but if that was it, you have my full approval. In fact I think we should try it again, just to be sure we got it right."

I could have stood there all night without complaint, listening to him murmur my name, his hands moving warm along my back and his lips so soft against my skin it made me shiver.

Finally, with a faint groan he said, "I think you need to go up," but he made no attempt to release me.

"I'll be hard pressed to do that if you don't let me go. Not that I wouldn't be perfectly happy standing just like this until dawn if that suits you, but I'm guessing we might cause an unwelcome stir as people arrive for services in the morning."

He let me go then, but he wasn't smiling. "From the first moment I saw you swinging that broom I knew this would happen." I wanted to ask what he meant by *this* but wisely refrained. It wasn't a time to interrupt. "I've never met a woman like you, Lou, and I don't know what to make of you."

"I'm not the mystery, John, you are. I'm plain Lou Caldecott, who's lived in Blessing all her life. Ask anyone who I am or what I'm like, and they'll be able to tell you. I'm exactly what you see. You're the one no one knows, the one with the secrets, not me." I reached up and put the back of my hand against his cheek. "And you know what? I don't care. I feel safe and happy when I'm with you, and that's all I need to know right now." He took my hand and kissed the palm gently, just a whisper of a touch.

"I don't know what to make of you," he repeated. His voice sounded hesitant and a little confused.

I started up the stairs and then looked back to see him standing there with one hand on the railing, still watching me intently. At that moment he looked oddly vulnerable, and my heart went out to him.

"Maybe you're trying too hard, John, and just missing the obvious," I told him gently before I opened the door and went inside for what was left of the night.

CHAPTER 9

The next morning I let Billy sleep while I went off to church. After a dreamless night I awoke refreshed, not at all as if I'd been up into the early morning hours. For me the relative quiet of a Sunday morning seemed a good time to think things through, to consider Lily and Paul Harper, to remember Sally's distress and acknowledge that we could not walk the streets of Blessing in safety anymore, and of course to reflect on my feelings for one John Rock Davis and what had happened last night between us. Maybe it was the moonlight or the music or maybe just me, more tired of being alone than I cared to admit. Maybe all I'd felt was a little night madness, meant to stir the soul for a moment and then disappear with the approach of daylight.

Sitting there on the hard wooden pew, the inside of the church already hot and stuffy, I eventually accepted the inevitable truth that I was not able to pay attention to any part of the service that morning. Instead, I spent the time trying to decide how I would broach the delicate subject of Paul Harper with Lily. Unfortunately, however I began the conversation with her in my mind, it always ended the same with Lily getting furious and telling me to mind my own business—which I probably should have recognized as the wise voice of God advising me to learn from previous experiences.

Later I checked in with Eliza, who told me Sally had shed a few more tears on her way to bed, that she had a swollen lip and a set of red handprints on both her upper arms but otherwise was fine, and that she finally dropped off to sleep more worried about her dress than anything else.

When I went to see Sally in the kitchen, she raised a wan face to me and tried to smile. "I'm sorry I was such a bother, Miss Lou."

"You weren't a bother at all. I'm just glad you're safe and sound." Her swollen and reddened upper lip made the rest of her little face look even more childlike. That a man three times her size could act so violently toward her shouldn't have surprised me but did anyway. What were we to do about it?

When I said as much to Eliza, she turned away from me, busying herself with something behind the hotel's counter. When she turned back to face me, she spoke briskly. "I don't think there is anything to be done. There were a lot of cowboys in town yesterday for the festivities, and Sally made the mistake of going off with someone she didn't know."

"It was one of Paul Harper's ruffians, Liza, and he can't be allowed to get away with that kind of behavior. You sound like you're blaming Sally."

"I'm not blaming anyone. That's my point. Yesterday was a day of high spirits and more than a little alcohol. Throw in Sally's pretty little face and some flirting, and one thing's bound to lead to another."

"High spirits! You didn't see her when I did. She was terrified. Bruises and a swollen lip and her dress torn nearly down to her waist are not high spirits, Eliza. They're criminal behavior."

"You're making too much of it."

"And you're forgetting that you're a woman. It could have been you in that alley."

Liza placed a hand on her distended stomach. "Believe me, it's impossible for me to forget that I'm a woman right now." Then she added in a cool tone, "You're always too quick to judge, Lou, as if you have all the answers. Sally was not seriously harmed, only shaken up a little, and who's to say it wasn't a good lesson for her to learn? Sally could use some growing up. A person can be too trusting as you of all people should know." The color rose in her cheeks as she concluded.

"What does that mean?"

"There's no use using that tone with me, Lou. You know you're a pushover for every sad story you hear and every pitiful person who comes to you with his hand out. You believe everything people tell you. When they take advantage of you, you don't seem to care, and you never seem to learn anything from the experience."

"I'm not going to argue with a woman in your condition, Eliza. We've been friends for too long, but I will say that when you and Steven came to me with your hand out, you were glad enough to take what I offered. I didn't hear any complaints about my trusting nature then."

She called my name after me as I left but I didn't stop. Pregnant or not, that was a side of Eliza I had never seen before, and I was taken aback as much by her tone and demeanor as by the words themselves.

Kate caught me as I passed by her shop on the way home. "I didn't get a chance to talk to you much last night, Lou. Come in for a little while."

"I'm on my way to Lily's, Kate, so I can only stay a moment. Now that I think about it, I hardly saw you last night either."

"I was there, but you were too busy on the dance floor to notice me. You looked beautiful, Lou. I was right about the dress, although I don't think it was the dress that accounted for that soft, lovely look on your face. Did you have a good time?"

"I don't know about the beautiful part, but yes, I did have a good time. Did you hear about Sally?" I told her how John and I had surprised the scene in the alley and how distressed Sally was.

"Will she be all right?"

"She has a swollen lip, but I think she was more scared than anything else. Oh, and her dress was torn, so I was wondering if you could stop by and help put it back together for her. Sally's such a little thing, I know it must have been frightening for her. Any one of us would have been scared." Then because it troubled me, I told her what Eliza had said. "I don't mind her criticizing me, Kate. She's right, after all. I do tend to be impulsive, and I could stand to be more discriminating in some of my business dealings, but for her to say that we should just let this incident go, that it was only high spirits and no harm was done, is wrong. I can't imagine what she's thinking."

Kate looked poised to say something, thought better of it and shrugged instead, adding simply, "I know how you feel, but since we can't do anything about it today, let it rest, Lou, and tell me instead how your evening went. Jim said you and your Mr. Davis had words, or what he really said was that you tore into him. Were you talking again by the end of the evening?"

I thought of the walk home and our time in the moonlight. "Yes, I would say so."

She chuckled. "Has anyone ever told you not to take up poker for a living? Your face gives everything away."

I probably blushed. "John and I did have a disagreement about Lily, and I handled it poorly. We talked about it later, though, and as far as I could tell, I was completely forgiven." At her knowing look I smiled. "I'm not giving you any more details, but I had a lovely night. The best I can ever remember. Now I'm on my way to talk to Lily about the very thing John and I quarreled over. I know it's going to end as it always does when I try to give my sister unsolicited advice. She's going to get defensive and haughty, and I'm going to get prissy and self-righteous. But saying nothing isn't an option, so if I'm the one with the swollen lip tomorrow, you can credit Lily."

"Why do you need to talk to her about whatever it is at all?"

"Because she's my sister and it's my duty."

"And what about her responsibility to you?"

"Kate, you know my father put me in charge of Lily with his dying breath. I can take care of myself."

"You think she can't?"

"We're going to repeat the same argument that John and I had last night if we're not careful, and since I'd rather not quarrel with every single person I meet today, I'm leaving. I'm not asking you to understand, Kate, just to be my friend."

She answered more soberly than I expected. "You make it hard for your friends, Lou, with those blinders you wear when it comes to your sister. Somehow you have to take them off so you can see what she's really like."

I wanted to tell my friend that she wasn't saying anything I didn't already know, that I was not blind to Lily's faults, that removing the responsibility and affection was not like getting a haircut. But I said none of those things, just left, running away from the second conversation of the day that made me both uncomfortable and confused.

By the middle of Sunday afternoon, I was willing to do almost anything except go talk to Lily about her association with Paul Harper. Was any harm being done, except on a personal moral level, and was that any of my business? If Lily was unhappy in her marriage, was it my place to butt in where I hadn't been invited? If Eliza and Kate were right about me and my thinking I was always right, it would be far better for me to stay out of Lily's personal life entirely. How was I entitled to give unsolicited advice? What John said was true. Lily was a grown woman with a husband and a home of her own, accountable for her own choices and decisions. Maybe my role was simply to love her. Still, there was my father's request, "Care for Lily. Promise," and I had willingly, freely agreed to the responsibility. How could I renege on that promise? I couldn't rid myself of the need to protect my sister. I couldn't *not* love her or stop myself from worrying about her, so with more reluctance than confidence I crossed the dusty street to Lily's back door.

Anna, Lily's cook, sat in the shade of the back porch, pretending to snip green beans but really napping and enjoying some respite from yesterday's hot work.

"Is Lily home?"

Anna nodded. "Just go in. I was out in the garden, but I know she's inside somewhere. I think in the parlor. I don't know where Mr. Fairchild is."

Calling Lily's name, I went in through the kitchen. When Father built the house he planted a stand of trees along the west side to shield the house from the afternoon sun, so the interior stayed relatively cool even on the hottest summer days. I passed the solid oak kitchen table at which Lily and I had done our lessons and where we had learned our first table manners. So many breakfasts there, with vague early memories of Mother, and clearer, more recent recollections of just the three of us, Father, Lily, and I, talking and laughing over supper. After Mother died, we never used the formal dining room that I could recall although I knew Lily and Gordon now ate all their meals there. I walked through the kitchen into the hallway and down the hall to the parlor, opening the double doors of the front room as I called her name again. Lily was there in the parlor, but she wasn't alone.

At first I thought I had interrupted her and Gordon and was hotly embarrassed, trying to stammer out some kind of apology as I started to retreat into the hall. Then I realized it was not Gordon standing there with Lily in his arms, it was Paul Harper. By outward appearances, I was the only one embarrassed. Harper had been kissing Lily quite passionately, one hand against her back pressing her into him and the other inside her dress, which was unbuttoned down the front halfway to her waist. Even as he kissed her, his eyes met mine, and I would swear they were amused, enjoying my discomfort.

Lily turned slowly in his embrace. "If you'd remember to knock, Lou, you wouldn't see things that offend your Puritan morals." She began to button her dress leisurely, still within his arms, and he purposefully bent to kiss the swell of her breast.

"Anna said you were in the parlor, and she didn't mention you had company. I called your name twice. You must have heard me."

"Mm-m-m, well, I was preoccupied." Lily stepped away from Harper and went to the oval mirror on the wall to finish fastening the buttons of her dress and then straighten her hair. None of us spoke as she did so.

Paul Harper finally broke the silence. "My dear, as much as I would enjoy hearing the conversation that follows, I think I'll be going." They shared a gaze in the mirror before he passed me on the way out, brushing by me too closely because he knew I would dislike it.

All that time I just stood there, rooted to that spot on the deep red parlor carpet as if I had become another piece of furniture.

"You needn't look like that, Lou, so mortified, so shocked, as if you've never seen a man and woman together before." I don't know what I expected from her, but it wasn't that cool, slightly sardonic look and tone.

"You're a fool," I finally said, surprised that I sounded as calm as I did. "Why are you risking your marriage, especially with a man like Paul Harper?" My last comment put color in her cheeks.

"You don't know anything about Paul."

"I know he's a thug wearing a thin veneer of civilization as a topcoat. I know he's power hungry and money mad and he has no respect for anyone or anything. He's responsible for the ruin of the *Banner* office and the fire at the Palmers' place, and he doesn't have anyone's best interests at heart except his own. Not yours either, Lily."

"He does some things very well, sister, but I won't embarrass you by giving you the details."

"What if Gordon finds out?"

She replied with a thick scorn that was startling because of the open hatred it revealed. "Oh Gordon. Precious Gordon. There's nothing to worry about with him."

"Lily, he could divorce you, and then you'd have nothing. Are you prepared to lose all this?" I flung a hand around the parlor filled with expensive furniture and the latest decor. "Do you really believe that Paul Harper loves you and will take care of you?"

She gave me a pitying look. "Little sister, you are out of your depth here. You don't know what you're talking about."

I went closer to her and took her by both shoulders. "Listen to me, Lily. Paul Harper and morality aside, you're risking everything, your status, your home, your clothes and jewelry, your trips east, your chance to be the governor's wife, everything. I can't believe you would do that for a simple infidelity, no matter how much pleasure you're getting from it at the time. I've always credited you with a certain mercenary practical sense about how to get and keep what you want. Have I been wrong all these years? If Gordon finds out about this, you could lose it all, everything you want out of life."

"If Gordon finds out," she repeated and laughed out loud, a grating, humorless laugh. "Gordon already knows everything." Lily pulled away from my grasp and stood in front of me, daring me to ask her what she meant, but I couldn't make sense of it and so could not respond. "For God's sake, Lou, stop looking like the farmer's daughter on her first visit to town. Gordon has one ambition, and that's to be the richest man in Kansas. Well, the richest man in the world, but he's willing to start with Kansas. Maybe he'll be governor or maybe he'll be famous, but all that's extra to him. Gordon just wants to be rich, and Paul Harper can help him get there. Paul has a plan, a grand plan, to make a lot of money and I mean a *lot* of money. Gordon wants to be part of that plan so bad he can taste it, so when Gordon tells me to be nice to Paul Harper, he isn't just saying invite him to dinner. Gordon means be very nice, as nice as it takes, as nice as Paul wants me to be. And I am."

"Gordon is your husband. No matter what his ambitions are, he wouldn't compromise you." But I knew the words were true by her expression and her voice and the loathing in her tone when she spoke her husband's name.

"Gordon and I are as practiced a pair of whores as you're likely to find in Blessing even if you count the Palace Saloon on a Saturday night. I admit he's better at it than I am, but I believe I'm enjoying it more."

"Oh, Lily, a man like Paul Harper. How could you?"

"Spare me your moralizing outrage. You think that taking what you want is something bad, but it's not. What do you think success is? How else do you get ahead? Paul will get what he wants because he's not afraid of anyone or anything, and I intend to stay right beside him."

"Do you really think he loves you?"

Lily gave me a pitying look. "What would you know about that, and what difference does love make anyway? I saw you last night in your new dress all starry-eyed because some man pays you a little attention. How long does that kind of love last, and what's it worth in the long run? Nothing. Paul doesn't realize he cares anything for me, but I know he does. For sure he loves the look of me and how I make him feel."

"Looks don't last," I said quietly.

"They'll last long enough to get me out of this town, this horrible, deadly dull, one-horse town full of horrible, deadly dull people. Paul Harper and I are two of a kind."

She seemed too defiant, as if she were convincing herself as much as she was trying to convince me, but that might have been wishful thinking on my part.

"No you're not. You're nothing like Paul Harper. You may be willful sometimes but you're nothing like him inside, Lily. I don't believe that."

"You should start believing it and stop crediting me with virtues I don't have and don't want." She was impassioned by rage and something unnaturally reckless and rebellious, and for the first time in my life, I feared I didn't know, had never known, my own sister. Perhaps I had created an image of her in my mind that had never existed at all.

"I don't know what to say to you. I wish Father were here. He'd know what to do."

"There's nothing to be done but wish me well."

"I can't. To wish you well would be to wish Harper well, and I can't do that. You're making a terrible mistake. Paul Harper is a bad man, Lily. There's something wrong with him inside, at the core. Why can't you see that? He'll hurt a lot of people before he's done, maybe you, and he'll still fail."

"Paul doesn't fail at anything, Lou, not at anything. When he sees something he wants, he takes it, and there's no one able to stop him. He wants your store and he'll have it."

"*Father's* store and he will never have it."

Lily walked leisurely past me out into the hallway. "If you were a gambler, sister, I'd make a wager with you on that. Never is a long time." Then she added over her shoulder as she started up the stairs, "You can see yourself out."

It was a while before I could do that, though, a while before I could take a deep breath and stop shaking and go out into the late afternoon heat as if everything was normal.

That night I slept so poorly I eventually gave up and went to sit in the chair by the open front window. The hot July night offered only a bare breeze that weakly stirred the curtains. From that vantage I could see across the street, past Lily's dark house to the ridge beyond and the small ribbon of moonlit road that reappeared in the distance.

Because I couldn't get the conversation with my sister out of my mind, I went over it again and again, from that first dreadful moment when I pushed open the parlor doors to her parting comment as she ascended the stairs. Hadn't she known, as I had from the very beginning, that Gordon Fairchild was wrong for her? Could I have stopped that union? But when had I ever been able to stop Lily from doing anything she chose to do? It was exactly as John said. My sister was a woman with a home and a husband of her own, all grown up and no longer in need of my advice and care. If she had ever needed me or if I had ever held any worth to her—and I had my doubts about that now—that time was long gone.

I tried to imagine how it would be to live with a man day after day and hate him, across the supper table, around the fire in the parlor, on the pillow next to you all the while hating the sight of him and the touch of him. What kind of toll would that take on a woman after a while, and what would she be willing to do to escape?

I felt little satisfaction knowing I had been right to dislike Gordon Fairchild. How could I ever have imagined that he would sacrifice anything and anyone, even prostitute his own wife, for wealth? With all the disdain I had for Gordon, I could never have sunk him to that depth. How had Lily felt when those words came out of his mouth, telling her to do whatever it takes, whatever Paul Harper wants? Was she glad to have her husband's permission so she could consort with impunity, or had she felt hurt and angry at the impersonal directive? Did she really despise Blessing, or was Blessing just a substitute for the man she had married? How could I have guessed, even in my wildest imaginings, what went on behind those closed doors across the street? Even as I sat there, still shocked and dumb with dismay, I knew I would never know the answers to any of those questions.

The night before and the time with John in the moonlight seemed like weeks ago. Cautiously examining my own feelings, I admitted that I still felt the same about him, still had a vivid memory of that moment when I knew that in John Rock Davis I'd found a man I could willingly, happily spend a lifetime with. But after the confrontation with Lily, I thought I should be more cautious. Nothing guaranteed that any woman couldn't end up like Lily, bound to a man who used her for his own purposes and hating the sight and sound of him. Yet Kate had been happily wed to her first husband, Francie Sullivan looked at her Lloyd sometimes with asperity but always with affection, Steven Hansen was as solicitous of Eliza now as he'd been during her earlier confinements, and there was that tangible, deep, emotional bond between Matthew and Mary Palmer. Some marriages were happy then. I pulled my thoughts up sharply at that. Thinking marriage when nothing had passed between John and me but a few moonlit kisses was unwise and presumptuous.

I fell asleep in the chair and was awakened a while later by the sound of a wagon in the street rattling into town, driven hard and fast. One man hunched forward on the seat with the reins in his hands. The night wasn't bright enough to allow me to identify the driver as he passed under my window, but I read something urgent in his posture that caused me to stand and watch the wagon's progress down the street. Once in front of Dr. French's office, the driver pulled up and leaped off the seat to bound to the door. I saw then that there was a second man in the back of the wagon, crouched next to a wrapped figure that bore a chilling resemblance to a shrouded corpse. Someone hurt, I guessed, someone who needs the doctor. Since I was now wide awake, perhaps I could help.

As I got closer to the doctor's office, I recognized the two figures as Jess McGruder and one of his sons, a family who continued to hold out against selling their tract of land on the eastern side of Blessing. The two men gently lifted the wrapped figure out of the back of the wagon, and I knew it must be the other McGruder boy. I caught up with them inside the doctor's office as they placed the young man onto the table in the back room. The unconscious figure was so pale he could have been dead. The two McGruder sons were not twins but so alike as to be identical, and I couldn't pretend to tell them apart. Their father always seemed a taciturn, gruff, aloof man who didn't seek or enjoy conversation and society. The three men came into town once a month for supplies and kept to themselves even then. At the store I had managed to catch both of the sons in a pleasantry or a smile one time or another, but never Jess.

I stood in the doorway feeling out of place and thinking I shouldn't have come as the doctor shooed the two McGruders out and closed the door of his surgery behind them.

"Mr. McGruder, what happened?" I asked.

He stood bleak-faced and grim, and it was his son who answered. "We was missing two head, and Pete thought for sure they'd gone down by the river. It being so dry, we've found them down there before often enough. He says he'll check it out. Be back by supper, he says. We'd had some trouble, some men who wanted us off the land, making mischief one way or the other, but we never thought it would come to this. I should've gone with him. I should've been there with him." The young man had to pause in his narrative. His throat tightened and for just a moment his lower lip trembled, and he couldn't speak. Behind him his father stood immobile by the surgery door. "When Pete wasn't back by dusk, we knew something was wrong, so Pa and I went out to find him. It took a while. He'd been shot off his horse and was just lying there. I never seen so much blood. We loaded him up and brought him here."

Behind him the door opened and Dr. French looked out to catch my eye and call my name. Milt French had cared for Billy's mother without charge during her last illness, and I knew him, especially from that time, as gruff but calm and capable and extraordinarily gentle. After I entered the back room, he closed the door behind me.

"You're not going to get squeamish on me, are you, Lou?" I sent him a wordless look that caused him to chuckle. "Good. I need you to press down hard on the pad I've put on his shoulder. The boy's lost a lot of blood and won't stop bleeding. I need you to put some pressure on the wound while I tie it up tight." Pete McGruder was as white as the sheet that covered him.

"Will he make it?"

Milt shrugged and repeated, "He's lost a lot of blood. The wound itself wasn't that bad, the bullet went clear through, but we've got to stop the bleeding." I took the heel of my hand and pressed it firmly against the thick gauze pad as the doctor continued to wrap a long strip of cloth under the boy's arm, around his shoulder, and over the wound. After the first layer, I supported Pete against my chest as the doctor finished. Then we laid him back down onto the table. I poured water over my hands and followed the doctor out into the waiting room where he was speaking to the other two McGruders.

"I can't tell you, Jess," Milt was saying. "He's lost more blood than most men could and live, but in his favor he's young and strong. I've got a bed in the back, and I'll need one of you to help me move him there. I gave him something to keep him quiet for a while so you two should get some sleep and come back in the morning."

"I'll stay with m'boy." Jess sat down on one of the straight-backed chairs in the waiting room. "Joe, you go help the doc move Pete."

"Mr. McGruder," I offered, "I could set up beds in the back room of the store for you and your son if you'd like a place to sleep."

"We're not going nowhere but here."

"I understand." I started to leave but turned back to say, "I think we should wire the sheriff about this."

Jess McGruder looked back at me, eyes red-rimmed and face bleak. "Nothing the sheriff can do now. I know who was responsible, but there's no way to prove it. I'll take care of it in my own time."

"You should let the law handle it."

"If my boy dies, I won't need the law to handle nothin'." Then he repeated, "I'll take care of it in my own time."

CHAPTER 10

In the morning I took ham, fresh biscuits, and coffee down to the doctor's office. The waiting room was empty and at my inquiring look, Milt motioned to the back room. "They're all back there."

"So the patient made it through the night?"

"I pumped enough laudanum into him to keep him quiet a good day. The bleeding's stopped, so we'll know by tomorrow what will happen."

When I took breakfast into the back, Jess McGruder gave me a stubborn look. "We don't need charity."

I took a deep breath for patience. "I'll make allowances for you, Mr. McGruder, because I know you're worried about your son. This isn't charity, it's neighborliness." I looked over at the bed where Pete McGruder lay, flushed and feverish. His breathing seemed too shallow, but for all he'd been through, I still thought the signs were good and said so.

"Obliged," McGruder replied, and I couldn't tell if he was thanking me for the food or for the hopeful words.

As I pulled the door of the doctor's office shut behind me, I nearly ran straight into John. He took my arm to help me catch my balance and for just a moment I had that familiar fluttery, unsettled feeling I'd come to associate with his proximity. Then righted again, heart and body, I said, "I'm sorry. I wasn't watching where I was going."

"Is everything all right?" He glanced at the doctor's signboard by the door, then fell into step beside me.

I told him about Pete McGruder's injury. "No one mentioned any names, but I know Jess McGruder is convinced Paul Harper is behind the attack and McGruder is not a man to make idle threats. If Pete dies, his father won't hesitate to confront anyone he believes is responsible. Jess and his other son are just farmers, though, and no match for the kind of men Paul Harper has with him." I opened the door of the store and turned to face John. "Would you be willing to help them?"

John stepped just inside the door before answering, so I was close enough to see how my words had driven the friendly expression from his face. When he spoke, he chose the words with slow care. "No. I already have a job, Lou, and it's not protecting your local farmers."

"I just thought—"

"You thought you might be able to take advantage of the tools of my trade, and being you, you also thought I'd jump at the chance to play the hero and save the world. It doesn't work like that, Lou. *I* don't work like that. I've learned over time that getting involved with the locals puts too much at risk, and I won't chance it. The job I've got right now doesn't include righting every wrong in Blessing, Kansas. I don't do what I do out of the goodness of my heart. It's just a job. You keep trying to make me out a better man than I am." John hadn't spoken harshly, but his words stung all the more because they were deliberate and thoughtful.

Later I'd have to take some time to think through what I had said that was so wrong, take even more time to figure out when and how I had developed the ability to antagonize everyone I cared about. At the moment, however, annoyed that he could make me feel childish and self-conscious with so little effort, I answered, "That's not fair. You know I wasn't talking about righting every injustice west of the Mississippi. I was talking about here and now, about my home, about Blessing and helping my friends."

"But not my home, Lou, and not my friends. Like I said, I've already got a job."

He seemed very detached, with no spark of warmth in those cool blue eyes. The person standing in the doorway was not the man made vulnerable by passion and moonlight but someone else entirely. From his words, I guessed he regretted getting involved with one local in particular, was sorry he had let down his guard with me, and was trying to regain ground he considered lost. But if he could act as if nothing had passed between us, I could, too. I took a steadying breath before I spoke so my voice would not reflect my hurt and disappointment.

"Well, that puts me in my place, doesn't it? Forgive me for presuming that you cared anything about Blessing. I can't imagine why I thought you might be willing to help." But I knew very well why I'd jumped to that conclusion and so did he. "Obviously I made a mistake in asking for your help. I doubt Blessing could afford a man with your level of expertise, anyway."

With a contrived smile I stepped past him, turned the sign on the door to read *Open for Business*, and pushed the iron doorstop forward with my foot to prop open the door. Business as usual, my actions said, and pardon me but you're in my way. John stood watching me, out of temper, I thought, although with him it was hard to tell, and besides, I couldn't figure out why that should be. I was the one who had embarrassed herself, and if I was hurt as well, I had only myself to blame.

"If there isn't anything you want, John, I have work to do," I told him, meeting his look eye to eye, raising both brows and cocking my head toward the door, as matter-of-fact as he, using the same cool tone.

Two women crowded past him to enter the store, and I could tell their presence kept him from responding. I turned away from him to greet the customers, wishing them a good morning and inquiring after families, and when I looked back he was gone. I regretted that I had said anything to John about the McGruders, regretted I'd asked his help without thinking it through beforehand. At the time the request had seemed an obvious solution to my concerns, but I had somehow overstepped as if my suggestion had mixed business and pleasure in a way he did not approve. I had assumed that John Davis had come to care about Blessing, even more, that he'd come to care about me and would be willing to help because of that. From his reaction I'd misread him on both counts. Despite my nonchalant demeanor, I knew John's quietly chastising words had left a bruise that would hurt to the touch for quite some time.

In two days Dr. French announced that, barring anything unforeseen and out of the ordinary, Pete McGruder would make a full recovery. On the third day, when I stopped at the doctor's office, I was surprised to find the McGruders gone.

"They packed that boy up in the back of the wagon and took him home. I'd say the McGruders are not much for town life." Dr. French gave a wry smile as he spoke. We both knew his was a charitable take on Jess McGruder's opinion of Blessing society.

"I doubt the patient was ready for that bumpy ride home," I responded, "and I can't see either his father or his brother having much nursing experience, but I think you're right, Milt. Coming to town was a necessary evil for them, and they couldn't wait to get out of here."

Late Friday afternoon I went looking for Jim Killian. "He's on his way back to Hays," Kate told me. "The new press is coming in a lot sooner than expected, any day now, so he's off to wait for it. The man's so excited there's no living with him, but for me, I don't care if that press ever gets here."

"How can you say that? You know Jim's got ink for blood and these past weeks without a newspaper to get out have been killing him."

Kate's face was somber. "*Not* printing isn't what's going to kill him, Lou. He'll print his first edition, and God only knows what he'll say. If it's something Harper doesn't like, what will happen then? We were lucky before, but what about the next time?" Remembering Pete McGruder, I knew my friend was right to be worried, and I had no answer for her. Kate gave her head a little shake as if to dismiss her worry, smiled, and asked, "What did you need Jim for?"

"I want to take supper out to the McGruders and check on Pete, and Jim's company would have been welcome. But they live pretty close to town and it's still early, so I'll be all right without him." I wouldn't admit to either of us that I was uneasy going east of town by myself.

"Lou, don't be foolhardy. Now is not the time to be going anywhere by yourself, especially in that direction. Ask John to go with you."

"This is not his home, and we are not his friends," I paraphrased stiffly. "I would rather ride through town naked than ask John Davis for anything, and I refuse to stop doing the things I've done all my life in my own hometown because I'm afraid. Besides, I'll take the rifle with me. I'll be fine."

She followed me to the door. "I hate it when you get like this, so hard-headed no one can reason with you. I'll go with you."

"Now there's an idea sure to strike terror in a desperado's heart," I said laughing, and then at the worried and frustrated look she gave me, added with more bravado than I really felt, "I promise I'll go straight there and come straight home, and I won't be gone long. We've got a good four hours of daylight yet, and I'll be home before dark. I'd take Billy along, but he'll have to mind the store the last hour of the day." Her expression remained unconvinced and I added lightly, "Worry about Jim. He needs the attention a lot more than I do."

I was right about the trip, which was uneventful and

perfectly safe both ways. I had stashed the rifle under the seat but never gave it a thought either coming or going. My only moment of disquiet happened when I pulled onto the McGruders' property. As I approached the house along the drive, Jess McGruder stepped out his front door, lifted a shotgun to his shoulder, and stood watching my approach through the sights of the gun. I was unsettled but had to believe he didn't recognize me.

I pulled up and called across the yard, "Mr. McGruder, it's Lou Caldecott."

When he put the shotgun down, I drove forward, stopped at the end of the drive, and clambered down from the seat. Young Joe greeted me and came forward to steady the team, but his father remained motionless, eyes narrowed, as I walked toward him.

"How's the patient doing?" I asked Jess, relentlessly friendly.

"Reckon he'll live."

"I'm glad to hear it. I was a little worried when I heard you left so soon." I put out a hand as if to ward off any argument. "I know he's your boy and it's your business, so I'm not interfering." I went to the back of the wagon and lifted out one large basket. "Joe, make yourself useful and get the other basket for me." I walked past Jess to the front door and responded to his baleful look by saying, "There's no use looking like that, it's not hospitable. This isn't charity, it's doctor's orders."

Three rooms made up the sod house, all of them surprisingly clean for bachelors' quarters, if spartan. I set the basket I was carrying on the table in the front room. "I brought some of Eliza Hansen's fried chicken and all the trimmings, fresh chicken noodle soup for the patient, a jug of lemonade, two pies, odds and ends I thought might tempt Pete's appetite. Of course, there's plenty here for all three of you."

Jess rested the shotgun against the wall behind the door. "No need for you to trouble yourself over us."

"I couldn't agree more," I replied pleasantly, "so it's fortunate it wasn't any trouble at all." On the wall hung a picture of Jess and a woman, he seated and serious, dressed in suit, tie, and high collared shirt, the woman, not quite smiling, standing behind his chair with one hand resting lightly on his shoulder. There was no mistaking her resemblance to Pete and Joe.

Jess followed my look and said stiffly, "The boys' mother, Jemima, on our wedding day."

"Yes, I could tell. Your sons favor her a great deal. If you don't mind my asking, what happened?"

I thought he might indeed mind, but he answered without hesitation. "She died of a fever almost ten years ago. After I buried her, we pulled up stakes and came west. Jemima favored the hills of West Virginia, but after she was gone, there wasn't nothing left for us there any more." I heard the understated grief in his voice and understood why he'd decided to settle on the flat plains of Kansas. Jess looked around the room as if seeing it through my eyes. "Place like this needs a woman's hand. Never been the same since she's been gone." The words were the most I'd ever heard him speak at one time.

"You've got two boys. They'll find wives some day although you could help that along if you'd bring them into town a little more often. It's not likely that young women will drop out of the trees for them."

I caught a glimmer of amusement in his eyes. "Reckon not."

I stood and put on my hat. "I don't mean to take up your time, Mr. McGruder. I was just being neighborly."

"If you'd like to sit a spell, I'll see if Pete's awake. Might be you could check on him."

I met Joe's surprised look with one of my own and promptly took my hat off again. "I'd like that fine," I responded and sat back down.

Later, I unwrapped Pete's bandages and, pleased with what

I saw, said, "I'm no doctor, but the wound looks like it's healing well. It's not red or hot or puffy. I'd guess all you'll have to show is a scar someday." Pete gave me a shy smile, not used to a woman around, and fell back asleep.

As Jess and I walked outside, I asked, "No more trouble, then, Mr. McGruder?"

He shook his head. "Not yet. If there is, we'll be ready for it this time." Joe came up riding one horse with another saddled behind him that Jess mounted. "We'll see you home, Miss Caldecott."

"There's no need to take that trouble."

"Couldn't agree more, so it's fortunate it's no trouble at all," he quoted straight-faced, making me laugh with surprise. Who would have thought this reticent, stone-faced man would have a streak of mischief in him? That would teach me to make early judgments about people.

"Just part of the way, then," I agreed. Truthfully, I was glad for the company as the evening darkened, since it was later than I had intended. They stopped at the foot of Pattycake and waited until I topped the ridge before they turned back toward home. I had enjoyed the visit more than I'd expected but regretted I had let it get so late. Kate would be worried and Billy, hungry.

Caleb stood waiting at the open stable doors, coming forward to take the reins and scold me. "I swear Lou, if your pa was alive, he'd take a switch to you for worrying folks like you do."

I climbed down from the wagon, then took the rifle from under the seat. "My father never took a switch to me in his whole life, Caleb."

"Which doesn't mean he shouldn't have," said John Rock Davis from the stable doors. He stood in the shadow of the doorway and behind him his big bay was saddled and ready to go.

"Coming or going, Mr. Davis?" I asked coolly and turned my back on him.

Caleb, who was leading the team and wagon past John into the stable as I spoke, looked back briefly to say, "We was worried. John was just going out to look for you," before he completely disappeared inside.

Behind me I heard John's long strides before he reached for one of my shoulders and turned me around to face him. "Don't ever do that again." His tone was clipped, and his blue eyes held no hint of warmth or friendliness.

I could only look at him blankly. "I have no idea what you're talking about."

"What were you doing going off by yourself? Were you thinking at all?" Deep inside me a little flame lit. He was worried about me, I thought with satisfaction, but that sentiment was best left unsaid at the moment.

I shook off his hand. "Kate knew where I was going and as you can see, nothing happened to me. I went to visit some friends, but you wouldn't understand that. As I recall, Blessing is not your home and these are not your friends, and since that's the case, I really cannot understand why what I do and where I go are any business of yours. You want to be careful you don't get involved with the locals, you know." My tone was even snippier than my words.

He scowled at me and I saw his lips tighten with anger, and then I don't know how it happened exactly, but my rifle fell to the ground and my hat got knocked off and I was in John Davis's arms being kissed like there was no tomorrow. Not anger at all, I thought contentedly, but something else completely.

"You must have figured out by now why I make what you do my business," he said softly over my ear and into my hair, both of his hands at my waist holding me as if he never intended to let me go. "I did my best to keep my distance, but I didn't bargain for the way I felt when you did the same. A man could lose his edge with a hard-headed woman like you."

"John, you say the sweetest things," I drawled. "I declare you'll turn my head with compliments like that."

He made a sound somewhere between a laugh and a groan. "What would you like me to say, that you have eyes like smoke and a smile that lights a room and hair that changes color in the sunlight? And then there's that mouth. Lord, Lou, your mouth." He ran his thumb along my lips and said in a husky voice, "You have a mouth that was made for one thing," and proceeded to demonstrate exactly what that one thing was.

A little later I finally answered, "Since you asked, yes, those are exactly the things a woman likes to hear now and then. For a man not given to flowery speech, you did just fine."

He didn't smile down at me as I had expected. Instead he said soberly, his arms tightening around me, "Promise me you won't go gallivanting all over kingdom come by yourself again. Promise me, Lou."

"I was not gallivanting, and I did not go all over kingdom come, but," this as he pulled back to glare at me, "I promise. Anyway, I agree it wasn't my most prudent decision. I was going to take Jim along, but he was out of town, and I had everything ready to go out to the McGruders, so it seemed silly to unpack it all. Then it got late because Jess McGruder got to talking, and that was so remarkable I didn't have the heart to stop him. I do promise not to put myself in danger."

There we were, John holding me so tightly against him I could feel his heart beat, his cheek against my hair and me resting so easily in the circle of his arms it was like coming home. Although dusk, the day still held enough light that Caleb, appearing in the stable doorway, saw what was happening, turned right around, and went back in.

"John," I said meekly into his shirt, "if I promise not to run away, do you think you could let me go? I admit this is delightful, but it's also a bit too public for me." He loosened his arms immediately, and I pulled his head down to mine. "Thank you," I said and kissed him one more time, just for good measure. Then I stepped away to pick up the rifle. "See, I did listen to you. I'm not as impetuous and foolhardy as everyone seems to think." We stood an arm's length apart, wordless and, I think, both surprised by the power of the other's touch. Finally I bent to pick up my hat, saying, "I have to go. I told Billy supper would be on the table two hours ago, and I need to stop and let Kate know I'm home."

Home in more ways than one, I thought to myself, watching the evening's shadow slowly darken John's face. But still we stood there, each reluctant to leave in the same way you hesitate when it's warm by the fire and you have to go out into the cold. Then I heard Caleb whistling unnaturally loudly and thought we'd held him captive inside the stable long enough.

"Good night." I wanted to say more, wanted to tell him that just then my heart was so full of him it didn't have room for anything or anyone else, but instead I repeated, "Good night," hoping he would somehow hear all the words I couldn't speak.

"Yes," said John simply, "it has been that." I wondered if he felt as suddenly disoriented and lost as I did, cut loose from the shelter of his arms. I couldn't tell from his tone, and his face was now completely in shadows. "You need to get home before it gets darker and later." He paused, then added, "You take care, Lou." Not the words of a lover, but I was more than content with what I heard there.

Halfway home I turned to see his darkened figure still standing and watching me, and I raised my hand in a small wave, but by then the night was too black to know if he responded.

CHAPTER 11

Jim Killian came home to Blessing, proudly bringing a new printing press with him. It was a hand press, a step down from what he'd had, but he was prouder than a new papa with it. If Kate was worried about the repercussions of starting up the paper again, she was wise enough not to admit her fears to Jim. Instead, we both went and did our duty by admiring the new addition.

"It will be good to have a paper again," I told Jim. "I once read that the newspaper is mother's milk to a town, and I believe that's true. Will you still publish on Monday?" He nodded without looking up, already so engrossed in what he was writing that Kate and I could have danced a polka around the room and he wouldn't have noticed.

Later, walking home, I spied Matthew Palmer pulling up in front of the store with Mary beside him in the wagon, and I hurried over to them.

"I'm glad to see you and know you're both safe, but Mary, I thought you were staying in Pratt with the children?" I gave her a hand as she climbed down from the wagon.

"We did take the girls over to Matthew's brother, but when

it came to Matthew leaving without me, I couldn't let him. So the girls are there, out of harm's way and in good hands in case something should—happen." I caught her small hesitation at the last word, thought of Pete McGruder, and knew she was right to believe something could happen. "I feel better now that I'm here where I belong," she finished, "but did he fuss!"

"And they say women are the worriers!" I said, and we went into the store laughing together. Billy was there and some other customers, so Mary and I didn't get to continue our conversation until the room cleared.

Matthew lowered his voice. "We heard about Pete McGruder. Bad business." He had a grim look about him that I knew was concern, not so much for him, I imagined, but because Mary was out there with him.

"It was bad business," I agreed. "If they hadn't found Pete when they did, he could have died. You need to stay in touch with us in town, Matthew, and with the McGruders, too. We all have to stick together."

"We check in with Jess and his boys pretty regular, and they're coming over to help rebuild the barn. Jess isn't the hard man you think at first," adding with a quick grin, "especially when Mary sets out a pan of fresh Johnny bread."

As they got ready to leave, I said, "Mary, don't be a stranger. I'll be worrying about you out there by yourself."

She was remarkably cheerful. "We put our trust in the good Lord, Lou, and he knows we got plenty of work waiting for us. Not much time left for worrying." She rested her hand on her husband's arm as he picked up the reins, and I saw in that gesture the reason for her content. Still together, so all was well. Remembering the security of John Davis's arms, I had a clearer understanding of how she felt.

As I stood on the store porch watching them leave, I glanced across the street to see Paul Harper's figure in the front parlor window of Lily's house, holding back the curtain, his gaze following the Palmers out of town. He saw that I had noticed him and turned his head to look directly at me. It was too distant to see his face in detail, but I had the uncomfortable feeling from his fixed look and the stillness of his pose that he was doing some kind of mental calculation. I wasn't sure if it boded ill for the Palmers or for me or for all of us, but I didn't like the immobility of his scrutiny. He was planning some deviltry that would benefit no one but himself.

A growing atmosphere of uncertainty and fear had crept into Blessing, fed by the unrelenting dry, hot summer. What was cause and what was effect I couldn't tell, but everyone, including myself, appeared more short-tempered, jumpy, and abrupt than usual as if we all knew some great and inevitable cloudburst must come and were afraid of what might happen when the deluge finally arrived. The strained atmosphere and blazing temperatures made for long, sultry July days and restless nights of little sleep.

I hadn't spoken to Lily since the Sunday I surprised her with Paul Harper. What could either of us say that had not already been spoken between us? We had had rifts before, but nothing like this deep and irreversible chasm that seemed to separate us now. It grieved me that we were so distant, but I had no remedy for the situation as it stood. Lily had moved in one direction and I another, and by that summer we had grown so far apart we might as well have been strangers.

I couldn't bear the sight of Gordon and went out of my way not to speak to him or even acknowledge his presence. He had offered once more to buy the store but did it with little enthusiasm as if he needed to go through the motions but knew how the conversation would end before it began. On his way out after that particular meeting, Gordon turned back long enough to state in his Doomsday voice that he had given me enough opportunities and was not responsible for the consequences of my stubbornness. As much as I wanted to laugh off his tone and his message, I couldn't. Too many untoward incidents had happened recently, and knowing that Gordon and Harper were conspirators forced me to take Gordon's pompous pronouncements more seriously.

One afternoon not long after my conversation with the Palmers, Billy and I were in the back room unpacking a delivery of hardware when I heard the bell on the front door announce a visitor.

"We're closed," I called out, then took a quick look through the doorway to see who had entered. My heart gave a loud thud, and I quickly turned to Billy, saying in a low voice, "Billy, don't ask why, just do what I say. Go as fast as you can and find John and tell him I need him right here, right away. It's serious. Go. Right. Now." At my sober, commanding tone, he gave me a quick, unexpectedly savvy look and left out the alley door without comment.

I knew instantly, just from the look of him as he stepped into the store, that Paul Harper was trouble that day. Something purposeful in his expression or in his determined pace told me he had not come to spar in the usual lazy and insolent manner he assumed in my presence. I stood immobile in the doorway that separated the store from the back room, eyeing the rifle that lay so alluringly around the corner and under the counter. After Harper turned and deliberately closed the front door, careful that the seldom-used lock clicked into place, he stepped behind the counter and moved close to where I stood.

"You and I need to have a talk," was all he said, but I couldn't mistake the menace, his eyes grim and glittering and no pretense of pleasantness in his voice. Despite my intention not to look away from him, my glance must have slid to where the rifle lay because he said, "You are not fast enough to get to it before I get to you."

I considered stepping back quickly into the storeroom and making a dash for the alley door, but he stepped closer, within arm's reach, and by hesitating I missed my chance. I'm not proud of it, but I suppose the dead weight of fear made me slow and momentarily helpless. I left myself no option but to brazen it out and hope John was not wandering the Kansas countryside, hope, too, that Billy would find him in time. Paul Harper's suppressed energy, the set of his shoulders, his unblinking stare all told me he was a man on a mission that somehow involved me.

"Talk away, Mr. Harper. You have my full attention." My cocky bluster didn't fool either of us. I backed up, not taking my eyes from his face and retreated into the storeroom, casually moving in the direction of the closed alley door. Harper followed, matching me step for step as if we were dancing and I had taken the lead.

"I have been too kind to you and way too patient, but I intend to remedy that mistake right now. I'm going to tell you exactly what I want you to do in a way you won't possibly misunderstand, and then you're going to do it. You're not going to argue with me—you're just going to do what I say. Understand that I want this store and you're going to sell it to me."

"No. I'm not."

"Oh, I think you are. That's the part I haven't been clear about. That's what you don't seem to understand. This isn't a decision *you* make. It's a decision I make, and I don't have the patience or time left to explain it to you any more. I've grown tired of the game, so you need to listen to me." He kept approaching, and I kept retreating until my back came up hard against the wall. Directly in front of me now, he trapped my chin between his thumb and forefinger in a pinch harsh enough to bring unwilling tears to my eyes. "You're a nuisance and a troublemaker, but your time's run out. I offered to make it easy for you. I would have enjoyed comparing you to your sister, and since I'd guess you haven't had a man in a long time, if ever, you might have enjoyed it even more." He brought his face very close to mine, green eyes cold with malice and a perverse pleasure at my discomfort. "She was a piece of ripe fruit who fairly fell into my hands, very willing and very talented, but you were something else. You promised the excitement of the hunt and the satisfaction of the kill, but sad to say, I have to cut the chase short. Your time's up. Today. Now." He leaned his full weight against me as he finished speaking, so that one of my arms was immobilized between us, but with the other I reached up to strike his hand away from my face. He caught my wrist and twisted it around behind my back hard enough to make me cry out. "I am not playing now. I'm telling you that tomorrow you will go over to the bank, and you will tell your brother-in-law that you want to sell me this store."

"Never," I spit at him and tried to bring up my knee with enough force to cause him some pain and make him loosen his hold. He made a convulsive movement against me, adjusting his posture to pin me even more firmly against the wall.

"Don't try it. You're not going any place I don't give you permission to go." He brought his face so close to mine I could feel the rough stubble of his cheek on my skin, all his weight pressing hard on me, one hand now circling my throat and the other continuing to twist my arm up behind me harder and higher. He gave a quick vicious jerk that caused me, despite my resolution, to give a wordless cry of pain. "I can hurt you very much," he said brutally, "and enjoy doing it." I was trying desperately to free my trapped hand, so I could push him away and relieve the almost unbearable pain in my twisted arm when abruptly his weight no longer pressed against me.

Thank God Billy had found John, I thought passionately, because it was John who had freed me, both hands to Harper's shoulders and a look on his face that would have brought any other man except Paul Harper up sharp. Harper turned, off balance, and John took hold of his coat lapels, lifted him partially off his feet, and pushed him hard into a stack of wooden boxes. Harper fell, and the boxes, too, scattering around him.

John stood so still and focused he almost didn't seem human, no sign of a breath despite the exertion, not a movement in him anywhere. Body and eyes both ice. In a voice I didn't recognize as his, John said, "You made a serious mistake just now. Your last one."

I thought with certainty that he would kill him, and the

knowledge made me sick with dread and repulsion. Billy watched from the doorway, and I didn't want him to see it. The violence would be something he would not forget, or I either.

At first Harper lay on his side, not moving. Then he shook his head slightly and slowly pushed himself up to stand, careful to keep his hands in full view. "I don't have a weapon on me." He carefully removed his coat, draped the garment over one forearm, and stretched his arms out straight toward us. "See. You want to kill me but you're not going to. Not an unarmed man, not in front of the boy, and not with her here."

John's eyes dropped briefly to Harper's outstretched hands, and then he repeated himself as if Harper had not spoken. "You made a serious mistake just now, so you need to understand this. If you even threaten to lay a hand on her again, if you make any move toward her at any time for any reason, I will kill you, and it won't matter what you're wearing."

Coolly, Harper made a pretense of dusting off his pants and tucking in his shirt. I didn't like the man, but I had to credit him with a kind of raw courage that, facing John's obvious fury and only one misstep away from death, did not allow his hands to tremble or his voice to shake. He had scraped a cheekbone against one of the wooden boxes, and the skin looked red and raw, trickling a thin line of blood down his chin that he made no move to wipe.

"It's Davis, isn't it? You're living up to your reputation, but don't forget you're just one man. I'd watch my back from now on if I were you. You never know who might be coming up behind you." He adjusted his coat over his arm, almost dapper, and reached for the door that exited to the alley.

I stepped closer to John, my shoulder pressed slightly against him, and Harper turned to speak to me as if John were not there. "Miss Lou." The familiar mocking tone was back, the one he seemed to reserve for me. With John standing protectively beside me, I thought Paul Harper must be either the most foolhardy or the most single-minded man I'd ever met. "You're the one making the serious mistake if you think a two-bit shootist with a fancy gun will keep me from finishing this conversation. I'm sorry we were interrupted. It was just getting interesting." Harper looked impassively at the two of us standing so close that John's slow, steady breathing tickled the back of my neck, and added coarsely, baiting, "I think I was wrong about you not having a man for a while. From the looks of the two of you, I'd guess you've been to his pump more than once."

I put a hand on John's arm and said his name in a low voice because I'd heard his quick intake of breath and felt his body stiffen with anger.

"You'll save all of us time and tears, Miss Lou, if you go talk to your brother-in-law tomorrow just like I told you. Then you might be able to sleep in peace. Until you do that, I wouldn't sleep too sound if I were you." Then he left, pulling the door shut as carefully as if he were a dinner guest who'd just said good night for the evening.

"Thank you," I said simply, turning to face John. He still stood immobile with fury, trying to control his anger the best he could. I felt as if I were looking at a stranger, at someone else behind those familiar blue eyes, someone impersonal and cold, someone so distant I couldn't reach him no matter what I said or did.

I took a calm, light tone. "It would have been wrong to take the law into your own hands, John, just wrong. It was awful before you got here but more violence would only have made everything worse. Harper just wanted to scare me, and," I forced a rueful laugh, "he did a good job of it. But it was an intentional encounter, calculated and premeditated for a specific reason. I'm all right." I put a palm up against his cheek, ignoring the painful throb in my shoulder, and said urgently, "Stop looking like that. You're frightening me. I'm not hurt." John came back then, from whatever fierce place he'd been, and reached out to put an arm around my shoulders and pull me against him. "*You're* the one that has to be careful now," I told him. "We both know he attacked Pete McGruder without warning, and now he'll be out for you, too. Harper doesn't want me dead. He just wants my property."

John asked without inflection, "And if you die, who inherits?"

His words took a moment to register and then I pulled away from him. "What an outrageous thing to suggest. Are you saying Lily would conspire in my death, so her lover can gain possession of a piece of property? That's preposterous. She's my sister." He didn't reply, probably because he realized there was nothing he could say that I wouldn't protest and deny.

I went to the doorway where Billy stood, uncertain, a little frightened, maybe a little excited by what he'd seen. "I did what you told me," he said.

"You did just fine. Thank you, Billy. You did exactly right."

That night, lying awake and unable to keep the thoughts and memories from spinning around in my head, I tried to consider objectively what John had hinted. Surely things had not degenerated so much between Lily and me that she would contemplate my death to get what she wanted. But with a shiver despite the summer heat, I remembered Lily's desperate desire to leave Blessing and unwillingly, in spite of myself, I thought that John might not be so far from the truth.

In the morning I made up my mind to contact the county sheriff about what was happening in Blessing. I had a personal complaint now, not a crime without witnesses and not just hints and hearsay. At the telegraph office I told the young dispatcher that I wanted to send a telegram to Sheriff Badger in Scott City. The boy stared at me, his Adam's apple bobbing up and down like a cork on a fishing line, as I wrote out the message. When I handed it to him, he set the piece of paper down on the desk next to him.

"I'll just wait here until you send it, Andy."

"Well, Miss Lou, I ain't gonna get to it for a while. I got some other work to do first." He didn't make eye contact, and I berated myself for having grown so suspicious. I had known young Andy all his life and couldn't think of one good reason to support the impression I was getting that he was reluctant to send my telegram.

"All right, but don't forget about it. I want it sent today, and I'll be back this afternoon for my receipt." He looked relieved that I wasn't going to press the point. Truth was, I was too tired and confused to be insistent with him just then. Fitful sleep and a nagging, terrible suspicion about my sister were taking a toll. I wished John had never made that remark about Lily. The idea he had implied was too ridiculous to consider, but I found myself considering it anyway, ridiculous or not.

As if thinking about her made her materialize, Lily visited the store that afternoon. Because of the other people present, she came up to me and said, too brightly, "I'm out of needles, Lou. Do you have any?" Wordlessly I brought out a packet and placed it on the counter. She met my gaze unashamedly, slipped the packet of needles into her pocket, and continued with the same breezy tone. "Didn't you tell me you got in a bolt of green gauze? Is it in the back? I was thinking of changing the veil on that old Easter hat from last year. Green would look nice for fall." She followed me into the back room.

"What do you really want, Lily? You have no more interest in green gauze than the man in the moon."

"I believe the man's dancing, Lou, or at least getting ready to. Paul told me you were seriously considering selling the store."

"Did he? Funny the tricks memory plays on a person. I don't recall saying anything of the sort."

Her eyes searched my face to see if I was serious. "Listen to me, Lou. Selling the store would be the smartest thing you could do." Then in a voice and tone completely unlike her, she took one of my hands in both of hers. "Do it, Lou. Please." I could have been mistaken, I suppose, but I thought I detected real concern and a kind of desperation in her voice. But I was aware of my own weariness, fear, and confusion as well, so attributing even a hint of affection to Lily might have been pure delusion on my part.

"Lily, can't you tell me what's going on? Can't you trust me? I don't understand why you feel I should give up my life and livelihood."

"Because if you don't, you may truly give up your life and not in the way you mean it."

Watching her face, conscious of the pressure of her hands, I remembered John's words and realized I no longer trusted her. That knowledge made my tone more caustic and suspicious than I intended. "Is that a threat Paul Harper told you to make?"

"Paul doesn't know I've come here," Lily answered indignantly. "I can't tell you anything except that the safest thing you can do is sell up and move away. Just do it, Lou. You're always so stubborn, and you always have to be right. You've never listened to me in your whole life, but this one time, I'm asking you to trust me. Everything will be all right if you just do the safe thing and sell the store to Gordon."

Because my sister had never before appeared so sincere or spoken to me so humbly or convincingly, I wanted to do whatever she asked. In our entire adult lives this moment was the closest Lily had ever come to expressing any tenderness or concern for me, never an *I love you* from her or anything remotely close, never a hint of an affection that I'd longed for most of my life. I wanted to believe she meant what she said, wanted to believe my sister loved me and was concerned about my well being, but I couldn't. I just couldn't.

"No, Lily," I replied, low voiced, withdrawing my hand from her touch. "You almost make me wish I could, but I can't do what you ask. I won't be forced to give up what I love."

"Then you've made a bed to lie in that you won't like," she retorted angrily. "You're being proud and stupid and stubborn, Lou, and I'm not responsible for anything that happens. I've done everything I could."

"Yes, you have," I agreed, "and no, you're not responsible. I hope that helps you sleep better at night."

"All I've ever been is an obligation to you, never a sister."

"That's not true."

"Oh yes it is. Think about it. Think how *you'd* have felt, passed along from father to sister without anyone asking you what you thought, as if you hadn't a brain in your head, as if you were helpless and lost, a perpetual child needing the constant care and admonition of your family. Think how you'd have rebelled at such a life."

"You know that's not how Father felt about you, and you must know I never intended to patronize you."

"I don't think you ever gave my feelings much thought, Lou. You were too caught up in the noble work of caring for poor, weak, shallow Lily. You convinced yourself you could be the perfect daughter by becoming the perfect sister." Seeing the past suddenly through Lily's eyes, I admitted there was some painful truth to what she said, but she wasn't entirely accurate or fair.

"You act like I was only playing a part all these years, but you're leaving out an important truth—that I loved Father and I love you, Lily. You were never an obligation. There's never been a day of my life I haven't loved you, even in the worst times. If I've acted the martyr, I was wrong and I'm sorry. I can see now how trying it must have been for you, and you're right, I didn't think about your feelings like I should have, but don't credit me with bad motives. There's never been a time I haven't wanted the best for you."

"You've always thought that what was best for me had to match what was best for you. You could never see farther than your own backyard, Lou, and your own set of small town morals. You never saw me as a flesh-and-blood person in my own right. You wanted me to be exactly like you."

"There are absolute rights and wrongs in life, Lily, when it doesn't matter whose backyard you're in," I responded wearily. This particular part of the discussion we had had before. "We make choices in life, and since we have to live with our choices, we should be sure they don't hurt others or keep us awake at night." At her uncomprehending look, I added, "We've talked about this before and I'm tired, Lily. I'm just tired. I don't want to talk about it any more. What's the use?"

Whatever trust had once been between us was completely, irrevocably gone. I hated that I couldn't believe she had come solely motivated by sisterly concern or that she sincerely cared about my safety, but I no longer recognized the real Lily or understood who she was inside or how she thought. My sister would forever be suspect. Lily must have realized that more conversation was useless, for without another word, she turned abruptly and walked out of the store.

CHAPTER 12

Time got away from me that day, and I didn't return to the telegraph office to check on the message I had sent to the sheriff in Scott City. After supper I spent the whole evening working on the account books and didn't recall my intention to go back and confirm that the telegram had been sent until I had closed the books and gotten ready for bed.

When I went into the front room to put out the lamp, I was startled by a knock on the door. The fact that I froze at the sound, my heart suddenly beating hard and fast, was an indication of how things had changed in Blessing. I had never been afraid of a knock on the door before, but when I heard John's voice saying my name, fear was replaced by the pleasure of seeing him.

"Just a minute." I threw a wrapper over my nightdress and went to the door to let him in.

My front room, which I had always considered to be of comfortable proportions because it ran the entire length of the store below, seemed to shrink as John entered. It wasn't so much the effect of his size—although he was a tall, broad-shouldered man—but more the way he carried himself, proud and strong. That visible confidence, which was as natural to him as the color of his eyes, accounted for the feeling of safety I had whenever we were together. That night, though, he looked troubled and not his usual unruffled self, a furrow of worry between his brows.

"There's no way around this," he began abruptly, standing just inside the door, not even removing his hat. "I need to go to Topeka and I'm leaving tonight. I've put it off too long already."

"Does this trip have something to do with the business you're on?"

"Yes, but it has to do with Blessing, too, and the sooner I get to Topeka, the sooner things may calm down here." He shook his head when I started to ask a question. "I can't tell you any more, Lou. Not now. I wish I could. But when I get back, I promise I'll explain everything."

"So you are coming back?"

I think my question truly astonished him as if it had never crossed his mind not to return and he couldn't believe that it had crossed mine.

"I'll be back. I have unfinished business here," he said with his slow smile, finally taking off his hat and tossing it onto a chair, stepping toward me with a look I read as an invitation, although it may have been a response to what he saw in my own eyes.

A little later we sat together on the overstuffed loveseat, my head on his shoulder, lonely before he was even gone.

"How long will you be gone?"

"I calculate six days at the most. I'll catch the morning train out of Hays to Topeka, and I think I can keep my business to one day, maybe two, while I'm there." Six days seemed an eternity to me, and I must have made some small sigh because he said, "I know. I don't like it either, but I've been thinking and there's something you can do while I'm gone. I want you to wait a day and then go talk to your brother-in-law. Tell him you're seriously considering selling the store. Ask him to go over everything again with you. Pretend you're confused about some of the details. Ask for a higher price. I don't know what else, but you'll think of something. Keep telling him you need a little more time to think about it and put him off as long as you can."

"But why?" I couldn't understand what such delaying tactics would accomplish.

"I want you to fill the time while I'm gone by making them think they're going to get what they want. If you do that, there shouldn't be a need for anything worse to happen." He added with a smile in his voice, "You've been practicing on Harley Johnson for a while, but now is the time to put your talent for making excuses to real work."

"I don't think I can stretch that out six days, John. How dense do I have to pretend to be?"

He turned and put both hands in my hair, letting it run through his fingers as a thirsty man might plunge his hands into a running stream, just for the pleasure of the feel of the water.

"Dense enough to stay out of trouble until I get back. Dense enough to make sure I've got someone to come back to. I never—" I waited for him to finish, but his voice grew rough, maybe with emotion, I couldn't tell, and he kissed me instead, which suited me just fine. "Don't tell anyone I'm gone, Lou. Not anyone. Eventually they'll figure it out, but thinking I'm still in town might buy you additional time."

I cannot remember, before or since, ever feeling as bereft and abandoned as I felt that night standing on the landing outside my door and watching John ride off into the darkness. All my life I had happily and proudly taken care of myself and in a few weeks everything familiar had been turned topsy-turvy. Just knowing he was not going to be near for a few days made me feel troubled and apprehensive. How had I come to exchange my blithe independence for this loneliness and longing? Now I understood the depth of the words and that uneasy tone in Mary Palmer's voice as she contemplated leaving her husband behind in Blessing. *We've never spent the night apart since the day we were married.* How easily a person could get used to having someone around, how comforted by a voice or a look or a touch. I had apparently lived contentedly without John Rock Davis for twenty-five years and yet, oddly, I couldn't seem to remember what my life had been like before him.

"I believe this will be the longest week of my life," I said out loud to myself before I fell asleep that night and didn't know the half of it.

The next morning I remembered yesterday's errand and went back to the telegraph office. Andy looked up when I pushed open the door, and a look of apprehension and unhappiness spread across his face. I knew instantly that he had not done what I'd asked.

"Any reply to my telegram yet?" Andy shook his head, speechless, eyes darting around the room as if he were deciding on the quickest escape route. "That's odd," I went on relentlessly, "since it was important, and I would have expected word back by now. You did send it out promptly, didn't you?" He seemed fascinated by a piece of paper on his desk and didn't look up. "Andrew," I repeated, "you *did* send it out promptly, didn't you?"

He finally raised a miserable face. "No, Ma'am."

"I beg your pardon."

"No, Ma'am, I didn't send it out promptly. I didn't send it out at all."

"Did you have a busy day, Andrew, or run out of time, or maybe you just forgot to send it?"

"No, Ma'am."

"Then you'll need to explain to me why you didn't do what I asked and what I paid you to do." Andy looked at me from under his visor in such a hangdog way that at any other time I'd have had to smile.

"Mr. Monroe said I wasn't to send any telegram you wrote out unless he saw it and approved it first, and when he looked at what you wrote to Sheriff Badger yesterday, he said I wasn't to send it. Mr. Monroe kept it and I ain't seen it since."

I didn't find Frank Monroe at his meat market, but if he thought he could keep me away by hiding out in his beer hall, he was sadly mistaken. It would take more than a foray into a den of alcohol to offend my modesty. Undeterred, I walked past the bar toward the small room in the back that Frank used as an office. Too early for the regulars, I paused in front of the lone patron, an old man with a dirty beard lazily sweeping the floor.

"Is Frank Monroe in the back?" I asked. He gave a fraction of a nod, and I went past him to knock on the office door. "Frank, it's Lou. I need to speak to you." When I heard no response, I knocked again. "Don't try to hide from me. I need to talk to you, and I am not going anywhere until I do."

After a moment Frank opened the door and ushered me into the stuffy office, saying in a placating tone, "Louisa, no one is trying to hide from you. You need to be more patient. I don't know where you got that peevish streak in you. Neither of your parents had it. Now sit down. Whatever is agitating you does not need to be discussed standing up." He sat down behind his desk and leaned back, lacing his fingers across his stomach.

I sat, too, calmed myself as I straightened my skirts, and turned on him a brilliant smile. "Frank, I can't tell you how this misunderstanding has upset me. I'm sure you'll be able to straighten it all out in a moment." My tone disconcerted him because he must have been expecting a tirade instead.

"What misunderstanding is that?"

"Andy at the telegraph office has the idea that you don't want me to send a telegram to Sheriff Badger in Scott City. Now before you get upset with him, I'm sure he just misunderstood your intent. All it will take from you is a simple word and my telegram can go out. After all, what possible reason could there be for you to interfere with my legal right to send a telegram to whomever I choose?" I met his gaze expectantly and innocently.

Because Frank had dandled me on his knee when I was a baby and had known me my entire life, his eyes narrowed warily. "I wouldn't call it a misunderstanding exactly."

"No? Then what?"

"Louisa, there are times when you act with more fervor, shall we say, than discretion. For you to attempt to engage the county sheriff in Blessing's internal affairs is not necessary or wise. You have overstepped your authority."

"Did you read my telegram, Frank? My *private* telegram?"

"I have anticipated such a telegram from you for some weeks, Louisa, since the Palmers' fire, in fact, when I could tell you were harboring imaginative suspicions that had no basis in fact. There is no need—and I forbid you—to drag Sheriff Badger into our dealings here. We have no problems. Our streets and businesses are safe."

"I was assaulted inside my own store, Frank."

"Nonsense."

"Paul Harper physically assaulted and threatened me, and I have no intention of tolerating his behavior. The *Banner* office was ransacked by Mr. Harper's thugs. Someone set fire to the Palmers' barn and nearly killed Pete McGruder, and you and I both know who's responsible. Something bad is happening in Blessing. We live in a civilized society, with laws for the protection of its citizens, and Sheriff Badger is the duly authorized person who enforces those laws. I fully intend to lodge a formal complaint against Paul Harper. It is beyond me why you would want to prohibit me from doing so when you're the mayor here, the person we rely on to maintain law and order. Besides which, for all you know, you and your establishments could receive the same kind of treatment as the *Banner* office or the McGruder boy."

"That will not happen."

Frank stated the words with such conviction that I leaned forward to stare him full in the face. "What have you done, Frank, that you can be so sure you and your businesses are immune from threat and violence?"

He had the grace to redden. "I am a practical businessman, Louisa. There is a cost to maintaining a safe business environment, and I am willing to pay that cost."

"I don't understand what you're telling me."

"You may talk all you want about civilization and society, but western Kansas is not New York or Philadelphia. These are still violent times and without our own law enforcement officer, we're at the mercy of roughnecks and hooligans. If I can purchase protection for my establishments, why shouldn't I?"

I sat quietly, trying to absorb what he was saying, and after a moment I understood. "You pay Paul Harper money to leave you alone, don't you? Harper extorts money from you under the pretense of protection when in fact he's protecting you from himself. Oh, that is rich, Frank."

"I don't like your tone, and *extorts* isn't the word I'd use."

"I'm sure it's not, but to paraphrase Shakespeare, a rose by any other name still smells. How could you be a party to that? How could you sell out? How could you betray the trust the people of Blessing put in you, the trust *I* put in you?"

Frank scowled, offended and sullen in his anger. "It's a business relationship between men that you wouldn't understand." I resented his patronizing tone hinting that because I was a woman I would be unable to fathom what he had done and why.

"You underestimate me. I understand very clearly about that kind of relationship, but Frank, what makes you think that in one month or three months or six months Paul Harper will be content with whatever you're paying him today? I guarantee he'll ask for more and keep asking for more. He knows he's sitting on a gold mine. You're a fool and you've made a pact with the devil."

"Then I'm not the only fool in Blessing, Louisa. From where I sit, it's people like you, people who confuse noble ideals on paper with real life who are the fools."

I stood up. "I understand now why you don't want the law involved. Badger might upset your apple cart. He might enforce the law and expect you, the mayor, to support him in his efforts. I'm glad my father isn't alive to see this day. Aren't you ashamed?"

For just a moment he did in fact look ashamed, but then the bluster returned. "Don't preach to me, missy. You would be wise to learn from your elders and consider the same approach. You're like your father that way. I told your mother the day she married him that Augustus Caldecott didn't have an ounce of practical sense and his head would always be in the clouds. You're just like him, always so busy thinking about how things should be that you can't see how things really are."

"Oh I see how things really are, Frank, I just don't like them. You may be able to keep me from reaching Badger today, but if I have to ride to Hays to send a telegram or if I have to ride clear to Scott City, I am contacting the sheriff."

As I left, Frank called after me, "Louisa, this is not the time for heroics." He was still speaking as I closed the door behind me and walked out past the bar and into the street, captive in my own town. What had Blessing become for me now if not a prison?

When I poured out the story to Kate, she sat very still, obviously unsurprised, with a guilty look about her. "Kate, did you know about Frank's arrangement with Harper?" At her continued silence, I cried, "What are you not telling me? You aren't part of this scheme, too, are you?"

"No, my little shop isn't important enough, thank God, not yet anyway, but it's common knowledge that half the establishments in Blessing pay Paul Harper what he calls a security fee."

"Who exactly?"

"Besides Frank Monroe, I know Harper collects from the Palace Saloon and the billiards hall. I've heard that Caleb, Levi Hoffman, and the Hansens pay, too. I'm sure there are others. Every Thursday Paul Harper comes into town, makes his little circuit of visits, and collects his fees." I remembered watching him go from storefront to storefront, remembered being curious about what he was doing.

"Why didn't someone tell me?"

Kate looked at me unhappily. "Because people know you, Lou. They know you'd be outraged and you'd scold them and they simply didn't want to have to deal with that on top of everything else."

I didn't know whether to be insulted or flattered. "Have I become the town shrew then?"

"More like the town conscience. Lou, you are the most honest person I know, and your heart is as big as Kansas. Everything is clear to you without any gray areas, and it's wonderful you're like that. People love you for it. But at the same time it can make folks uncomfortable, especially when there's a chance that you're right and they may be wrong. People just found it easier to go along with Harper and not make a big issue of it. I don't know what I'd do if the subject was forced with me. I'm not brave and I don't want anything to happen to Jim." She got up and opened a desk drawer, displaying a derringer small enough to fit in her palm. "Jim got me this and told me to keep it handy. I think I could use it if I had to, but I hope it never comes to that."

I couldn't say a word, still adjusting to the fact that I, so certain that I knew my town and the people of my town, so sure of my pivotal place in Blessing, so proud of my relationships and my history here, had not known what had been occurring right under my nose, had been completely and purposefully kept in the dark. The realization seemed somehow shaming to me, as if I had failed my friends, as if they needed something essential from me that I could not, would not provide.

When I stood up, still not speaking, Kate said hastily, "Lou, don't be angry with me."

"With you? Never. I just can't believe that in two months so much has changed, or do you think Blessing wasn't ever what I thought it was?"

She looked at me kindly and shook her head. "I'm sorry,

Lou." Sorry for Blessing or me or herself I didn't know and hadn't the heart to ask.

That evening I made a mark on the page of my journal, indicating one day past and five to go before John would be back. In a world that seemed to be ever changing, he was the one constant I was clinging to for dear life.

I faced the next day with dread. Although I had promised John I would visit Gordon and pretend I was serious about selling the store, I so much did not want to go through the exercise that I nearly persuaded myself to wait another day. Pride mostly, I suppose, but since talking to Lily, I held Gordon in such disgust that I could hardly bring myself to look at him. Now I must pretend to be the cowed woman brought to her knees by the brute force of a crude scoundrel. The idea went against every bone in my body, every breath I breathed, but I had promised John I would do it, and I would not break a promise to him. The fact that his plan held some merit also didn't escape me. I would never have thought of such a tactic myself because I didn't possess the shrewdness of intellect to think matters through so dispassionately. I'm a poor chess player for the same reason, with a weakness in strategy that my father used to tease me about.

"Your heart always leads your head, Lou. You might consider reversing the order some time and see what happens." Then he would move one playing piece and then another, and the game was over, and I had inevitably lost. Now, though, the time had come to take my father's advice, strategizing literally for all I was worth.

I greeted Mr. Cuthbert as I passed him and went to stand in the open doorway of Gordon's office. My brother-in-law raised his head from his work in that maddeningly pompous way he had and said my name, lilting the end so it came out as a question.

"Gordon." I went in uninvited and sat down across from him. "I've been thinking about your recent offer to buy the store, and perhaps I was precipitous in my rejection of that offer. I know you are well aware of my sometimes too-hasty decision making, and I hoped we might discuss the proposition further." I looked at Gordon, trying to appear wide-eyed and hesitantly smiling, the picture of an uncertain woman. He returned a look that at first held surprise followed by deep suspicion, and then in his way, his overconfident and self-important way that must always be superior to me, he smiled a victory smile.

"How wise of you to change your mind, Louisa. How very astute. I didn't think you had it in you," his voice a purr of satisfaction. I wanted to smack him.

"I'm a practical woman, and I recognize a certain inevitability to the situation now, but I have several questions, and I want to revisit the price you offered." We spent two hours together discussing the sale and going over a list of questions I had composed the evening before. I had done my homework, pretending to be unhappy with his previous price, running through endless lists of the store's contents, and comparing the building and the land to comparable properties in the area. Finally I gathered up the stack of papers and stood. "You've given me a lot to consider, Gordon. I'll need a little time to think all this through."

He stood also. "A *little* time is all you have, Louisa. Come back tomorrow, and I'll draw up the final papers."

Tomorrow was sooner than I had planned. "I'm still a working woman, Gordon, so I doubt a day is enough time for me to do all the necessary calculations and comparisons."

"You can trust my judgment, Louisa. I am practiced in these matters."

Condescending prig, I thought, but outwardly said, "I'll try to find time tomorrow afternoon," and he had to be content with that.

Before I went back to the store, I stopped at the *Banner* office to visit Jim Killian. He was working at the press, shirt sleeves rolled above his elbows.

"Is your darling up and running now, Jim?"

"Yes, dearie, and a piece of magic it is." He flourished a practice run printed sheet, once more in his element and happy.

If ever a man were born to the printed word, it was Jim Killian.

"I'm here as a paying customer. I want to place an order." I told him about my conversation with Frank Monroe and the following talk with Kate. "Will you run off enough flyers to pass out to all the business establishments in Blessing? I think it's time we called a town meeting. Make it tomorrow night after supper so Eliza and Steven can come, to be held in the back room of Caldecott's General Store and Dry Goods. Promise an interesting discussion and say whatever you need to so people will show up."

"Are you sure you want to do this, Lou?"

"I'm not sure about much any more, but I believe it's time to clear the air. Do you think I'm making a mistake?"

Jim examined me soberly, thinking the matter through. "No, maybe it is time. I can't disagree with you, so consider the flyers on the house."

"I'll send Billy over after supper to pick them up, and he can deliver them in the morning. Then we'll see what happens. You'll come, won't you? I need someone I can count on for support."

He gave a wicked Irish grin. "Oh, I wouldn't miss it for the world, darlin'. If nothing else, it'll make good press."

That night I looked west out my front window and for the first time in a very long while saw clouds building along the horizon. The air seemed to crackle, and I had a subdued but very real sense that a long-awaited change in the weather was approaching. Nothing definite yet, but I saw rain out there and this time believed it might actually reach Blessing.

I made another mark in my journal that night—two days past and four to go. John should have arrived in Topeka today, I thought, picturing his tall figure stepping off the train, and he'll be back home in Blessing—maybe not just my home, maybe home for him now, too—before long.

Saturday morning, I thought when I awoke, the day I had to meet with Gordon and once more act the simpleton. I was completely at a loss as to what to say to stall further. I thought I would continue to protest the price and obstinately demand more money. Greed was something Gordon understood, and I held out a slim hope that he would assume I was motivated by the same cupidity. Since tomorrow was Sunday, the bank would be closed, which would allow me to stretch the transaction out into Monday. Hopefully John would be back sometime Tuesday, and I could then drop the pretense with Gordon entirely. With a touch of luck, everything would work out, but in my heart of hearts, I was certain something unnamed was simply being postponed.

The Palmers and the McGruders came into town for supplies that morning. Matthew told me that Jess and Joe were helping him rebuild his barn and all had been quiet.

"I smell rain," he commented, and the furrows of worry that had built up across his forehead and between his eyes seemed to disappear for a time. Mary took a moment to enjoy the bolts of colored fabrics lying out, then with a sigh asked for simple things, vinegar, sugar, flour, and coffee. I tucked some peppermints down in the side of the package because I knew she favored them.

"I know you miss the girls, Mary. Maybe since it's quieted down, you could bring them home."

She shook her head. "It's quiet now, Lou, but I have a bad feeling we're not done with the trouble yet." Her uneasy gaze met mine, and I knew exactly how she felt. Maybe it was just the approaching rainstorm that had put me on edge, but I didn't think so. Something bigger was brewing.

Jess McGruder returned the baskets I had used to deliver the food and, more voluble than usual, volunteered that Pete was on his feet and eating again. They were all staying pretty close to home, he said, except when they were working on the Palmers' barn, and Mary Palmer was a "passable" cook, who made sure none of the McGruder men went hungry. A veritable torrent of words but now so natural that neither of us gave it a thought.

When I asked where Joe had disappeared to, Jess said,

"He's met some little girl who works over at the hotel. Thinks he's sweet on her." He gave me a bland look. "I don't think she fell out of no tree either."

His comment made me laugh. "I should hope not. If it's Sally, she's such a little thing she'd hurt herself falling out of anything. She's a nice girl, Jess, and a very good cook. If you're not careful, you're going to find yourself domesticated out there."

He looked as if the prospect wouldn't be unwelcome. I recalled the spotless sitting room with his wedding picture on the wall, that gentle smile on his wife's face and her hand resting intimately on his shoulder. Sally would be good for all of them, and a couple of grandchildren running around the place wouldn't hurt either.

Early in the afternoon I took a deep breath, freshened my cheeks with a splash of cool water, and went over to the bank. It did not have regular Saturday afternoon business hours, but Gordon had unlocked the door and was waiting for me. The day felt hot and muggy, hopeful harbinger of a rousing prairie thunderstorm, but even in the most uncomfortable weather Gordon never appeared mussed or wrinkled. He had spread the sale papers out on his desk and with a minimum of words and no greeting tried to hand me a pen. Ignoring the gesture, I sat down and gathered all the sheets, reading each one methodically, line by line, slowly and carefully.

When I finished, he commented impatiently, "It's exactly what we discussed yesterday, Louisa. I need your signature in three places."

"You know, Gordon, I've had a chance to go over the contents of the store, look at my books more thoroughly, confirm what similar properties might be selling for, and I don't think you're offering quite enough money. Not quite enough for all you'll be getting." I rested my hands in my lap, making no movement toward the pen or the signature line on the document he held.

"It's exactly what we discussed yesterday, Louisa," he

repeated, "and it seemed attractive enough to you then."

"You know us women, we change our minds at the drop of a hat. Could you go over some of the details with me again? I'm not sure I quite understand them all." But even as I said it, I knew I'd said too much, even for Gordon. I had gone too far.

He stared at me so long that I became fleetingly uncomfortable, and then a wave of red spread up his neck to his face from his perfectly starched shirt collar to his thinning hairline. His words were slow and thick with anger. "You have no intention of selling your store, do you? You've been playing me for a fool."

"Don't be ridiculous. Why would I do that? This is a big step for me, and I just need more time to be sure I'm doing the right thing."

He went on as if I hadn't spoken. "You've been an embarrassment and a hindrance to your sister and me since the day she and I were married and it will stop." He spit out the last three words venomously, then stood up with such force that his chair spun away the desk and collided with the wall. "Get out." When I tried once more to convince him of my sincere intentions, he interrupted me. "You have always been a selfish, condescending little bitch. I was the fool for thinking you had changed. Get out."

I stood as well, openly scornful and furious. "My, my Gordon, you're forgetting your manners. I may be selfish and condescending, but at least I've never sent my wife on a whore's errand."

He responded to my glare by crashing both his palms down on the desk. "Get out and don't think you can come crawling to me later asking for my help."

"There are few guarantees in life, but that's one you can take to the bank," I responded, matching him in tone and bluntness. "You're a disgusting excuse for a human being, Gordon, a shameful husband, and a rotten branch on our family tree. I should have locked Lily in her room on her wedding day and never let her out. I wish she were still there."

LILY'S SISTER

Leaving the bank, I was aware that I had undoubtedly made things worse, but at that moment I didn't care. I had attempted what John had asked me to do, could tell him that I had done it with good intentions and to the best of my ability, and if I wasn't successful, so be it. There was just so much pretentious posturing a person should have to tolerate, and that Saturday afternoon I had reached my limit.

CHAPTER 13

Following my instructions, Billy had delivered the handbills to all the merchants in Blessing, announcing a town meeting to be held in the back room of my store Saturday night after supper. I had a full house. Frank Monroe, the undertaker Levi Hoffman, both Hansens, Caleb from the stables, Carl Pomeroy, who owned the Palace Saloon and the billiards hall, the barber George Marks, even Milt French showed up. I could tell that many were there against their better judgment and so were a restless and unsettled group.

I stood up to speak without preamble or introduction. "Most of us in this room have known each other a long time, and we've stuck it out through some rough years. We all have a considerable investment in Blessing and a mutual reason for keeping our town respectable and secure. You know that people aren't going to want to settle their families someplace that isn't safe. Besides that, there's not a one of you here I don't count as a friend. That's why I wanted to get together to talk about what's happening in Blessing."

"What do you think is happening?" asked Pomeroy.

"It's obvious that a bad element has taken over our streets,

Carl. We've had vandalism, threats, assaults, arson, and attempted murder in our midst, and we never had anything like that before Paul Harper came to town. I know that some of you, maybe all of you, are paying him to leave you alone, but giving in to that kind of force doesn't solve the problem."

Frank Monroe, hands grasping his lapels, stood to offer his rebuttal. "That's where you're wrong, Louisa. It does solve the problem. None of us here except Killian has had a bit of trouble. That arrangement you condemn has kept them out of our establishments and away from our customers. It's a cost of doing business, and I consider it money well spent." The group murmured their agreement.

"Then you're not thinking into the future. I said this to you before, Frank. Men like Harper are not content for long with the going rate. You're going to end up paying through the nose and why should you? You worked hard for that money, and I can bet you had plans for it other than lining Paul Harper's pockets."

"Lou's right." Jim stood to speak. "I can tell you from my experiences in Boston that this will go from bad to worse. Once you've got a tiger by the tail, it's damned hard to let it go."

"Well, this isn't Boston. What's our alternative? I had my fill of fighting in the war. Look what happened to your place, Killian. If that happened to me, I'd never recover." The speaker, George Marks, had just refurbished his barbershop with new chairs and fancy mirrors at considerable expense.

"We should let the county sheriff know what's going on. That's what he's there for. He's got deputies and his jurisdiction includes Blessing," I suggested.

"Sheriff Badger is seventy miles away," Frank pointed out to the room. "He can't be around when we really need him. The moment he leaves, we'll be worse off than we started. What if Harper got wind that we did what he told us not to do? Blessing would look like Lawrence after Quantrill before Badger could even get here."

"We're not without resources," I protested. "If we stick together and protect each other, we can stand up to those bullies until help comes. We don't have to be Bat Masterson. We just have to be prepared to support one another."

A number of simultaneous conversations buzzed in the room, so at least they were considering alternatives to the present situation. A good sign, I thought hopefully, but then Eliza Hansen stood, pushing herself up from the chair with one hand and grasping Steven's arm with the other.

"We are not fighters," she observed scornfully, "and to suggest that any of us could hold our own against Harper and his men is foolhardy. What we pay Paul Harper is nothing but an investment. Steven and I are investing in peace, safety, and prosperity, and we're not prepared to play the part of some hero that Louisa has read about in a nickel drugstore book." Just like that everyone stopped talking.

Liza looked at me with open disdain. "What risk do you take, Lou? Harper is thick with Fairchild, who's married to your sister. Nothing is going to happen to you with that kind of insurance policy, but the rest of us aren't so lucky. We aren't just talking businesses and money in the bank, either. I have a husband, two sons, and another child ready to join the family any time now. Why would I even consider taking risks with them?" She looked around the room. "All of you here have more than business establishments on the line. You have families to protect, and that's what you should be thinking about. What we pay is a small price to be able to sleep in our beds secure and unmolested." She moved heavily out of the room, followed by Steven, who looked back at me with an expression of some shame. Others began to drift out as well, making no comment, ordinary people thrust into extraordinary circumstances, now uncertain and afraid.

Milt French stayed a moment. "Harper once said to me that he was surprised how often I was out on the prairie by myself, making calls. He asked if I ever got nervous being so unprotected. He's never said anything since, so I didn't give it much thought. Now I wonder if I should be expecting a visit."

"What will you do if he shows up, Milt? What will you tell him?"

He shrugged, considering it. "I've taken an oath to heal, Lou, not to harm. I saw all the fighting I ever wanted to see in the war." At my steady look he added, "I lived through one war and God knows I don't want another, but sometimes I think you can't avoid it and maybe that's what we've come to in Blessing."

Later, Jim, Kate, Billy, and I sat on the front steps of the store without talking, desperately trying to fan some life into the stifling, still air.

Kate commented, "Now that I think about it, Lou, I haven't seen John around lately."

"He's away for a while," I answered carefully, "but there's no reason a lot of people need to know that. I expect he'll be back soon."

"It's a funny thing we've got here," observed Jim. "People you've known all your life aren't really who you thought they were. They've turned into strangers." He was sitting a step above Kate, who rested comfortably against him.

"Not everyone," Kate said softly, and he laid his hand on her crown of braids.

"No, mavourneen," he agreed, "not everyone."

I watched them walk off together, hand in hand, conscious of my own solitude in a way that was becoming more and more familiar to me. It was disconcerting to feel lost and unhappy in the midst of everything that had once represented a familiar, comfortable life. I hadn't realized that missing someone could make a person feel so incomplete and not quite whole, so absolutely miserable.

Billy looked inquiringly into my face. "Fiddle tears?"

Putting an arm around his shoulders I gave him a quick, hard hug. "Yes, nothing but fiddle tears."

Before I went to bed I added a third mark to my journal. Three days to go before John was back in my life, and it still seemed like forever.

Since neither circuit preacher made it to Blessing that Sunday, we had to do without formal services. Usually we had one or the other, so it was a peculiar circumstance to have both small churches closed and quiet. Ominous, in a way, as if even divine providence had deserted us. No melodies and hymns, no pump organ, no singing voices floating from the church windows. The Sunday morning silence unsettled Billy and put even him on edge—he was happiest when he was surrounded by music.

The morning air that Sunday was so incredibly heavy and sticky that it was impossible to move without sweat beading along your forehead or trickling down your back. The only redeeming feature was the gray and cloudy sky, which obscured the sun and kept its heat from intensifying the discomfort. We were all aware of the potential dangers of a violent summer storm and so kept a keen eye on the darkening clouds as they bunched and swirled around us. Whole towns had been destroyed by the hail or the ferocious winds that came out of this kind of weather, and the flat Kansas prairie offered little protection from either. Recently neighboring Coffeyville had borne the force of a twister that had damaged so much of the town it was still in repair. If we were fortunate, Blessing would have only some intimidating thunder and lightning followed by much-needed rain.

It was too hot to cook, so I spent the day puttering in the store, straightening displays and planning orders to send in the next week. Now on the downside of summer, it was not too early to start planning for the needs of fall harvests and winter protection. After a while, though, I found it increasingly hard to concentrate on the task at hand and eventually stopped entirely to simply sit back, close my eyes, and listen to Billy playing his fiddle.

Blessing itself seemed to become as still as the air. No

traffic rattled in the street and little activity showed from any of the storefronts or homes. I had the sense of many people waiting quietly behind their walls for the imminent storm. By evening I could hear distant rumblings of thunder and clearly see far-off flashes of lightning as dusk turned into night. Rain for sure and moving in our direction. I finished my journal entry—past half now, only two days left before John was home—and blew out the lamp. I didn't dress for bed, intending instead to lie down and try to sleep until the storm finally reached us. Then I was sure its noise would awaken me.

Some time not long after midnight something did awaken me, but it wasn't the storm. The thunder and lightning seemed right over us, and the wind was blowing so fiercely it had threatened to pull the curtains off the rod before I closed the window, but I had been hearing the noise of the storm for a while and sleeping fitfully through it. Different sounds, sounds not connected with a summer thunderstorm, jarred me fully awake. Below me in the store I heard a great deal of thudding and crashing going on and even, coming simultaneously with a loud crack of thunder, the unmistakable shattering of glass. I sat up, suddenly and completely awake, my heart thudding in my throat. I knew someone was downstairs making mischief, but Billy was downstairs, too. What if he had been hurt? I pictured Pete McGruder lying on the doctor's surgical table, his face as pale as the sheet over him. What if Billy lay downstairs, injured and bleeding?

The gusting winds made a lamp useless. Besides, I knew every inch of the store by heart and could have found my way through it blindfolded. Going down the outside staircase from my rooms, I hesitated for a moment, trying to plan which entrance to the store to use. The noises seemed to come from directly under my sitting room, from the front of the store and not from the rear storage room where Billy slept, so I entered through the side alley door into the back. Each brilliant snap of lightning illuminated the entire area as clearly as if it were noon. If I could see, I could also be seen, so I moved stealthily along the alley wall until I reached the door. Once inside the windowless storage room, I shut the door behind me and made my way to the corner where Billy usually slept. My eyes had adjusted to the darkness enough to see that his bed was rumpled but empty. I said Billy's name in a whisper in case he was hiding nearby, and when he did not respond, I pressed motionless against the wall to listen. All I could hear were the noises of the storm, although I felt certain I was not alone in the building. The door that connected the back storeroom, where I stood, to the front of the store was open and I could clearly detect the harsh, strong, ominous smell of lamp oil. If Billy lay unconscious in the darkened building and someone set the place on fire, the boy would not survive.

I moved slowly along the wall to the doorway, avoiding unopened crates and several stacks of boxes, and called Billy's name in a low voice once more, then tripped over something in the doorway.

"Billy!" I cried, forgetting to whisper. I had tripped over his legs as he lay behind the counter, half in, half out of the doorway. Saying his name again, too loudly for any secrecy, I crouched to put a hand on his chest. He was breathing, thank God. Standing upright again, I turned back into the doorway to grab hold of Billy's legs, so I could drag him fully into the back room with the thought of pulling him to safety out the alley door. He was dead weight and much too heavy for me to lift or maneuver around or over the counter that stood between us and the front of the store. Suddenly, silhouetted by a bright flash of lightning through the front windows, a figure rose up right in front of me on my side of the counter so close I could smell his breath. He must have been crouching just beyond where Billy lay, waiting for me to appear. The man was recognizable by the cap he wore and the shape of his head. His unexpected presence startled me so that I screamed and tried to back away from him quickly, stumbling and falling against the counter. Busy trying to catch my balance, I never gave a single thought to the rifle that lay so tantalizingly close. The man said nothing, but with the full force of his fist he hit me along the side of my face, slamming me back against a wall of shelves with a hard jolt. I slid down to the floor, unable to catch myself, unable to do anything but collapse in a heap in the dark, trapped between the counter and the wall. For a moment I was completely immobile, too stunned and hurt to do anything. When I tried to push myself up, my head seemed to split with a blindingly violent pain and I fell back down, retching and sick. Something trickled down my cheek and I realized helplessly that I was bleeding, but I couldn't move, not even a hand to my face. I felt him still standing next to me, watching, and as I tried once more to rise, he kicked me in the side, hard enough to make me lose my breath, so that doubled over from pain and nausea, I could only breathe in shallow, harsh gasps that seemed in the dark room to be as loud as the thunder.

The man I knew to be Cobb moved away, and I could hear the slosh of liquid and smell the lamp oil closer and more pungent. Through all his violent activity, he never said a word. I knew with a separate, rational, and conscious part of my mind that he was going to fire the place, set it ablaze with both Billy and me caught in the flames, and yet I could not move at all. The awful pain in my head and the panicky feeling of not being able to catch a deep breath would not allow it.

I must have lost consciousness for a while because when I came to, I was enveloped by blackness. Lying behind the counter on my back, it took me a moment to realize that the blackness was really thick, acrid, choking smoke above me. I got to my hands and knees, willing the pain in my head away, and then reached for the counter to pull myself up. The counter's edge was searing to the touch, so that I jerked my hand away quickly, pain shooting across my palm. Almost disinterestedly, I watched fire lick along the floor and the side counters and creep up the walls and the boxes stacked on the shelves there. The heat was terrible and the smoke so thick I gasped and gagged. There was a moment when, terrified and panicked, I thought, This is it. I'm going to die in this inferno.

If the smoke doesn't kill me, the fire will. But that despairing thought lasted only a moment. Out of nowhere, I pictured John stepping off the train in Hays, impatient to be back in Blessing, finally having someplace and someone to come home to. I couldn't fail him.

Crouched low under the smoke and holding one arm across my mouth to try to breathe more easily, I grabbed hold of one of Billy's ankles with my hands and began to pull him slowly, excruciatingly into the back room and toward the side door that led into the alley. The flames had not yet reached the storage room, but the smoke was just beginning to spread there, and I had to bend to keep under its suffocating cloud, ignoring the pain in my head and neck and the nausea that threatened to overwhelm me. All the while I was talking to the boy, although he couldn't hear me.

"Come on, come on, come on," I heard myself whisper, my words coming out in small, shallow gasps. I scraped his body along the wooden floor, colliding with boxes as if we were both drunk. "Help me, Billy." He made a moaning sound as if responding to my plea but didn't come to. At first I couldn't find the door and sobbing, had to let go of Billy so I could feel for the knob. Then, because his body lay too close to the threshold, I had to drag him back away from the door before I could finally jerk it open. Through the doorway I inhaled a full breath of clean air, ignoring the sharp, knife-edged pain that angled up from my ribs toward my shoulder. Outside, I was instantly surrounded by the furious and continuous cracks of thunder and snaps of lightning that seemed so close I ducked by instinct at the sound. Taking hold of both of Billy's ankles, ignoring the pain in my head and my hand and my chest, intent on survival and nothing else, I yanked the boy through the doorway and into the alley. In the white blaze of the lightning flashes, I could see that Billy's left forearm bent at an unnatural angle and that he had an enormous bump on his forehead, swollen so big it seemed his skin must split.

Leaving him lying in the dirt, I stumbled down the alley to

the street to see flames leaping from the broken front windows of the store. The fire had a voracious appetite, and nothing could have stopped it except the imminent grace of God, now well on its way to Blessing. On legs that would no longer support me, I fell to my knees and lifted my face to the heavens, not able to think or plan or move one step farther.

From the street, Jim Killian saw me and shouted my name. Cradling a rifle in one arm, he crouched down next to me, grasping me by a shoulder and looking directly into my face.

"My God, my God, Lou, stay still," he said urgently. I heard the shock in his voice and wanted to reassure him, wanted to say, It will be all right, Jim. The flames won't spread. Everything will be all right. But I couldn't speak. I wanted to tell him that Billy was in the alley and needed Dr. French's attention and that I had a terrible, splitting headache, but that we were both alive and nothing else mattered right then. When I tried to speak, though, my throat felt painfully raw, and I couldn't force any sound out. So instead I said nothing, just closed my eyes and lifted my head toward the sky just as the heavens opened above me and blessed, blessed torrents of rain gushed and beat against my upturned face. Showers of grace had finally arrived and not a moment too soon.

CHAPTER 14

A bout all I remember after that is Milt French's calm voice and being hoisted into strong arms, and I only remember that because of the pain. I have a vague recollection of waking once, feeling as if I were swimming up from the bottom of a deep, dark pond, troubled, frightened, wanting to cry out but unable to make a sound, the way it is in nightmares sometimes. Kate's dear face hovered over me, saying something soothing, hushing me. When I tried to grab her hand, my own hand was wrapped in something bulky, and I couldn't make it work the way it should. Kate forced some foul liquid between my lips, and I was as determined not to take it. Although I couldn't have named them, I knew there was something I needed to know and something else I was urgently waiting for, something I would miss if I fell asleep again, something that I dared not miss. So I remember fussing as if Kate were a threat to me and trying to push her away, all unsuccessfully, because I eventually slept without dream or nightmare for a long while.

I awoke to that confusion a person feels when he has slept very deeply and for a few seconds after awakening has absolutely no recollection of where he is. There's no panic in the moment, only a comfortable confusion, a certainty that if one lies very still and is patient, everything will sort itself out. So I opened my eyes and did just that, looked around the room as well as I could, tried to identify whose room it was, tried to remember why I was there and not in my own bed. Memory came back slowly, the smell of lamp oil, the sudden figure rising up out of the darkness in front of me, the sharp, crackling noise of the fire, the dense smoke, pulling Billy along the floor like a sack of grain, every moment of that horrific night. I recalled Billy as I had last seen him, lying still as death in the alley, and pushed back the covers, determined to find him, but trying to sit up made me clutch my head from the splitting pain, and I realized the palm and fingers of one hand were wrapped in gauze. Kate, sitting in the rocking chair next to the bed where I lay, got up, and gently pushed my shoulders back down to the pillows.

I started to speak, made an unintelligible croaking noise, swallowed, and tried again. This time I said, "Billy?" in a rasping voice hardly recognizable as my own.

Kate held a glass of water to my lips and helped me drink, then said, "Dr. French is looking after him. He'll be fine, Lou. His left arm is broken, but Milt says it should heal fine, and he has a big goose egg on his forehead, but with that hard skull of his, there's no concussion. Unlike you."

I tried to look around but found that the effort to move my eyes made my head ache. "Where am I? What time is it?"

"You're with me, Lou, safe in my room. Jim stood watch all night, so there's nothing to be afraid of. And it's late Monday night, bedtime for most folks." Except I'm just waking up, I thought, still confused but certain everything would be all right now. I was with Kate, in her snug rooms behind her shop, no fire, no smoke, no danger or fear. Billy was alive and I was alive and everything would be all right.

"It rained, Kate," I said inconsequentially, "a lovely rain."

"Yes, Lou, it was a lovely rain," she agreed, and then I slept again.

The next time I awoke I knew exactly where I was and I felt

immeasurably better. I had vague aches and pains all over, but my head didn't hurt, and I could move my eyes without the nasty, nauseous feeling I had experienced ever since Cobb landed his first blow. I looked over at the rocking chair, expecting to find Kate there again, but she was nowhere to be seen. Instead, John was sitting there, his head against the back of the chair and his eyes closed. He looked exhausted, his face rough with lines of worry and fatigue that did not smooth out even in sleep. I wanted to reach out and touch him, to run my fingertips along his cheek and soften his expression, but I hadn't the energy to do it just then. Still drowsy, I turned my head and lay quietly, my eyes fixed on that weather-roughened, lean, loved face. This must be day six, I thought contentedly and smiled to myself.

At my slight stirring, John opened his eyes and caught my gaze on him, caught my smile, too. He leaned forward to place one large palm over my bandaged hand. "Well, Sleepyhead, it's about time you woke up," speaking with such tenderness that the sound of his voice brought unexpected tears to my eyes. Fiddle tears again, I thought. I must be weaker than I realized if such a prosaic sentence could make me cry.

"Is it still Monday?"

"Tuesday afternoon."

I tried to think where all the time had gone. "When did you get back?"

"The train pulled into Hays around midnight last night, Monday night. I got back to Blessing around four this morning." That explained the harsh lines of weariness on his face.

"You haven't been sitting in that chair nursemaiding me since then, I hope."

"Not all the time, no. I stopped by the doc's office to see how Billy was coming along and spent some time with Jim Killian."

I frowned, trying to recapture the moment. "Jim came to help, I think. I remember him crouching down next to me and then it started to rain." With my left hand I felt the stitched cut along my hairline, then lightly fingered my tender and puffy cheek and bruised eye. "I guess it's a good thing I can't see my face. I must be a sight."

John's hand tightened on mine. "You're alive. You look beautiful to me."

I pushed myself up slowly, carefully swinging my legs over the side of the bed, waiting for a clanging in my head that didn't come.

"Kate left me in charge, Lou. If she comes back and you're not resting in bed, I'll be in serious trouble."

"Not the first time, I bet." I laughed, then gasped at the sharp pain along my ribs, now bound tightly with gauze and tape. He stood up immediately and came forward to put an arm behind my shoulders for support. Because he was so close and I could no more keep myself from doing it than breathing, I took my bandaged right hand and pulled his head down to mine so I could rest my cheek against his. That close he said my name in a hoarse whisper, his voice catching in his throat, telling me so much with that one soft, broken word, telling me he'd been afraid of losing me, telling me he'd been thrown off balance by the intensity of his need for me. I understood everything he didn't say.

"I know," I murmured in return, comforting him, at that moment able to read his mind. "I was frightened, too, but you're home now and everything will be all right." We rested against each other in a posture that should have been awkward but felt perfectly natural and comfortable, and for a while had no need for words.

Later, wanting to grin but finding it too painful, I teased, "You're not the only strategist. I needed a way to get you closer, and you have to admit my idea worked." Then, without planning to, I rested my head against his shoulder and added in a whisper, "You won't go away again, John, will you, at least not for a while? I don't think I could bear it."

Sitting on the edge of the bed next to him, I felt him tense at my question, but his voice remained lightly conversational. "No, I'm not going anywhere."

We sat in comfortable silence a while longer and then I roused myself to say, "Would you hand me that wrap and then help me stand, please? I'm really much better, and if I have to lie here one more moment I'll go crazy. Lend me an arm into the kitchen, and then you should go get some sleep yourself. You look all in. Have you slept at all since you got off the train at Hays?"

With my good hand holding onto his arm, I walked unsteadily into Kate's little kitchen and plopped ungracefully onto a chair at the table. I winced as I sat, clutched my side, and said without thinking, "That's where that man Cobb kicked me," and then because of the look on John's face, wished I hadn't said anything.

I knew instinctively that he would be inclined to some terrible vengeance and realized that, whether he lived or died in the attempt, his taking a personal, violent revenge would be intolerable for me and change everything. I understood that the war and the solitary, sometimes violent, intervening years of John's life had given him instincts that were foreign to me and at odds with what I believed. I didn't fault him for that. I hadn't lived through a bloody war, then spent a day searching among ruined and mangled bodies only to find the one person I loved in the world dead on a filthy battlefield. I hadn't wandered without home or roots for fifteen years, growing older, more reserved, and more solitary as time passed. I had enjoyed a much different life and sometime soon, as soon as I was stronger and not prone to weak tears, I would try to make John understand how deeply held were my beliefs in the civilizing influence of the rule of law and the power of forgiveness. But not now, not now. Now I needed to have him close, needed those blue eyes watching me with undisguised tenderness, needed to rest my hand on his muscled arm and feel safe again.

"I'll get some sleep later." Pulling up and straddling a chair, he watched me, obviously out of his element. "If Kate comes back and finds you out here, Lou, she'll have both our hides."

"Nonsense. I'm not a person who needs to be babied. I have a few bumps and bruises but nothing that won't heal. I'm perfectly fine." My weak and breathy voice belied my words, so I added hastily, trying to keep a calm tone, "Is the store burned to the ground?"

"No, there's a lot left standing. When I got in, I stopped long enough to be sure the fire was out." His dispassionate tone told me more than he knew. Stopped long enough to control his shocked panic and fear, I thought, long enough to see if two charred bodies lay among the ruins. "Once the rain started Jim said it came down heavy, so it put out the fire before it reached the back room or brought down the ceiling. It'll still need considerable repair, though." I found the picture of John standing alone in the drizzling rain staring at the blackened storefront more than I could bear, and I changed the subject. "Did you get your business all settled?"

"Yes, but not soon enough or you wouldn't be sitting there in the shape you're in." He paused, wanting to say more but unsure how to express it. A man not given to flowery phrases, he had once told me, so I understood why he spoke so carefully, a formal man to whom emotional speech did not come easily. "I promised I'd tell you everything, Lou, and I will, but I need to say something first. When I rode into Blessing and saw the store, I didn't know what to do or where to turn. I felt like someone had hit me hard in the stomach and I couldn't breathe. It felt like my heart even stopped for a minute. I knew right then that if anything had happened to you, the sun wouldn't rise for me any more, not in any way that would matter to me. I didn't know a woman could make a man feel like that. I'll carry the blame for what happened to you all my life because I should have been with you, taking care of you, and I wasn't." I started to protest but he went on doggedly, his voice ragged with feeling. "There's never been anyone in my life who means what you mean to me, Lou, and there never will be again. I should have been here to protect you and I wasn't. I'm asking you to forgive me."

My darling, I thought, willing him to understand, I don't need you in my life to protect me, only to love me, nothing else, just love me. Then, pained by such humility from a proud man, I answered quickly, resting my good hand on his arm, "You don't have to ask and there's nothing to forgive. If you blame yourself, you're blaming the wrong man. We both know who was responsible." I tightened my hold on his arm. "There was a moment that night, John, with the smoke so thick I could hardly breathe and the flames spreading, that I wanted to give up. I thought Billy and I would just die there and that would be the end of it. It would have been so easy. My head felt like it had been hit by lightning, I couldn't catch my breath, and I was so tired I didn't know how I could take one more step. And then I had the strangest thought. Out of nowhere I thought, This is the fourth day and John said he'd be back in six days and I have to live. I have to be there when he comes home. He'll be expecting me. Then I grabbed hold of one of Billy's feet and just started dragging him along the floor like a sack of seed until we were both in the alley and out of danger. So in a way you *were* there. You were there all the time. You just didn't know it." I never imagined that blue eyes, usually so cool, could flare with the fire of warmth and emotion I saw on his face.

"I love you, you know," he said quietly, the words a natural part of that conversation, no fanfare and maybe not much of a surprise by then, but for a moment my heart still stopped at the magnitude of the gift he'd given me.

Then my breath returned and I answered with a smile, "Yes, I know. Now tell me about your business and what's been going on. I survived the fire but curiosity could kill me for sure."

"I've been working for the railroad, for Cy Peterman's railroad."

"I met Mr. Peterman at Lily and Gordon's," I exclaimed. "I liked him."

"Cy remembers you, too. He's quite a man, rich, powerful, shrewd, and careful. He sent me on ahead confidentially to gather information about Blessing and get the lay of the land. Later he asked me to stay on a while longer. Cy reads people pretty well, and I think he began to have second thoughts after visiting your brother-in-law."

"Second thoughts about what?"

"Cy was thinking seriously about putting in a railroad spur from Hays southwest to Blessing. It would have run east of town. He thought he could connect with cattle coming up from the south, from Texas and Oklahoma Territory, and easier than them backtracking to the railroad at Wichita. It would be good business for him and good for Blessing, too, or so he thought. But somehow Paul Harper got wind of it. Cy thinks maybe through Josiah Leavenworth, the banker, but he can't be sure."

My mind was racing ahead. A railroad spur south to Blessing would have changed everything about the town, brought increased traffic, customers, merchants, travelers, and trainloads of homesteaders. No longer could I have quoted Father, "Not boom or bust, just Blessing." The railroad line would have meant boom for sure, with all the prosperity and the headaches that came with a boomtown. Look what happened to quiet Dodge City when the railroad arrived.

"Cy was prepared to buy out all the land east, especially northeast of Blessing, and he would have paid well for it. He's a fair man."

"But then Paul Harper came to town," I said thoughtfully, "taking advantage of the drought, the hot summer, and the hard times, buying up that land for pennies on the dollar."

"Thinking he could inflate the price, sell it to the railroad, and make a killing." John's choice of words made me shiver.

"And with a foothold in every major business in town, he'd have easy income from every merchant who was willing to pay for the peace." At John's questioning look I explained Paul Harper's menacing security plan and how he had begun extorting money from the more prosperous businesses in Blessing. "And you can bet his price would have gone up as business and traffic increased. I told Frank Monroe that Harper was sitting on a gold mine, but I didn't know the half of it. Why does he want my store so badly?"

"You ever been in a boomtown, Lou?"

"No. I've just read about them in the papers."

"Only the saloons do better business than a general store when the railroad comes to town. They both rely on supply and demand. When you buy things cheap and sell them high, you can turn a nice profit pretty fast. The store would be located close to the line, too, practically the first thing people see when they step off the train. Harper realized the possibilities early on. Besides, you were becoming a problem to him, urging the homesteaders to stay, extending them credit, encouraging people to stand up to him, unwilling to give him what he wanted. It turned into a contest of wills."

"It did get personal, didn't it? Gordon was a part of the scheme, too, John. Lily said he wanted in on the deal with Harper so badly he'd have done anything. Do you think that's how Harper got the money to buy the land?"

"That's my guess. I knew things smelled bad as soon as I got here, and it didn't take long to figure it out. I couldn't send telegrams from Blessing and keep things quiet, so I had to go to nearby telegraph offices to get word to Cy. I should have gone to Topeka sooner, but I couldn't make myself leave you. That was my weakness and my fault, and it almost got you killed. Finally Cy decided he and I had to talk face to face. He'd made up his mind about something, which is what this last trip was all about."

"And?"

"The railroad isn't coming to Blessing after all, Lou. Cy Peterman has no intention of paying three times what the land's worth, and he doesn't want to deal with a man like Harper. He's thinking now that he might put in a spur to Great Bend or Pratt."

"Does that mean you'll have to go there?" I asked, trying to sound nonchalant.

"The Kansas Pacific Railroad and I have parted company.

On good terms, mind you, but I'm done there."

I wanted to ask about John's future plans, but it wasn't the time or place for that. "What does that mean for Paul Harper then?" I asked instead.

"He'll find out that the railroad's passed him by. Cy intends to make sure your brother-in-law gets the news real soon. Harper will be out more than he can afford, with a lot of land on his hands that I don't think he'll get much for, not with the government giving acres away up north and practically paying people to settle in the Dakotas."

Oh Lily, I thought, you won't be going anywhere after all, not the way you planned, and I felt grieved for her, not gloating or triumphant. She wanted out and away from Blessing so badly she'd have sold her soul. In fact some might say she did, and now the exultant departure, the glorious future she had counted on wouldn't happen. Poor sister.

"Lou?" John touched my cheek gently with the back of his hand.

I shook my head and tried to smile. "Just thinking. Problem is, Harper's still here and we have to deal with him. All along I've wanted to get a hold of Sheriff Badger in Scott City, and I'd still like to do that. You know I don't believe in vigilante justice, John. Once I file charges, Badger's the law and he should handle it."

Before John could reply, Kate came into the kitchen. "I thought I heard voices. I put you in charge of the patient, John Davis, and I surely didn't expect to see her sitting at the kitchen table."

He took the scold meekly enough, but I said, "It's no use blaming John, Kate. There's no way he could have kept me from getting up." I stood to give her a weak hug of thanks. "How have you gotten any rest with me in your bed?"

"I slept in the chair just fine. You were so restless at first I was up all the time anyway. Not that I could do much good since I wasn't the one you were fretting over." Kate glanced at John. "I don't know where the six days came from, but she was awfully worried about you coming back in six days and missing your arrival." Then she turned back to me. "Dr. French finally gave you something to calm you down, and then Jim and I took turns watching you until John got here."

I asked hesitantly, "I don't suppose Lily's come by to see how I am, has she?"

"No."

"I guess I was expecting too much, wasn't I?" I tried to shrug as if it didn't matter and sat down again. "I want to get the smell of smoke out of my hair, Kate, and do you think you have a dress close to my size? I'm not quite up to parading around town in a nightdress, especially one cut for a woman a head shorter than I."

"I don't think you're up to parading around town at all," she answered indignantly. "You have a concussion, two cracked ribs, six stitches, and a burn, not to mention a bruise on your face that's turning a lovely shade of indigo. Milt French told me to keep you down and quiet for at least three days."

"I need to see Billy and I need to see the store, and I'll do that dressed or looking exactly as I look now. But I'd be very appreciative if you'd help me get presentable." I ended meekly and gave her a beseeching look.

Kate turned to John and said his name, as if importuning him to take a side, but he held up a hand. "I know a battle I can't win when I see it and I am not commenting." He got up to leave and without embarrassment leaned down to kiss me on his way out. Quite a concession, I realized, from a "fairly formal man."

"I'm going to catch some sleep over at the Hansen House, Lou. I'm that close if you need me." As soon as he was gone, I felt suddenly exhausted and sore as if John had taken all my energy with him when he left.

Kate said, "I've never seen a man look like he looked this morning, standing outside my door in the darkness, rain running off his hat and him soaked to the skin. He had a look about him so still and fierce I didn't recognize him and was frightened for a moment. It was like he didn't really see me at first. He just wanted to know about you. The first words out of his mouth were, "Is she alive? Are she and the boy alive?" When I told him you were a little the worse for wear but alive and sleeping in the back room, that ferocious stillness just melted away, and he was the man I remembered. He followed me back here and stood in the doorway watching you sleep, and he just drank you in. That's the only way to describe it. Like a thirsty man, he just drank you in. You need to hold onto that one, Lou."

Oh, you're preaching to the choir, dear friend, I thought, as if I'd ever let John Rock Davis go anywhere without taking me along.

Later, with my hair washed and spread out to dry, Kate and I struck a deal. I'd be on good behavior and sleep a while. When I woke up, she'd help me dress, we'd go over together to look at the remains of the store, and then someone would bring Billy over to Kate's later that evening. By then I was more tired than I wanted to admit, so she got no argument from me about anything.

I awoke around suppertime, catching the smell of something cooking in the kitchen and hungry for the first time in a number of days. After I dressed, Kate and I had something to eat before we went outside.

Walking from the kitchen through her workroom to the front door, I caught sight of myself in the mirror and stopped in my tracks. The woman in the mirror was not the same woman who'd been reflected there the night of the Fourth of July dance. I went closer, shocked by the thick, black, puffy stitches along my hairline and the ugly, purple bruise that spread from the corner of my eye down across my cheek to the corner of my mouth, every mark appearing even darker against my unnaturally pale complexion.

"This is worse than I thought."

"Dr. French says everything will fade," Kate responded calmly, "and while you may have a small scar from the stitches, you can cover that with your hair. Be glad you're alive. That's how the rest of us feel."

I recognized the wisdom of her words and turned briskly away from the mirror, saying with a slight smile, "What a sensible woman you are, Kate. Now let's go see the other ruins."

CHAPTER 15

K ate and I stepped out into early dusk, the long days of summer already a memory and autumn lurking just around the corner. Gone, at least for a while, were the heat and the dust and the parched air of the past weeks, replaced by a breeze refreshingly light and, for August, almost cool. Water still pooled in several places in the street, rippling when the breeze touched it. In the early evening light it seemed everything had been washed clean, even the weather-beaten storefronts.

I was pleased to discover that the store wasn't as bad as I had imagined it. Although most of the front was gutted and there was nothing left to salvage there, except for a fine layer of soot and the still-bitter smell of smoke and oil, the back room had no real damage. The only exception was the scorched and blackened doorframe where Billy had been lying. I had to turn away when I saw that, remembering the moment when I had stumbled over his legs and then that shocking figure rising out of the darkness in front of me, wordless and patiently malevolent. That paralyzing moment would haunt me for a long time.

Outside, the steps to my rooms were intact, but Kate was right to caution me not to go upstairs. "Jim says to strengthen the store's ceiling first, otherwise it might not support you and you could fall straight through to the room below."

I stood in the middle of the store and looked around. "It could have been worse," I said finally, and she gave me a sober look.

"Oh yes, Lou, it could have been much worse."

Billy came over to Kate's that night, his arm tightly bound and in a sling. He stepped inside the door and stood there a little sheepishly, smiling at me.

"Broke my arm," he said, patting the sling as if it were a badge of honor.

"I see that. How's your head?" I reached out a hand to brush his hair off his forehead, overwhelmed with affection for him and with gratitude for his being alive.

"All right." He put his good hand up to the bruise on his forehead and frowned a little. "Can't remember what happened."

"That's all right. Sometimes it's better that way."

He looked at me, still confused. "Can we go home now?" he asked, his tone pleading and a little lonely.

"Not right now, but we will go home, I promise," and my promise seemed to set his mind at ease.

Caleb made up a bed for Billy in the stable while I remained at Kate's. "I can't take your bed," I protested, acting more fretfully than was usual for me.

"There's room for both of us," she answered, "if you stop that restless fussing you do while you're sleeping. If you keep that up, you'll kick me right onto the floor." She felt my forehead. "I think you might be a little feverish, probably did too much today. Why don't you go lie down? I'll come to bed later." But try as I might, I couldn't sleep. Eventually I wandered back out into the kitchen where Kate sat at the table reading, her glasses perched at the tip of her nose. Watching her undetected, I thought she was dearer to me than any sister, a true friend who could never be replaced. She looked up at me in the doorway, surprised and then concerned.

"What's the matter?"

"What will happen, Kate? What will we do? I can't sleep because I'm frightened." I think my words shocked her, since I'd never admitted such a thing in all the years we had been friends.

"No one will hurt you here."

"I'm not frightened for me exactly. I'm afraid of what will happen to Blessing, to all of us. I think something terrible is right around the corner, and I don't know what to do or how to stop it."

"Maybe you can't stop it. Maybe you shouldn't try. Some things just happen, Lou, as natural consequences in life. If it's John you're worried about, don't be. I've never met a man better able to take care of himself."

I couldn't explain to her the dread I felt, the fear that John would be implacable in vengeance, that he would kill and become no different in my eyes than the very men he scorned. Or worse, that he would himself be killed and I would have to go back to life as it had been, trying to reclaim a past contentment that had vanished the first time I saw myself reflected in John's eyes. I must be feverish, I thought, because this frail uncertainty was not typical of me. Or maybe this is how love makes a person feel, this constant concern, this vague sick feeling, nothing like the dreamy emotion of one of Shakespeare's sonnets. Whichever fever was the cause, I felt worried and afraid and not myself at all.

The next day Dr. French pronounced me well on the way to recovery. He took the bandages off my hand, which, while red and tender, hadn't blistered and so would not be open to any risk of infection.

"The stitches can come out in a week or two, and your girlish complexion will return in no time." He felt my cheek. "I was afraid at first that the cheekbone was broken, but I think now it's just badly bruised. Watch your ribs and take it easy for a while, but there's no reason you can't be up and about."

The prognosis cheered me and while Kate worked, I went down the street to see Jim. He was scribbling like crazy at his desk but looked up and brightened when he saw me. His brogue was especially thick, so I knew my appearance must have brought on a touch of Irish emotion.

"So you're up and about, Lou darlin', and back to your old self. Faith, you gave me a scare."

"I can imagine I was a sight. Still am for that matter."

"Oh, a fury. You looked like an avengin' fury that night, roundin' the corner with your hair streamin' and blood runnin' down the side of your face. Nothin' I'll soon forget."

"I wasn't feeling like an avenging fury, but thank you, Jim. If you hadn't been there, I don't know what I'd have done." I went over to plant a light kiss on his cheek. "You're a true friend."

He turned back to his tablet, embarrassed. "That's what friends are for, eh? Anyway, your man's already thanked me enough for the both of you."

"Jim, what day does Harper do his collecting? Isn't it Thursday?"

"That's what I understand."

"And isn't that tomorrow?"

"Yes."

"So what's going to happen?"

"Lou, this is something you shouldn't be worrying about. You've had a rough time and you aren't quite yourself. God knows I'd never dream of telling you what to do, but my advice, just my friendly advice, darlin', is to go back to Kate's and lie low for a while until you're stronger."

"I think you're avoiding my question," I accused.

His eyes crinkled into a smile. "Now you're sounding like your old self again." But that's all he would say.

At the Hansen House, Sally said as she saw me, "Oh Miss Lou, I was that worried about you. That was awful about your store and Billy hurt, too. Are you both all right?"

"Yes, we'll be fine. What about you? Still stepping out with Joe McGruder?"

She gave a shy but self-satisfied smile, nodded, then turned a pretty pink. Her happy, heart-shaped face did wonders for my spirits, even put me in a good enough temper to talk to Eliza, who stood behind the hotel desk.

"Liza, you should sit down. You make me tired just looking at you. Are you sure there aren't two in there?" She was in that last stage of pregnancy when a woman seems to list along from side to side like a ship out of water.

When Liza looked at me, I think she was shocked at my appearance, but she quickly hid the expression. After a brief, awkward silence she laughed. "More like four, the way I feel. How are you and Billy?" From her tone I knew she was remembering and regretting the recent town meeting and her words about my supposed protected status.

"All right. Bruises, bumps, and broken bones, but we'll be fine. I was looking for John." She didn't bother to ask who I meant.

"I saw him head off toward the telegraph office."

Still too lame to hurry anywhere, I stopped outside the telegraph office to catch my breath and through the window of the telegraph office saw John in conversation with Frank Monroe. Frank appeared red-faced and flustered. Andy was clicking away a message as John, looking slightly amused, stood between Frank and Andy as if he were a wall keeping them apart. In a moment John laid some coins on the counter and Andy handed him a receipt. I sat down on the bench outside the door to wait. There was something so uplifting about Frank Monroe getting any kind of comeuppance that I needed to savor the moment.

Frank came out first, walking too fast, looking more chagrined than angry, as if he'd been caught doing something wrong. When John came out, he was folding the paper receipt and tucking it into his shirt pocket. He saw me and sat down next to me on the bench.

"Nice morning."

I agreed absently, eyeing him. "Frank didn't look happy."

"We had a little disagreement, but he finally saw things my way."

"About—?"

"Yesterday I sent a telegram to Sheriff Badger, Lou, like you wanted, but I didn't get an answer. Today I sent a message to Cy Peterman, asking him to use his influence to get Badger here right away. Frank Monroe is worried about what might happen because of that."

For a moment I felt lightheaded with relief and gratitude. I recognized the concession that John had made, knew he'd done it for me, not from his own inclination or persuasion, and was humbled.

"Thank you."

We sat there side by side in the morning sunshine, not touching, just looking out at the street. Finally John said quietly, "I know what I am and what I do troubles you, Lou, so I'm trying to play by your rules, but whether Badger gets here soon or not, there will still be hell to pay. I don't know the man, but he'd better be good at his job."

"John, tomorrow is Harper's collection day. What will you do if Badger doesn't get here by then?"

He shrugged. "We'll have to wait and see, but I won't do anything to shame you."

"I'm not worried about you shaming me!" I was angry that he'd even think that. "I'm worried about you getting killed."

He responded mildly, "I don't plan on that happening, but I think the time has come to reach an understanding with Mr. Harper."

"You can't do that by yourself."

"I can if I have to. I've done it before." Then, as if to pacify me, he added, "But I don't think I'll have to tomorrow." He wouldn't explain further, and I had to be content with knowing he was a careful man of experience and necessary caution, not one to lose his head or be led by sudden impulse to a deadly indiscretion. "Jim Killian and I have some business to attend to this afternoon, so I may not be back until later this evening." Since his return, John had been letting me know his itinerary almost to the extreme, and I believed he did it for his own peace of mind as much as mine. When I stood, he did, too.

"You're a man of secrets sometimes, John."

"Part of my charm?" This with a smile.

"Oh, charm," I said in a low voice, meeting that blue gaze with a steady look and a little smile of my own, "doesn't begin to describe it."

When I got back to Kate's, I borrowed one of her old smocks, plaited my hair into a thick braid, pinned it up off my neck, took broom and bucket, and headed over to the store. Kate wasn't happy with me, and I had to remind her that I had received the go-ahead from the doctor.

"That's not exactly my recollection," she responded with uncharacteristic sarcasm. "I heard Milt tell you to take it easy for a while."

"I am taking it easy, but I have nothing but time on my hands and that's worse than the cracked ribs. I'll be at the store and I promise I won't overdo."

My simple plan turned out to be more work than I had imagined. The August heat had returned, the soot refused to be picked up with one sweeping, and using water to clean only created a nasty kind of muck that took several scrubbings to remove. Still, as I worked in the back storage room, cautiously pushing boxes around, taking note of what I had stored there, making some headway against the soot and dust, I began to feel hopeful about the future. The day passed without my paying attention to the time, and it was only when I found myself squinting into the interior of the room that I realized it was late. I surveyed the results of my efforts with satisfaction.

"Time to call it a day, I think," I commented aloud.

Standing in the open alley door John said, "More than a day, I'd say," but because I hadn't heard or seen him approach, I stood petrified at the sudden sight of his unexpected figure, a twilight shadow in the dimming light. My heart thudded into my throat and beat out a furious rhythm that wouldn't allow me to catch a breath, and for a sudden blinding moment I remembered with vivid clarity the pure terror of Cobb rising up in front of me. The memory brought me close to panic.

John must have seen the fear on my face and was instantly contrite. "I'm sorry, I didn't mean to frighten you. I should have let you know I was here."

My voice shook more than I liked, and it took me a moment to gather my wits so I could speak normally. "I'm just jumpy. I'll get over it," and because I had never spoken to him of the details of the fire, I added, "I expect it will take time, though. That night when I saw Billy on the floor in the doorway, I forgot to be cautious. I said his name out loud and rushed over to him. I was paying so much attention to making sure he was still alive that when that man Cobb reared up in front of me, I was caught completely off guard. It was almost a relief when he hit me because I was so frozen, so absolutely terrified, that I couldn't move and at least the pain got my mind turning again. I've always been proud of being practical and unafraid and not given to flights of fancy. Lily accused me of thinking I'm superior to others, and after Sunday night I'm ashamed to say I believe she was right. I admit I've secretly scorned folks who are afraid or timid, but that was false pride. I needed to learn that I'm just as human, no better and no different from anybody else. I guess I deserved to be humbled. I didn't know I had it in me to be that scared."

John didn't come any closer, just watched me soberly from the doorway, giving all his attention to my lengthy confession. When I finished, he said, "No, you didn't deserve to be humbled, and only a fool wouldn't have been afraid. You're a lot of things, Lou, but you're no fool."

"Sometimes I wonder about that, but I need to leave that night in the past. It's over and done. Anyway, I've had an idea. It'll take a while to get the front of the store rebuilt and everything back in order there, but why can't I run the business out of the storeroom until then?" I got excited thinking about it and began to move around the room. "See, I could put a counter up here and have some shelves put in all along this wall that would give me plenty of storage space. That wouldn't take much, and I think I could make myself a little room back here in the corner for the time being, maybe one for Billy, too. I'd just need to throw up a couple of walls. I can't stay at Kate's much longer. Poor woman—she needs her own bed back." When he didn't respond, I turned to look at him.

"Business as usual?" he asked without inflection.

"It will never be business as usual, John, not after what happened, but business, certainly. What did I say that was wrong?" I could tell from his expression that something in my words had pulled him up short.

"Nothing to talk about now. Kate sent me over to make you come home—as if anyone could make you do something you didn't want to do." His tone was ambiguous and proved his words false because even the hint of disapproval I thought I detected in his voice had the power to make me feel remorseful and unhappy.

"I know I can be headstrong," I admitted, "but I hope I don't act like I always have to have my own way. If I do, I'm sorry. Lately I've realized that I'm too much like Lily in that regard. It's not a becoming trait in either of us."

At that his odd, pensive mood disappeared. "The only way you're like your sister is in looks. Otherwise you have nothing in common that I can find."

"Really?" I asked, my attention arrested. "I don't think I look anything like Lily."

"Someday I promise we'll discuss that at length but not now. Kate is keeping supper warm, and it never does to keep the cook waiting."

To which I responded brazenly, "You might want to keep that in mind for future reference, John."

CHAPTER 16

Thursday morning when I crossed the street and walked back to the store to continue cleaning, I was struck by the quiet. A breeze swirled a small tornado of dust down the street and shook the leaves on some of the trees by Lily's house, but other than that, Blessing lay still as death. This is the day Harper comes to town, I thought, and people are afraid.

Sunday night had forced me to look at life from a new perspective. I better appreciated people's fear, understood Eliza's matter-of-fact scorn for my advice to resist Paul Harper, even understood why Frank Monroe thought he could make a pact with the devil. But understanding did not mean that I condoned a compromise with wickedness or that I would do, say, or recommend anything differently than I had before. Years ago, Father had told me "Right is right, Louisa. On some issues compromise is not an alternative." At that particular time he had been speaking of holding the union together and abolishing the national shame of slavery, but I could guess that he would make a similar application here. Once I had asked John if he thought it mattered what we lived and died for. I knew now that for me it did matter and hoped that John had come to his own answer and his own peace.

Midmorning John stopped by long enough to ask me to promise I would stay off the street for the afternoon.

"I can't promise that. I'd be lying if I did. But I can promise I won't get in the way."

"That's not good enough." He frowned, his expression stern.

"It's the best I can do," I replied stubbornly.

After he left, I was brought up sharply by the realization that if something happened to him, something terrible, our last words would be that abrupt, quarrelsome exchange. He'd only been looking out for my welfare after all, and I had reacted as if he'd asked me to do something difficult or distasteful. I hadn't even inquired about Sheriff Badger, and John had asked for the sheriff's help only because of my influence. At that moment I could not imagine what he saw in such a shrew. Ashamed, I decided to find him to apologize, thinking with weak humor that I was certainly getting enough practice at asking his pardon for my stubborn streak and my willful tongue. I went over what I would say, how I would laughingly remind him that as long as he was busy being annoyed by me, he at least wouldn't be bored and should consider that a positive.

I hurried outside, feeling for no reason I could name an urgency to find him and tell him I was sorry, let him know his concern for me meant more than I could share, that he had become as much a part of my life as air or sunshine, that I couldn't imagine living without him. All those thoughts tumbled around in my mind, and I picked up my pace, the clicking of my shoes against the boardwalk practically the only sound to be heard anywhere in Blessing. No children playing, no dogs barking, no greetings from doorways, no rattle of wagons, no sound anywhere except for the subdued and distant rumbling I heard behind me, the sound of horses cantering, certainly more than one. When I turned to see four of Harper's men riding down the main street, my first agonizing thought was, Too late. Too late to tell you I'm sorry, John, too late to mend fences, too late to say I love you.

I pressed back against the nearest wall and watched the men pass, laughing with each other, oblivious to the fear and consternation they were causing, clearly full of themselves. Harper wasn't with them, but Cobb was, and although he didn't see me, just the sight of him caused me to panic in a way that made my hands tremble. I stepped away from the wall to follow their progress and watched them stop in front of the saloon. So simultaneous it was almost comical, the men ceased all talk and movement. They had just become aware of John, who stepped out from the saloon's doorway and down into the street. His concentration on them was so fixed, so calculated and deliberate, that the contrast with his genial, relaxed tone came almost as a shock.

"No need to get down, gentlemen. There's no place for you here any more."

"Yeah?" said the handsome one with the long hair, Oba, the one who had accosted Sally the night of the dance. "Who says?"

"I do." John just stood there, deceptively casual, arms loose at his side, half-smiling, watchful and waiting. At that moment, I found him terrifying.

"Oo-oooo." At Oba's mocking response, the other three laughed. "I believe the man's trying to scare us, boys." Oba turned his head as if to say something to the man next to him but instead suddenly reached down to yank the pistol out of the holster looped to his saddle. Faster than any motion I have ever seen, so fast I honestly could not believe it had happened, Oba was looking directly into the barrel of John's Peacemaker, his own weapon still partially sheathed. John's arm was stretched out so still and so straight it almost seemed the gun was just an extension of it, all one piece of flesh and blood and metal. None of the men was laughing now.

Cobb, his horse prancing restlessly, said, "You can't get all of us. One man, no matter how fast, one gun, no matter how good, is still just one."

"Well," John responded pleasantly, "that's where you're wrong."

As he spoke, an extraordinary thing happened. From the corner of the saloon, Jim Killian, rifle butt firmly against his shoulder, said, "Not just one man. You'd better look around." Frank Monroe stood beside Jim, a revolver out and poised. Across the street I saw Caleb holding the old blunderbuss shotgun he'd had around for ages. Steven Hansen stood ready with a pistol in front of the Hansen House, and I saw Carl Pomeroy, and George Marks, and even Levi Hoffman dressed in funereal black, who I don't think had ever held a gun in his life. An armed Jess and Joe McGruder, grim and ready, stepped out of an alley, Matthew Palmer beside them. The men of Blessing lined the street, a sight I never thought to see. How John and Jim ever accomplished such a feat, I didn't know, but from the looks on the riders' faces, I wasn't the only one surprised.

"Hey," said one, his hands splayed before him, "it was just a job."

"You need to find a different job, then," said Jim Killian.

Frank Monroe spoke with the bluster he couldn't help. "We don't want you around here. You're not welcome."

"Tell you what," said John, so slowly the words came out a drawl, "we'll give you a chance. Be real careful, keep your hands in plain sight all the time, and ride out. One chance is all you get. You ever show your faces around here again, we'll hang you, if you live long enough to make it to the noose." Then he swung his arm so his revolver aimed directly at Cobb's chest. "Except you. You don't go anywhere."

Cobb's three companions looked at each other. Oba said, "Sure. We'll take you up on the offer." With deliberate movements, he reined his horse back from the rail, and all three of them rode slowly to the end of the street. Except for

John, who kept his eyes on Cobb, the men of Blessing watched the riders until all that was left of their departing figures was distant dust.

And still John stood there motionless, his eyes locked with Cobb's, his arm outstretched and steady, his gun now aimed at Cobb's head. I heard the ominous, telltale click of the hammer as he cocked the weapon, and even at my distance I could see the sheen from the sweat on Cobb's face. Jim Killian spoke John's name loudly, but I don't think John heard him at all.

I thought I should do something to stop John's obvious intent. I should step out and call his name, tell him this wasn't the right way to settle things, tell him we lived under a rule of law precisely for men and moments like this, tell him I didn't know if I could bear the touch of an executioner. But I did and said none of those things. I only stood there, hardly breathing, my eyes fixed on John's profile, willing him back from wherever he was with all the energy I could find. I watched the struggle in him, the desire to pull the trigger so strong I could read it in his face and in every taut muscle of his outstretched arm and steady fingers. I remembered the implacable ice in him, saw again the deep, quiet, fierce center that had made him momentarily unrecognizable, even frightening, to Kate. All that Cobb saw, too, and surely knew he was only a movement away from eternity.

Then, his decision made, John said to Cobb, "Get down. Take all the time you need. Make sure I know exactly what you're doing with your hands every second." After Cobb dismounted, Caleb brought out a rope from the stable and tied the man's hands behind him. "Badger should be here today or tomorrow," John continued. "He can take you with him. But don't give me an excuse to kill you because it wouldn't take much." I knew he was right, that it still wouldn't take much at all, but for me the worst was past.

We all exhaled at the same time. In a sudden spurt of energy, all the men began to move, look around, and talk to each other, clearly relieved but proud of themselves and maybe surprised, too. Eliza came down the hotel steps, holding the railing to support her bulk, and took her husband by the arm. Other women appeared, too, but I ceased paying attention to them. John had turned to see me standing there, one hand at my throat, my eyes on him with a message of pride and love I wanted him to know as clearly as if I had shouted it across the distance between us. I could tell by his expression that he hadn't known I was there. My darling, I thought, how could you not have heard me standing here, when my heart was speaking to yours as loudly as a ringing church bell? But I didn't speak and I didn't move. "A formal man," he had told me, so not one to appreciate a headstrong female publicly flinging herself into his arms, but I wanted to and I believe he knew it.

Jim Killian called to John, "Four down and one to go. I wonder where Harper is." At his remark, as clearly as if he had said Lily's name, I knew exactly where Paul Harper was. Did Harper know by now that the railroad wasn't coming to Blessing? Did Lily know? If she didn't, would he tell her he was broke and on the run, or would he maintain the pretense and lure her away with him, use her as he chose, then abandon her without a pang of conscience when he was tired of her? Regardless of what my sister believed, I knew she was out of her depth with Paul Harper. He would only hurt her.

I couldn't dismiss all the years of worrying about her, protecting her, stepping into the gap for her. Picking up my skirts, I turned and ran back down the street, back toward Lily's house. Somehow I knew it could be my last time to see her. The pain in my side from my wrapped ribs slowed me down, and when I reached the house I was breathing with a harsh, gasping sound that announced me before I arrived. The front door was locked and the curtains drawn. The house looked empty. Running to the rear of the house, I saw a wagon with two large valises loaded in the back. At that moment Lily, dressed for traveling and beautiful in a gleaming black silk suit, came out the back door followed by Paul Harper. Her flaming hair was pinned up under a charming hat with a silver feather that curved around to kiss her cheek, and she sparkled in the sun like diamonds. She looked so radiantly happy, so glowing, that I thought her the most beautiful thing I had ever seen.

Harper carried a large traveling bag and Lily's tapestry rose satchel that had been our mother's. They came down the steps, he speaking something from behind and she laughing over her shoulder in response. Neither saw me until I stepped forward.

"Lily," I called and went to the foot of the path, standing between them and the wagon. They both stopped.

"Did you tell her?" I asked Harper scornfully.

Lily, seeing my injured face for the first time, half turned toward him. "You told me she hadn't been hurt."

Harper dismissed me with a hand wave. "It looks worse than it is. A bruise, is all. An accident."

I stepped closer, my eyes fixed on his face to be sure I could read his expression. "You've heard from Peterman, haven't you, and you know."

"Know what?" Lily asked, not as confident or radiant now. Something in my tone or his ferocious curse in reaction to my words had alarmed her.

"The railroad isn't coming to Blessing, Lily. All he's got is a lot of worthless land that he'd be lucky to give away. His men just took off for parts unknown, and there's no more extortion money to be had. He knows he's bankrupt and wanted by the authorities, besides, and he wasn't going to tell you any of that. I bet he reminded you to bring your jewelry, didn't he?"

She turned to look back at him. "Paul?"

He spit out the words with vicious fury. "She'd do anything to have you stay in this God-forsaken place. She'd say anything. The only excitement your sister's ever had has been through you. If you go, she'll wither away, a dried up old maid with no life and no future without you. Don't believe a word she says. I have money to burn, Lily, enough so we can live the way we both deserve. We were made for each other and you know it."

I took another step closer, commanding her to listen to me, to hear the love and sincerity in my voice, to know that I had always had her best interests at heart and always would, to recognize that in a special way, she and I were two sides of one coin and should not be separated.

"Mr. Peterman knows everything, Lily. He knows about the whole scheme, and he won't be a part of it. The railroad is passing Blessing by. John worked for Peterman. That's why he was here, to scout things out. How would I even know any of this if it weren't the truth? There's no railroad money in this man's future. He hasn't got a future or anything to offer you but heartache and homelessness. Oh, Lily, your home is here. Don't go."

I looked at her, and she met my eyes and knew from what she saw there that I spoke the truth. When I moved toward her, Harper said to me, "Don't take another step." In his hand he held a small ivory-handled revolver pointed squarely at my chest.

Lily said, "Paul, no," and took his arm, but he shook her loose and pushed her away.

"You go wait for me by the wagon," he told her, never taking his eyes off me, "while I finish up a little business here."

"Don't go, Lily," I begged again. All my energy was focused on her. The gun might as well have been invisible. "There's no life for you with him. Stay here with the people who really love you. Blessing is your home and always will be. It's where you belong."

"We can still have it all," Harper countered, speaking to Lily but continuing to watch me, the little gun in his hand implacable and unwavering, aimed at my heart. "You and I were made for each other, and nothing should keep us apart, not your dry stick of a husband and not this desperate spinster sister of yours. Do what I say." His last words came out harshly enough to make Lily turn and stare into his face.

For a minute she stood indecisively and then in the following moment it was clear, at least to me, that she had made a decision. She's not leaving, I thought triumphantly. I've won.

Aloud I said, "You bastard, she's not going anywhere with you." He knew it, too.

Behind me John called in a clear, carrying voice, "Don't do it." I understood the calm rationality of his voice, knew he did not want to risk harming Lily or me. All he could do was call again, "Don't do it, Harper. You're a dead man if you move."

Harper laughed. "I'll take my chances," he said and pulled the trigger.

Because my eyes were on Lily and hers on mine, I saw her consciously, deliberately take a step forward, move herself between Harper and me at exactly the moment he fired. She crumpled without a sound. From a distance came two more quick pops, followed immediately by two bright red spots that appeared on Harper's white shirt front as if he had been suddenly spattered with paint. He fell backward, sprawled across the porch steps, instantly dead.

I remembered all that later. At that moment I saw and heard nothing but the figure on the ground dressed in black silk, the white lace down her bodice staining red, the charming feathered hat thrown from her head, the thick, glorious auburn hair falling down across her shoulders now the color of blood to me.

"Oh, Lily," I cried. I stumbled forward, falling to my knees next to her and scooped her up in my arms. A delicate froth of blood bubbled at the corners of her mouth, but her eyes were open, the gold flecks pronounced in the sunshine, and she knew me. "Oh, Lily, don't go. I'm sorry, I'm sorry. This is my fault. It should have been me. Hang on, my darling. It will be all right." It's what you say even when you know it won't be all right—as if you truly believe that the sheer force of grief and longing and hope can make things right again. Desperate to speak, my sister reached up a hand and caught her fingers in my hair, pulling my head down closer to hers.

"Hush," I whispered, my lips against her hair. "It will be all right, love, it will be all right. I'll take care of you. Haven't I always?"

I felt John crouch down next to me, heard him say my name as if from a distance, but I shook his hand from my shoulder, oblivious to everything but my sister, my dazzling, dying sister. She tried to speak, failed, then breathed haltingly into my ear.

"Lily, I'm sorry it wasn't me. Please don't go. Don't go," I cried again, as if she were choosing to punish me by her leaving. But by then it was too late. She had already gone.

CHAPTER 17

In time all grief fades. That's the merciful way God arranged it, to spare us reliving each bitter, painful incident with the same intensity we first experienced it. Life would be unbearable if it were not so. But even now, years later, I cannot remember that Thursday afternoon, can't even write the words, without once more feeling the same sense of loss and abandonment, the same searing guilt I felt holding my sister's lifeless body in my arms. If I had allowed her to leave, she might well be alive today. How could I have foreseen that my need to care for Lily and protect her would lead to her death? I carry the blame still, knowing I was the one intended to die.

As a true indicator of Gordon's prominence in the community, no one gave him a thought until hours later when he came staggering down his front steps, dazed from a long gash in the back of his head that he had received from a fire poker at the hand of Paul Harper. By then Sheriff Badger and his deputy had arrived from Scott City, in time to write up a report about Lily's and Paul Harper's deaths and to take custody of Cobb.

Badger was a burly man with a large walrus mustache. He asked me what happened, and I told him exactly as I remembered, able to speak without any discernible emotion. He wrote it all down, and without need for judge or court declared Lily's death murder and Harper's death justifiable homicide. Badger took Cobb back to Scott City with him, saying I might have to come and testify at his trial there. But as it turned out, Cobb was wanted for killing a family in south Texas, so the Rangers came and took him back there to stand trial for that crime. Later I heard that although he had been found guilty and sentenced to hang, he died of a broken neck falling from his horse while trying to escape. I suppose John could have saved a lot of people a lot of trouble, but I'm thankful he didn't.

I buried my sister on Saturday, and everyone in town except Gordon attended her funeral, just as they had Father's. No speeches, of course. I wanted a quiet service. I told Kate bluntly that I had no intention of attending if Gordon would be there, and we both knew I meant it. That he should sit in that big house free and blameless, pretending that he was not as duplicitous as Paul Harper enraged me. I knew better and could not accept the injustice. Gordon chose to play the wronged and aggrieved husband, however, and did not attend his wife's funeral, so I was able to go after all.

At the church it became obvious to me in a clear, unemotional, and absolute way that my sister was really and truly gone. Until then I still half-expected to see her in my doorway or hear her lilting voice call my name. I laid that wild, desperate hope to rest at the funeral along with Lily. Whoever, whatever, lay in the coffin at the front of the church, it was not Lily, and I felt no need to weep for that chalk-faced, still figure of pale beauty and no brilliance. Besides, if I wept at all, someone might have thought I mourned the loss of a flawless face or a mane of autumn hair or eyes that glinted gold, and that misapprehension would have made mockery of my grief. What dimmed my world was the absence of Lily's diamond sparkle and that inner bright energy of mischief and wit that could so captivate. That was what I saw absent in the casket, what I realized was truly gone and could never be replaced, so tears were a useless and misguided affectation. Through the funeral, later even, standing at the edge of the grave, watching her lowered into the stolid, unappreciative ground, I had no need for tears and did not indulge in them.

I must have said all the right things, but I have no strong recollection of that time. As soon as I could, I escaped to the store to resume my plans for setting up business from the back room. Billy healed quickly and was able to help me move and unpack boxes and put order into their display. I hired a carpenter to build shelves, a new counter, and a small sleeping room for me in the back until I could again sleep in my own bed. Once my upstairs rooms were refurbished, I planned to move Billy out of the stable and into the back room I vacated. In no time the carpenter began serious work on renovating the front of the store and strengthening the ceiling. It felt strangely comforting to work and plan, to start early and stay late and watch the store come together around me. "Can we go home now?" Billy had asked, and again and again in my heart I promised him and myself, Oh, yes. This is our home. This is where we belong.

Eliza Hansen gave birth to a baby girl she named Louisa. I was touched by the gesture, knew it to be an apology of sorts, but one Liza would never put into words. At the christening I was charmed by the chubby little newborn with a head full of midnight-black hair. Standing beside me at the side of the room, Eliza tried to offer discrete sympathy about Lily, but I met her concern dispassionately with a cool, "Thank you," and then deliberately moved away to congratulate Steven on the addition to his family. I was determined to pick up my life in Blessing as it had once been and to put all that had happened behind me. It seemed pointless to discuss the past.

Through those early weeks after Lily's death, John's presence seemed distant in a way I couldn't explain and found troubling, as if he drifted somewhere on the periphery of my life but left no real impression. He stopped by daily to talk and was always there if I needed him, but I don't remember him touching me once during that time and I know I didn't give his restrained behavior a second thought. He wasn't less dear to me and I did not cease caring for him, but something was gone, or more accurately, some previous connection we had shared seemed lost. I thought he must have changed, but I didn't understand why or how and was unable to make sense of it or find the right words to talk to him about it. All I could do was keep working to reconstruct the way my life had once been. Without consciously forming the thought, I believed that if I could somehow restore my past and recreate that world, I could recreate Lily as well.

Milt French visited periodically, asking what I considered to be impertinent questions about my sleeping habits, my appetite and bodily functions, and shook his head disapprovingly at my responses. I assured him that he didn't have to worry about me—I was fine. If I was losing weight, it was only because of the physical exertion of putting the store back together. My body was healing nicely, thank you very much, and I didn't feel at all ill.

Then one day toward the end of August, John came into the store. He stood for a moment, his hat in his hands, his posture oddly helpless and ill at ease.

"Sit down a minute, Lou."

I did so obediently, my hands folded in my lap, looking at him expectantly. He sat across from me, our knees

almost touching, and reached to take both my hands in his.
I could tell it was hard for him to speak. At first all he did
was look down at my hands, examining my palms as if he'd
never seen them before, gently stroking them with his
fingers, thoughtful, reluctant to begin, grieved, it seemed to
me.

"I think it's time for me to leave," he said finally.

"Leave? Where are you going?"

"Away, just away. Cy Peterman says he might have a
job for me over in Pratt, where he's putting in the railroad
spur we talked about, so I might go there. I'm leaving the
day after tomorrow."

"Why do you need to leave, John? I don't understand."
I was honestly puzzled. What he said made no sense to me.
Why would anyone willingly leave Blessing? As much as I
tried to understand his words, I couldn't. He might as well
have been speaking a foreign language.

In as gentle a voice as I'd ever heard him use, he told
me, "My darling girl, there's no place for me here." At my
blank look he added, "I can't be the person that I guess you
need. It's Blessing, not me, that you want. You need a
storekeeper or a farmer, somebody that will fit here in
Blessing, but I can't be either of those things. At one time I
believed I could make you happy, but now I don't know
what it would take to do that. You told me that good
always follows bad, that it's a matter of holding on and not
giving up while you wait, but I can't hold on and I can't
wait. I can't watch you like this any more, Lou. I'm not a
strong enough man to handle it." His humble admission
struck me wordless, as wordless as that first moment when
I'd met him in the alley, when he had stepped into my life
and with one blue-eyed look had had my heart. "I'm going
away, but I'll let Jim know where I am, so if you need me
for anything you only have to wire me. If you ever want me
back, I can be here in a heartbeat." He lifted my hands and
dropped a kiss on one palm and then the other, then leaned

forward to kiss me on the mouth, fully, firmly. As much as a part of me wanted to, I couldn't respond to anything he said or did, as if I were frozen, all of me, inside to out, mind, heart, and body paralyzed. "Not that long ago you asked me not to go away again, and I told you I wouldn't. I meant to stay and try to be whatever you wanted me to be, but now all you seem to want is the past back, and I can't give that to you. I was never a part of your past, but God knows I never wanted anything more in my life than to be part of your future."

He stood up and put on his hat, waited a moment for me to speak, waited for something I couldn't give, waited longer still, and then at my continued mute stare walked away, gently closing the door behind him.

After John left I sat there for a long time, long enough for shadows to form in the room around me. I felt as if some hard shell covering me were cracking slowly and so completely that soon I would be terribly, dangerously exposed, exposed to air and light, to love and life and loss and joy and sorrow, to the emotional risks of living that could be so terribly painful. I was shaking and afraid. Sitting there in the dark, I began to cry without sound and without conscious thought or prompting. Tears welled up in my eyes and spilled down my cheeks into the corners of my mouth and then into my lap, hot and salty tears, not a cool and blessed rain falling on my face this time but tears that scorched and seared. I made no attempt to wipe or prevent them. I sat there well into the night, not moving, weeping and unable to stop.

I must have crept into bed sometime because I awoke there the next morning exhausted but exhilarated, feeling as if some kind of fog had lifted, more clear-headed than I had been in many, many days. I realized that I had several tasks of enormous, momentous importance to accomplish in a fairly short time. I put on my dove-gray dress with the white collar and rearranged my hair. In the mirror I looked too pale and my eyes were shadowed and swollen from tears, but my hair covered the scar along my face, all the bruises were nearly gone, and I could pinch color into my cheeks, so I was presentable enough for the business I had in mind.

First I went to talk to Frank Monroe. We had a serious conversation, then shook hands over a hastily written agreement that I signed without a doubt or tremor or regret. After that I retraced my steps to the big house across the street, the house of my childhood, and pulled the bell. When Anna answered, I asked to speak to Gordon and waited in the hallway inside the front door until he came.

He was very surprised to see me, not pleasantly. "What do you want?"

"I want my mother's jewelry," I announced calmly, "every piece of it."

I was prepared for him to refuse, to tell me to get out, and I think he wanted to. But I was also prepared to expose his deceitful partnership with Paul Harper to the general population, and I think Gordon realized that, as well. He stepped to the side and motioned up the stairs.

"You know where her room was," Gordon said, as if he could not bear to say Lily's name. "I haven't touched it since." From the foot of the steps behind me he added as insult, "Be sure that's all you take." I kept walking, oblivious to his rudeness. He had lost the power to upset or enrage me.

For as long as she had been married, Lily had had a room of her own. Pushing the door open, I thought, Not me. My husband and I will never sleep apart. Inside it seemed she had never left. Gordon had closed the door and done nothing to the room as if Lily's absence was insignificant to him, as if she had never existed, but her room gave vibrant testimony to her life and personality. Her scent was everywhere. All her things seemed to be exactly as she'd left them, and for a minute I buried my face in her dressing gown that still lay casually on the bed where she'd thrown it. How delectable she had always smelled! The room's elegant disarray reminded me of Lily herself. I could imagine her standing before her wardrobe on the last day of her life, deciding what to pack, pulling out one thing after another, and throwing the rejected items onto the bed and floor.

The stunning emerald earrings Gordon had bought for her as a wedding gift remained in her jewelry box. How she must have loathed her husband to be willing to leave those expensive baubles behind! I recognized the unusual woman's timepiece Lily had worn the night she'd entertained Cy Peterman, its lily-shaped pin imbedded with amber and glowing a rich butter-gold that had perfectly matched the gold flecks in her eyes. For a moment I desperately wanted the watch as a keepsake, but then I dropped it back in the box. My grief for Lily would dim the amber's glow. Surely Gordon would not keep the timepiece, its distinctive lily shape too obvious a reminder, and perhaps the pin would one day rest on the breast of a woman who was loved and so regain its warmth and sparkle from her happy heart. The fanciful thought brought both tears and a smile.

The items I was interested in nestled next to the more expensive pieces: my mother's single strand of pearls, a small floral brooch of aquamarine that had belonged to my mother's mother, a golden link bracelet my father had purchased as an anniversary gift for his Becca, and a modest gold wedding band. Nothing near as grand as the remaining contents of the jewelry box, but all that was important to me. I chose to believe that my sister had left our mother's jewelry behind for me to have. Someday I will have daughters, I thought to myself, and they will wear these things.

Gordon waited at the foot of the stairs, watching me

descend, Anna hovering in the background. I know he wanted to ask to see what I had taken, but even he wouldn't stoop that low with Anna as witness. As I passed him, I turned in the doorway, as tall as he, eye to eye. I had planned to say something scathing, something hurtful, so he would always know in what contempt I held him, but at that moment I was overwhelmed with the oddest pity for him, this miserable, miserly, small-hearted man, who despite all the years he had lived with her, had never really known his wife at all.

"Oh, Gordon," I said softly, "what have you lost?" If he thought I was speaking only of Lily, he was mistaken. I never saw Gordon again. Somewhere I heard that he remarried a rich, older widow from Wichita, whom he brought back to Blessing. For all I know they still live in the big stone house my father built for my mother. For all I care.

I went to see Kate next, popping in to interrupt her as she sewed tiny stitches along a seam. "Kate, have you seen John?"

She glanced up, looking at me almost as if I were a ghost and then beamed a wide smile. I believe she was tempted to get up and hug me, but she contented herself with saying, "Welcome back, stranger. It's been pretty dull without you."

"Was I really that bad?"

"You shut us all out for a while, Lou, but it doesn't matter now that you're back with us. Try the *Banner* office. I think John was on his way to talk to Jim."

I saw John through the *Banner* window, half sitting on Jim's desk and smoking a small brown cigar as the two men talked. I would have to get used to the tobacco, I told myself with a slight smile, but knew there were worse vices. When I pushed open the door, they both stood in unison and at attention. An endearing sight but comical enough to make me laugh.

"I'm not the queen so you can sit down again. I don't need an honor guard." A little silence followed my remark as if neither of them knew what to say. I looked at Jim. "I know it's your office, and I have no right to ask, but do you think you could close up shop and go away for a while?"

His leprechaun face lit up. "Darlin', I'm parched," he said and was gone.

I pushed the door shut, pulled down the blind, and turned the lock for privacy. Then I went up to John and took hold of the lapels of his coat, a hand on each side.

"Listen to me. I don't want a farmer and I don't want a storekeeper and I don't expect you to be either one. I just want you. I offered the store to Frank Monroe this morning, and he bought it, lock, stock, and barrel. I asked for his best price and I didn't quibble. I took his offer on the spot." John was as quiet as I had been yesterday, not taking his eyes from my face. "We can go anywhere and do anything you want. I've got an idea, but it's only an idea, and if you don't like it, we can do something else. It's fine with me if you want to go to Pratt or live in a tent in Mexico or settle under a train bridge in Kansas City, I don't care. It doesn't matter to me. Just take me with you." Then I put my arms up around his neck, watching something come to life deep in his eyes, and pulled his head down to me so I could whisper right against his mouth, "Just don't think about going anywhere without me."

Later he spoke in a dazed tone I smugly considered all my doing. "We can rule out a train bridge in Kansas City, but that tent in Mexico is beginning to look pretty good." Then, more seriously, "How can I ask you to leave your home, Lou? You've never wanted to live anywhere but Blessing."

"I know that's what I thought and I know that's how it seemed, but here's what I discovered last night after you left, John. Here's what I didn't understand until then. All this time I believed Blessing was my home, but I was wrong. Home isn't a place at all—it's people. Sometimes it's just one person. For me, home is you. Wherever you are, that's home."

Later still, after words and promises no one needs to know but the two of us, John asked, "So what's this idea of yours?"

"I've been thinking about that place you've got in Wyoming Territory. I'd like to see it. We could go there and if it suits, we could settle and raise our family in Wyoming. I told you I've never seen real mountains and I'd like to. It's cattle country, isn't it? We could ranch. I can ride pretty well and I'm not afraid of hard work. We'll just have to be sure we have a couple of sons to help out. There's only one rule as far as I'm concerned."

"What's that?"

"I don't want to sleep apart from you for even one night. Not one, not ever. That's the rule."

He pulled me to him and asked quietly, "Is the man in the moon dancing, Lou?"

"My darling, he's been doing a jig up there for quite a while now. Poor fellow's probably all tuckered out."

John laughed out loud and kissed me passionately, both our hearts keeping step together and dancing with the same joyful abandon as that faceless man who lived up in the night sky.

"John." He held me so tightly against his chest, I had to push away to look at him. "You know you get Billy along with me. He's sort of a free bonus. I can't leave him behind. What would he do?"

"I'm only marrying one of you and it isn't Billy, but I never expected anything different than to take the boy along with us if he wants to come."

"Thank you. And there's another thing I've been wondering."

Something in my suddenly meek tone gave him pause. "Yes?"

"Isn't Wyoming suffrage territory?"

"I seem to recall that women have the vote there."

"Good," I said contentedly, giving him one more kiss before I left to start packing. "I believe I'll fit right in."

EPILOGUE

This is where fairy tales leave off, I guess, where two people live happily ever after and that's the end of the story. But because life is seldom like a fairy tale, there's always more to the story than you think, more grief, and if you look for it and hold on to it, more joy, too.

We were married in the German Lutheran church early in the evening of the following Sunday. Just the four of us were there with the preacher, John, distinguished in dark suit and tie, and I, with Kate and Jim as witnesses. Afterwards the Hansens hosted a small reception in the lobby of the hotel for us, nothing grand because I was in mourning, just a time for well wishers. Billy played the fiddle, the first time since his injury, so he was still a little tentative with the bow, but no one commented. It was obvious he was playing from the heart, and that made up for any missteps. The boy acted excited about the move to Wyoming, but I had my doubts that he really understood what the distance and the changes would mean. Well, I didn't really understand it either, so that made two of us.

I was most surprised to see Jess McGruder there, dressed properly in jacket and pin-striped trousers. In an unexpectedly warm gesture, he took one of my hands in his and held onto it.

"You was good to my boy and I'm obliged. Ain't one of us don't wish you happy." Then he turned to John standing next to me and said as sternly as if he were my father catching the measure of a suitor, "A man needs to take the responsibility of a woman serious. I don't want to hear she's unhappy or that you're not treating her right. If I have to make the trip to Wyoming Territory, I will."

John responded seriously, "Yes sir, I understand," closer to sixteen than he'd been in many years.

Toward the end of the evening, I pulled Jim and Kate aside to say sternly, "No practical jokes, no noisemakers, no pans clanging under our window, no serenades at the door in the middle of the night. That would be hard to forgive. Promise?" Jim hesitated until Kate nudged him and nodded, understanding. Women never found that sort of activity as entertaining as the men did.

Once the door of our room closed behind us, John and I just stood at a distance, looking at each other like strangers, the night just ahead and the future as far as we could see. Then I turned my back to him, holding my hair up off my neck with one hand.

"I always have a hard time with these buttons. Would you get them for me?" His hands were warm in my hair and against the back of my neck, his lips warm there, too. As promised, there was no chivaree, but I wouldn't say our wedding night in the best room of the Hansen House was uneventful.

We left the next morning, pulling out of Blessing with my dowry money from the store along with my mother's jewelry secure in a strongbox under the seat and Billy in the back of the wagon, tucked in among boxes and a few pieces of furniture I could not bear to leave behind.

Hardest was my goodbye to Kate. "Oh, Kate," I said, hugging her, my voice breaking, "I'll never have another friend as dear to me as you. I'm going to miss you more than I can say. Will you plan on coming to visit Wyoming as soon as we're settled and can put a roof over your head?" Kate cried, too, and promised to visit, but while we've written faithfully for years, we haven't seen each other since that day. In all the time since leaving Blessing I've met countless people, known many neighbors and had good women friends, but there's never been as faithful a friend or one as dear to my heart as Kate Wilhelm. There never could be.

John and I headed west, and so we didn't pass the store and the big house that faced each other on the opposite end of town. I, taking a lesson from Lot's wife, didn't look back then and have never looked back since, never had a regret about my decision or a moment's doubt that I made the right choice.

We arrived in Laramie, Wyoming, in mid-September with the weather already beginning to chill. When we pulled up in front of the house—a charitable description—it was clear the place needed a lot of work inside and out. John and I sat on the wagon seat looking at the cabin in silence. Even Billy was speechless. The front door hung on one hinge, and the whole building leaned lopsidedly away from us as if our approach had startled it. I took a quick look at my husband's face, surprised a rare look of consternation and doubt and something almost like shame there, and before he could say anything, I leaned over to give him a quick kiss on the cheek.

"Home at last," I proclaimed cheerfully and climbed down from the wagon, not waiting for his help. "Billy, come on. We're home now and it's time to unload." I flashed John a brief, shared smile, glad to see that previous look on his face replaced by something else, something fierce and proud, as if he were remembering, as I was, that wherever we were together was home, and that was all we'd ever need. John worked like a man possessed to get the place snug before winter and was still hammering during the first snowfall. We've added on to the house three times since, so that now it's large, comfortable, and rambling, warmed by a huge stone fireplace that takes up almost one entire wall. We have plenty of room for all the generations.

When we bought our first herd and brought it up from Ft. Collins, I rode right along with it, scandalizing my neighbors by riding astride in men's pants. Folks needed a while to understand that I wasn't one to stay behind and that my husband approved, encouraged, and desired my company. Until we could afford to hire help, I rode in the roundup, helped with the branding, and even strung fence, all with John Thomas, our firstborn, strapped to my back in the way I learned from our Indian neighbors.

Not that we didn't experience terrible times, times to grieve the soul and question Providence. Our first daughter, Blessing, died of scarlet fever a week after her first birthday, and we buried her at the foot of the mountains under a stand of pines that reached to heaven. John built a second side to the porch so that even in the worst weather, I could step out and see her little grave in the distance. Blessing's death was the only time I ever saw my husband weep, a sight that so affected me I knew I must overcome my own grief to console him. Our first child, a son, was my husband's pride and namesake, but when our daughter was born, I saw a side of John I never expected. Certainly I loved that little girl, but he was totally captivated from the beginning, a besotted and protective father charmed by her every smile, wrapped around her baby fingers and loving every minute of it. Blessing she was named and a blessing she was, more of a treasure to her father than if she'd been spun from gold. I can still see him bending over her cradle, reaching down one of his fingers for her to grasp, then turning to look at me with an expression I'd never seen before.

"She has your eyes, Lou. Isn't she something? She's already captured her first heart." For a man not given to fanciful language, John told me an awful lot with those few words.

His still and furious grief at Blessing's death was painful to see, and for a while it seemed I lost both husband and daughter. But we held faithfully to each other for mutual and tender comfort, conceiving Becca from our anguish, and Becca has been a joy since the moment she came squalling into the world. A healthy, happy, loving girl, our Becca was as accomplished on a horse as she was on the dance floor, and pretty besides. She chose a good man for her husband, a minister, and they live close by in Laramie. Becca wore my mother's pearls on her wedding day, and whether it was the glow of the pearls or my daughter's radiant face, something stirred tears.

"I'm just happy," I told John when he whispered his concern, but we both knew it wasn't that simple.

Our seventh winter in Wyoming, the snow came early in September and stayed well into May, huge drifts of it, with a wind that howled mercilessly against the house and temperatures of relentless sub-zero cold. Despite my years of living through the harsh winter winds of Kansas, I had never experienced anything like that winter. It was all I could do to keep John Thomas and Becca warm, and I worried for John as he prowled restlessly and silently from window to window, looking out at the unrelenting snow. He would come to bed and we would sleep with the children close for warmth, Katherine beginning to stir inside me and I unable to share her presence with John because I knew another child would worry him even more. Slowly the children's breathing would calm, warmed in the hollow between John and me, but I could tell, even in the darkness, that my husband was nowhere near sleep. I would rest my hand against his face to bring him back from wherever he'd gone, knowing he was lying there, thinking purposefully through the future, considering alternatives, ruthless to protect us and our livelihood.

By late spring, countless carcasses appeared in sickening repetition as the snow melted, so many steers frozen to death that we lost over half the herd. The bitter winter of '87 drove some of our neighbors out of the cattle business all together, but we started building up our herd again without even needing to discuss the decision. Our family lived on little in those years, but we were rich even then. If we're successful today, it's because of John's unrelenting determination to provide for his family and the sheer grueling hard work he put in day after day without complaint. He gives more credit than is due to my Caldecott head for business, but I admit the cattle trade is not much different from a mercantile enterprise, and I have always had an aptitude for commerce.

For a few years John headed Laramie's Cattlemen's Association, but he resigned when the range wars against the homesteaders and sheepherders turned deadly. Truth to tell, the other cattlemen of the county demanded John's resignation, a fact I proudly declared I would fly like a flag over our house if I could figure out a way to do it. My husband counseled compromise, collaboration with the sheepherders, and respect for the rule of law, a voice of thoughtful reason from a man with a violent past, a man who would not be partner to the slaughter and the bloodshed of those years. I always believed John took a peaceful stand because he had long ago had his fill of slaughter and bloodshed, that he remembered searching for his brother, body by ruined body on a bloody Virginia battlefield. Those were sad, shameful years in Wyoming history, filled with brutality and the unconscionable butchery of both men and animals, really the only time I secretly thought John would suggest we leave and settle elsewhere. Thank God we stayed and held our own, went into Laramie together, pleasant and casual, business as usual and nothing shameful on our consciences. The sheepherders found only safety and protection when crossing our land for higher pastures, but I cannot say the same for some of our neighboring cattlemen, who loathed sheep and refused to believe Wyoming held enough grazing land for all. Now in splendid irony, John Thomas has almost convinced his father that we ought to run sheep along with our cattle, and I am in full agreement with our son, if only to give our neighbors a reason to talk about us again.

Our first year in Wyoming Territory was so much harder and so much colder than I ever imagined or expected, so much for both of us to learn, always early mornings and late nights, physical exhaustion and never-ending work that aged us from the start. But in some respects, that first year was wonderful, too, snug in that little house, Billy's concerts free for the asking and the kitchen dance floor all to ourselves, John and I talking and planning our future, learning about each other and loving what we learned. We still bring up that time, especially when it's late at night, and with the children away to school or to families of their own, just the two of us in the house again.

"How did we ever do it?" I ask, serious about the question but still with a laugh in my voice, remembering. "Neither of us knowing a thing about raising babies or a family or even cattle, and no one around for miles to help or give advice. How did we ever dare? We were two greenhorns for sure."

John seldom laughs in return, only pulls me closer. After all these years, he's accustomed to a tall woman and knows how to curve himself against me exactly right, so that I feel safe and protected.

"You made it a home, that's how we did it," he says against my hair, his arms tightening around me, still able to surprise me with his depth of feeling. He remains a formal man not given to flowery speech, and yet for all his reserve, I have never felt anything but deeply loved.

Those first years of our life together I had brief, sharp longings for the Kansas prairie, but I kept them to myself. Although in most other areas John came to know my thoughts as intimately as his own, from the beginning I was careful to keep from him any sign of that poignant homesickness. I knew my unhappiness always troubled him. But even today sometimes, looking out at the mountains from our front door and circled by hills all around, I feel walled in, too surrounded and enclosed. For just a moment I would give anything to see the great unbroken, flat horizon of wheat fields from my childhood, hear the plaintive do-do-dooo of the prairie chickens as they call to one another across the plains, see the random rows of sunflowers bent by the prairie wind, their open faces following the sun. My children will never know those things as part of their memories, and I feel it's their loss. But I would change nothing, trade nothing, do nothing differently, and if John awoke tomorrow and said he wanted to move to Arizona or Austria, it wouldn't matter. Without a second thought, I'd start packing.

This last winter seemed longer than usual and with the extraordinary circumstance of time on my hands, I decided to put the story of Blessing, Kansas, down on paper. I've shared with the children how their father and I met, and I've talked affectionately of Blessing, of my parents, and of Lily, but this winter I began to set down the details of that long ago summer as I remembered them. I've been scribbling for months and I'm almost done. I'm twice the age I was when I first met John, stouter than I wish with gray streaking my hair and a touch of arthritis in my hips and hands. John and I will be grandparents soon, with Becca's first child due in the spring. Our oldest, John Thomas, who's worked beside his father since he was old enough to sit a horse, was married this past fall and lives nearby with his bride. I consider our new daughter-in-law and the coming grandbaby to be perfect anniversary gifts.

John surprised me with his own present, a trip to San Francisco to celebrate twenty-five years of marriage. I saw an ocean for the first time and heard my first opera, surrounded by velvet curtains and chandeliers that twinkled like diamonds, just as Lily described. We rode in cable cars and horseless carriages, stayed at the Palace Hotel, explored Golden Gate Park, and ate at Delmonico's on Market Street. John said he enjoyed watching me more than any of the sights of California, and it's true that I felt and acted eighteen again. The trip was a wonderful experience of a lifetime, but I hadn't changed all that much in twenty-five years. Lily was still San Francisco, and I was still small towns and sunflowers, content, even eager, to be home in Laramie again.

When I began this writing last fall, I hardly knew how to start. I had to rekindle memories by unearthing my journals from those years, but as I read, the memories began to flow

---

with such a rush that there were times my hand couldn't keep up with my thoughts. I'm almost done with the telling, and for all the heartache and loss, the words that escape me are the ones to describe how blessed my life has been and still is. How could I ever have imagined that I would be so loved? I've been careful not to take what I have for granted, and I believe John feels the same.

I have a cherished memory of him coming in at the dark end of a cold, late fall day, stomping fresh snow from his boots and shaking his coat out just inside the door. He had rested his rifle on a rack high out of the children's reach and turned back to face the room, his face lined with fatigue and cold. Becca was hopping up and down in front of him, saying "Papa" over and over again, because from infancy she had loved her papa with a focused devotion and was not above demanding his attention through sheer, shrill repetition. John Thomas was standing by the table, waiting patiently for his father to notice and commend the sums he'd been working on all afternoon. I had given John a quick, distracted kiss by way of welcome, then taken a fussing Katherine from my hip and thrust her into his hands so I could use both of mine to scrape the stew from the bottom of the pot before more of it burned.

"Thank you," he said.

I turned quickly from the stove to look at him. After more than seven years I recognized something different in his tone, but thank you for what, the abrupt present of a wet baby? Or thank you for a supper of burned stew and tough biscuits after he'd spent a long, cold day looking for ungrateful, wandering cows? Thank you for Becca's doll, extended with both hands in her insistent way or for John Thomas's sheet of arithmetic problems or for a cranky wife who had been feeling sorry for herself all day? I tried to picture the kitchen through John's eyes, a room redolent with the smell of burned stew and a baby that needed changing, cluttered with toys and dishes still dirty from the morning, loud with Becca's incessant chanting. I had been short-tempered all day, still round-faced and too heavy from delivering Katherine, prone to tears without warning, housebound and restless from the weather and the children, perspiring from standing over the stove with my hair coming out of its pins all which ways like a common floozy.

Grinning to himself at his own private thoughts, John transferred the baby to one arm and then crouched down to pick up Becca with the other. Straightening with a girl balanced on each side, he took a moment to approve John Thomas's work. Then, shaking his head a little, grinning as if he'd seen something too incredible to believe, he said, "Thank you," again, said it across the room, across the kitchen clutter and the noise of children, caught my gaze with his sky-blue eyes and said it just to me. So I don't believe he's taken any of our life for granted either.

With Blessing sleeping safely under the pines, our four remaining children, John Thomas, Rebecca, Katherine, and Augustus, are part mystery, part joy, four bright, spirited, and strong-willed individuals. Gus, the youngest and still at home, recently turned fifteen, and I see in him my father's sharp intellect, humor, and perceptive ability to probe and consider several sides of an issue before he arrived at what was right in his own heart. My Gus had an early curiosity about politics and government, and while I concede that it may be a mother speaking, I believe he would someday make a fine governor. I consider all my children special in their own right, but of course I have a bias.

Katherine—to my disappointment she never allowed *Kate*—worried me for a while, honey-haired but still like John in appearance and certainly like him in temperament, introspective and sometimes too quiet. Katherine's away at Kansas Medical School now and has chosen her own future. Whether we're ready for a woman doctor in the family remains to be seen, but the times are different in this new century, so why shouldn't Katherine be exactly what she wishes? Who could have imagined that women lawyers would be pleading cases before the Supreme Court or that an independent journalist named Nellie Bly would make a solitary circle around the globe in just seventy-two days? From childhood Katherine has been fearless and determined in the pursuit of her dreams, and her father and I couldn't be prouder of her.

Billy is still here. He's worked right beside us through all these years, never complaining, always eager to please, gentle with the children, grieved by Blessing's death and mourning her in music, a dear and integral part of our family. Had it not been for Billy, I might never have met John, so I will always be in his debt and nothing I can do could ever repay it. He's "Uncle Billy" to our children and will be the same to theirs. When the children grew up and the house became too quiet, Billy asked for a bed in the bunkhouse, where the camaraderie of our ranch hands made him feel at home. God bless him. Billy fiddled us through some very hard times.

Kate wrote to say Jim Killian died suddenly, clutching his chest and falling across his desk mid-word, still grasping his pen. I telegraphed immediately that she should come to us, but she moved instead to Topeka to be with her sons and grandchildren. We continue to write and promise to visit. Kate must be at least seventy now, but when I picture her in my mind's eye, she always looks like she did twenty-five years ago, wearing a sea green dress and her braids wound around the top of her head like a coronet.

Every evening for the past week I've been telling John I'm almost done with this testament, but I keep writing and he's stopped asking. I've been thinking of the past a lot, of course, and trying to recall what I expected from my life or from this marriage. Not that it matters because even in my wildest dreams I couldn't have imagined that my life would be what it is. I didn't expect that after twenty-five years I would see John, now silver-haired, crossing the yard to the house with his easy stride, nodding thoughtfully at something Gus is saying, and still feel that butterfly of love and desire fluttering low in the pit of my stomach at the sight. I suppose I thought the time would come when a feather touch from his hand along the back of my neck would stop making me shiver, but to this moment it reminds me of our wedding night and has exactly the same effect on me as it had then. John wears glasses when he reads now, and I laugh to see him tuck the wires behind his ears with a mild expression of disgust and disbelief. Neither of us can believe how the years have flown. In the morning he's slower to rise and groans a little more loudly when his feet hit the floor, but I believe those blue eyes are bluer than ever and he has the same grave, sweet smile that starts somewhere deep inside behind his eyes until it finally lights his whole face. Someday in God's good time, although I hope not for many years, we'll be buried side by side under the stand of pines where Blessing lies, and we will not sleep apart even then. I love that man.

Love. Love brings me to Lily, gone all these years, resting next to our parents in the little Kansas cemetery behind the Lutheran church at the edge of town. Darling sister, who so desperately longed to leave Blessing but never did and never will. At first, I wanted to share Lily's story and give her a memorial of sorts, but now I think the telling has turned into so much more, a story of right and wrong, of sacrifice, loss, and healing, of time and generations and family. A story of home.

I watched my daughters carefully in their early years, half-fearing, half-longing to see Lily in them, but she wasn't there. Katherine was like John and Becca my exact image, but I could not find Lily in any of my children.

At first I dreamed of my sister regularly, sometimes crying out her name, waking with tears and the need for my husband's wordless comfort, mourning the exchange of her life for mine, guilty and grieving over the unjust substitution I had forced on her. But the intensity and frequency of those dreams are long past. Lily still visits my sleep, but since this writing, I awaken with joy at her memory in a way I never did before, embrace her image, and welcome her sparkling, laughing voice as if it were early morning music. Perhaps that means my guilt at her death has been replaced by something else. Perhaps at long last I accept Lily's final decision as a choice she willingly made, a choice she could live—and die—with.

There's a part of Lily I will never understand, a part foreign to me, but I've come to see that she and I were as individual then as my own children are today, no matter that the same two people brought us into being. I can accept that now and be thankful for all the years Lily was in my life, thankful even for the painful times, and thankful for the gift she gave me as she lay dying, a gift dearer than life, although she gave me that, too. The moment remains as vivid to me now as if it had occurred just yesterday.

Reaching up to catch my hair in her hands, Lily pulls my head down so that my ear is against her mouth. I am saying her name, but somehow I know she wants me to be still as she tries to speak. I can't understand her and I try to quiet her.

"Hush," I say. "It will be all right," but Lily is concentrating hard, intent on saying something and so tries to speak again.

"Love you," she gasps. I lean closer, and then because my sister is afraid I did not hear her and so I will never know, she somehow finds the strength and a last breath to say unmistakably, as clear and unmistakable as these words I write on this page, "I love you, Lou."

LILY'S SISTER

Meet Hope Birdwell, daughter of a San Francisco prostitute, former servant in a rich man's house, and early twentieth-century homesteader:

Lou Davis rode over to see me on my second Friday in Wyoming. She rode astride, which I'd never seen a woman do before, dressed in men's pants, a hat, and a short, heavy coat.

"Hello, Hope!" she called, sliding off her horse. "You've had a week to get settled. How are you doing?" I was glad to see her warm, friendly face.

"Just fine. I haven't had a chance to thank you for your generosity. I've put everything you sent to good use."

She waved my words aside. "No, thank *you* for taking some of those old things off our hands. That little wooden table was what we used our first years in Wyoming but we outgrew it, and I've had it stored in one of the barns. There was too much sentiment involved for me to discard it all together so I'm glad you found a place for it." She stepped inside the cabin but stopped in the doorway at the sound of the lambs baaing in the shed next door.

"Poor little bummers," I explained, laughing at her expression. "Do you know Fergus Campbell?" She nodded. "Well, he stopped down by the creek for lambing and I'm helping out. I'm learning a lot about the sheep business." I watched her face carefully because Fergus had talked about the animosity between sheepherders and cattlemen and I wondered if, despite her kindness, she harbored bad feelings. But I saw only a smile there. Together we walked down to the flocks.

"I haven't seen you in at least two years, Mr. Campbell," Lou Davis said when she saw Fergus. "I hope everything's well with you."

He wore a felt hat that he removed out of respect. "Aye, Miz Davis. It's been a warm winter this year and I can't complain. I trust you and your family are prospering."

"Becca's a bride and Katherine's off to medical school. John Thomas swears he'll die a bachelor, Billy is still fiddling, Gus is preparing for the University, and John and I are getting older but not necessarily wiser." She gave a little chuckle. "If that's not prospering, I don't know what is and like you, Mr. Campbell, I can't complain. I'll let John know you asked after him." She took a deliberate look around at the restive sheep. "I see you've enlisted Miss Birdwell's help."

"I can't convince her to roam with the flocks, though. She insists on staying in one place."

"Home is very important to a woman, Fergus. That's why there are so many solitary herders." Her next words were interrupted by a ewe's loud, urgent, and distinctive bleating and with an apologetic shrug, Fergus left us.

Later over tea, Lou invited me to her home for Sunday dinner. "I could stop by and get you for Sunday services if you'd like, as long as the weather holds. John and John Thomas will be pulling calves, but the preacher's our son-in-law so at least one of the family should make an appearance at church. Then you could come for dinner afterward. We'll be sure you get home before evening. With both of my daughters away, I'd welcome your company." Lou Davis had a way of doing kind things and somehow making you think it was you that was doing her the favor. She reached across the table and put a hand over mine. "Are you sure everything's all right, Hope?"

I said yes, then felt tears pricking at the back of my eyes because I couldn't remember another time when anyone had expressed the same heartfelt concern or asked me such a question without expecting something from me in return.

"Fiddle tears," Lou commented, and at my blank look smiled. "We've always called sudden, quick tears you don't expect fiddle tears. As I recall, Uncle Billy inspired the phrase years ago, and now it's become a family tradition." Then she rose, saying calmly, "I've got to get back or they'll send out search parties. If you need anything, Hope, you only have to ask. I'll see you Sunday."

from *Waiting for Hope* by Karen J. Hasley

If you enjoyed *Lily's Sister* and would like to read about the next generation of the Davis family, watch for *Waiting for Hope,* the second book of the series, available soon. Find out additional information about the author, the series, or the next publication at www.karenhasley.com.

Printed in the United States
78280LV00002BA/139